BODY IN THE SQUAT

SQUAT

A Merseyside murder mystery

DIANE M. DICKSON

THE BOOK FOLKS

Published by The Book Folks

London, 2022

© Diane Dickson

ISBN 978-1-913516-85-7

www.thebookfolks.com

BODY IN THE SQUAT is the fourth standalone title in the DI Jordan Carr mystery series.

A list of characters can be found at the back of this book.

Prologue

The house at the end of the terrace had been a family home. Four children, now and then a cousin or a brother who needed somewhere to stay. Noise, parties and life. A couple of weddings and one sad funeral.

After the older three had moved, there were incidents. Noise at night, a fight in the garden, the neighbours complained about the youngest one's behaviour. The council became involved. They counted empty bedrooms. It didn't matter to the men in grey that a family had grown up there. It didn't matter that it was full of memories and the only home the sons and daughter had ever known. The house was too big and the old woman and her one 'special needs' child were moved to a flat. There were tears but it didn't matter. It had never belonged to them.

A couple of families moved in, moved on, and then it was empty for a while.

It should have been boarded up and secured but the squatters got there first and even afterwards they prised open the ill-fitting windows and clambered inside.

They were followed inevitably by drug dealers, and then addicts and itinerant people with nowhere else to be.

Then, after a while, there was a change, subtle and quiet. Not so many rough sleepers looking for warmth. Not so many addicts spaced out on the damp grass in the back. But there were comings and goings, noise and disturbance.

The people using the house at the end of the terrace became a part of the scenery, neighbours sneered and tutted, but it was what it was and there were other things to think about, other problems to solve.

The local boys called out names as the women walked past. They drew graffiti on the walls and windows, lewd images, and once they left a dead cat on the step. For the youngsters it was fascinating. They were drawn to it, sneaking behind the walls, creeping through the garden. Until the day they looked through the window. Until the day they saw the blood.

Chapter 1

Detective Sergeant Stella May stared down at the flimsy paper in her hand. She turned it over to look at the back. She checked her phone again and shook her head.

"Mam, hiya. It's me."

"Yeah, I know. Your name comes up on the screen. Duh." Her mother laughed. "Anyway, what's to do? Have you seen the time? I was off to bed."

"Yeah. Sorry. I just wanted you to do me a bit of a favour."

"At eleven o'clock at night. Jesus, queen, what on earth?"

"Sorry, Mam, but can you just check the lottery numbers for me?"

"What? The lottery. Honest to God, girl, you're away with the fairies. Just look them up on your phone. Anyway, what are you mithering about lottery numbers for at this time of night? Go to bed. You have work in the morning. Haven't you got scallies to catch?"

"I know but can you just do it?"

"Oh, for Pete's sake. All right, just a minute."

She read them out. Stella took a breath.

"Listen, Mam. What I'm going to tell you, keep it under your hat, yeah? I mean don't go telling Aunty Vi or Peter. Only, it looks like I've won."

"Aww, queen. I'm made up for you. I suppose you mean more than just a twenty-five or whatever. How much do you think? Do you think it'll be enough so you can get a new car? That old banger you're driving isn't a good look for a detective. I thought you'd get something new when you were promoted. Our Peter'll be able to see you right. He's got a mate."

"No, Mam. It's not like that."

"Oh. What a shame. Never mind, love, treat yourself to something nice. You could do with a new jacket."

"No, Mam, listen. I think I've won it. Well, not all of it. The big prize. I've got the other one, the five and a bonus. I think it's going to be a lot. I had a look. Mam, I think I might have won over a million pounds."

"Oh."

Chapter 2

Stella's head was pounding. She hadn't slept. At first, she'd spent the time clicking on lottery results pages. She even watched a recording of the draw on the website. Everywhere she looked told the same story. She'd won. A lot. She read the tiny writing on the back of the ticket. Apparently, she couldn't just go back to the offy and hand it in the way you did with a ten-pound win. She had to tell people. She'd clicked the box for no publicity, but she still had to tell people. The thought made her feel sick.

It was ridiculous, she knew that. She saw that. She should be leaping about screeching. She'd won the lottery. What was the point of buying a ticket if you didn't throw a wobbler when you won? Open the fizzy whit oh no, scrap that, open a bottle of real champagne and ¸ aste half of it squirting froth. You should ring your mat¸ , have a party.

The trouble was she had known she'd n¸ ¸er win. People like her never won. It was a thrill to get a¸ enner, a giggle to get a bit more – even that had only ¸ppened once. But, no, you weren't supposed to win.

She liked her life. Since she'd been at sch¸ ¸l, she'd known she wanted to be a copper. Now, she wa¸ doing it. She truly was.

She'd burst with pride at the passing out p¸ ade and couldn't wait to tell all the aunties and uncles wh¸ ¸ she got her promotions. Now she was in plain clothes. A¸ etective. She loved it. Yes, it was a dark and nasty world s¸ netimes. Yes, there were things that wrung your heart a¸ d seared your soul. But then, nurses had that. Social wo¸ ¸ers had that. Even teachers these days had that. But ¸he was making a difference. She was. There wasn't any ¸ing else to make her this happy and, sitting on a beac¸ all day, living in a posh house, poncing about in design¸ dresses, wasn't her.

She put the ticket inside one of her books and ¸ut it on the shelf. She tried to sleep. It wouldn't stop. R¸ ¸nd and round all night. So, now here she was. Very ea¸ y in the morning, heading to a house in Kirkby and ¸ big-deal drugs raid.

The DI from St Anne Street, a tall black bl¸ ¸e called Jordan Carr, was in overall charge of their role i¸ it. He'd just been transferred to Serious and Organi¸ d from Wavertree where he'd made himself noticed.

He'd come to talk to them a few times in th¸ last few days. Told them how important it was that ¸ ¸ey kept things quiet. No letting things slip in the pub, ¸'d said. But he'd said it with a grin. Dunn had been deep in conversation with him and there'd been meetings ¸n closed rooms. Briefcases and uniforms. Heavy stuff.

Before DI Carr had come on board, they'd been watching addresses for weeks. Besides the dealers, they were going to net people traffickers, pimps, and all the scum who collected around the drug world. They had gathered information and waited. They could have had the mules and prozzies in ones and twos at any time. But the idea was to swoop in and clear up as many as possible in one day.

It wouldn't be long before it started up again but for a while at least the drugs on the streets would be reduced. If drugs were harder to come by there was more chance of friction between the dealers. With friction came mistakes and with mistakes came arrests. Stirring up the hornet's nest was seen as a good idea, somewhere, so now the troops at the sharp end waited in the damp, cold morning trying to believe they were going to make a difference.

Chapter 3

Today, when she needed to be on top form, Stella was dizzy with tiredness.

DIs Dunn and Carr were together beside the big black crew bus. Dunn frowned at her.

"You alright, Stel?" he said. "Looking a bit rough round the edges there."

"Yeah, I'm good, boss."

"If you're not ready for this, say so now. It's too late when you've cocked it all up."

"I won't. I wouldn't. I'm okay, boss."

"Well, see you are. Don't try anything clever. You've got your tasks, that's what you have to do. No heroics. Right? And don't get in everybody's way."

"Yes, boss."

She had thought she was getting used to him. He was cranky sometimes, most of the time really. But at least Ian Dunn treated everyone the same. Well, usually. This was a bit different. He wasn't talking to any of the male officers this way. Maybe she looked worse than she thought. She pushed her shoulders back and lifted her chin.

He was obviously dead keen to make an impression himself and decided it would be at her expense. A couple of the other blokes were watching, wiping grins off their faces when they saw her looking at them.

DI Carr asked her quietly, "Ready to go, Sergeant?"

"Yes, sir." So, she'd been noticed – not in the way she would have hoped for, but she'd been noticed.

"Excellent," he said.

She'd just let it go. Just suck it up. It was worth it; part of the deal. Dunn was, after all, the boss, and Carr was his boss and so it went on. They turned away and Carr clambered into his own vehicle and drove off. Other places to be.

They waited in the grey morning. Tense and primed.

* * *

Now, it was happening, she had to be on the ball. The yelling had started, they'd brought out the door ram. The armed team were fast shuffling forward. She just had to wait until they'd made it safe and then it would be time to do her part of the job: scraping up the dregs and making sure they had a solid case for the CPS. Everything by the book. She readied herself. The hard part of the investigation was over, and now it was time to gather them in.

Chapter 4

From her position near to the people carrier Stella could see the squad inside. She could hear them as they moved from room to room. "Clear. Clear. Clear." She could see the torch beams sweeping the walls. Outside they were waiting for the yells of outrage and screams from the women.

There was nothing.

One by one the dark-clad figures trailed out through the front door. It wasn't long before the ugly truth became obvious. The house was empty. All the planning, all the anticipation, and they had nothing.

DI Dunn stomped down the narrow front path. He spent a few minutes in animated discussion with the head of the tactical firearms unit. They shook hands and turned from each other. Neither looked pleased.

Dunn snarled at the group milling around the cars. "Right, you lot. Get yourselves back to the station. There's going to be some blowback from this, make no mistake."

One of the detective sergeants asked the question. To the relief of the rest of them. "What happened, boss?"

"Nothing happened, Brian. Nothing at all. The place was empty. No drugs, no girls, no money. Nothing. Cleaned out and gone."

Stella watched the CSI team, white suits rustling as they carted their boxes of equipment into the empty house. They'd go through the motions, acquire fingerprints, probably drug residue and hair but it would only be any good if they had someone to match it to. That obviously wasn't the case right now.

She slid her notebook into her pocket and shrugged out of the stab vest. She'd come with DI Dunn. Now she glanced around to see who else might have room in their car, but everyone was going back in the same seats and there was nowhere for her. Perhaps the best thing would be to hang about and try to cadge a lift back with one of the patrol cars, but she'd look a bit pathetic.

"Stella, when you're ready."

The dilemma was taken out of her hands by the DI. She ran across and slid into his 4x4. He slammed the door and pulled away. A few of the locals standing watching gave them the finger but it was habit more than anything else and they both ignored it.

"I don't sodding believe it," Dunn said. "They were there last night. According to the intel they'd been there for weeks. New girls coming in and being sorted. They'd been tracked from Dover. How the hell did they know? The whole place was cleaned out. All they left was their rubbish, bottles and pizza boxes."

"Plenty of DNA eh, boss."

He didn't answer her.

On the ride back to the station they listened as reports came in of the successes elsewhere. Dunn was livid. He muttered and cursed under his breath.

"If this comes back on us, Stel, if it turns out that one of ours let them know, I'll swing for them. I will.'

Chapter 5

The rest of the day was tense and difficult. Dunn stalked around the incident room scrawling on the whiteboards and shaking his head. It had taken weeks to plan the raid and Kirkby had come away with nothing.

It was almost end of shift when DI Carr arrived. He'd been doing the rounds of the other stations under his wing. Congratulating them on their success. Flying the flag for Serious and Organised.

He stood by the door and waited for quiet. "Right, that didn't go quite the way we'd hoped," he said. "You're embarrassed, I'm embarrassed. I have to go and explain how come we spent all that money and we've come up with nothing. But the only thing we can do is go back to the beginning and see what we can salvage. We have the identities of most of the major players. We've got an all-ports alert out for the ones who may try to leave the country and we're working with colleagues in Eastern Europe in case they do slide out and turn up back at home. Our colleagues in other forces, from other stations, have access to information." He glanced at the maps on the wall.

It could have been a dig, it could have just been him laying down the facts but DI Dunn, standing beside him twitched his shoulders and scowled at the room in general.

Carr continued, "The girls will have been moved on to other towns. Possibly London so we've liaised with the Met. Also, Bradford, Manchester, Newcastle, and Birmingham. The information is on HOLMES. They may have given us the slip this time but it doesn't mean we're giving up on them. They should have been there. The intel we had was sound. They weren't, why not? It's a total cock-up but we'll get the bastards." He stopped to let his words sink in and then stalked from the room.

* * *

For a while nobody quite knew what to do. There was some paper shuffling, a couple of uniformed officers sloped off to the canteen and the civilian clerks made a start re-organizing the whiteboards. People found other places to be, away from the miserable atmosphere.

Stella tidied up some files in her computer and then went back to paperwork she'd been doing a couple of days ago. A convenience store robbery which had proved easy to wind up because the thief was the nephew of the owner. The time investigating had been wasted because, once the old man had been told, he withdrew his complaint. There was talk of the police bringing a prosecution themselves. There had been a weapon involved. An iron bar brandished in front of the young woman manning the counter. But she'd been got at, probably paid off and told if she complained she'd lose her job. So, the CPS had advised that they cut their losses and close the case.

She glanced around the nearly empty room, the door opened, and DI Dunn beckoned her over with a crooked finger.

"Where is everybody?"

"I'm not sure, boss." She glanced at her watch. "It's pretty much end of shift."

Dunn sighed heavily. "Okay, what are you working on right now?"

"Just finalizing some paperwork, boss."

"Right. Get yourself back down to Westvale. There's a report of some sort about a squat. Kids up to no good, looking in windows and making up stories, more than likely. Not much detail. It came in while we were all wasting our time chasing shadows. The details will be on your tablet by the time you're ready. Requisition a car. Yours is a bit ramshackle. A patrol unit is already on the way."

* * *

A small crowd had gathered by the time she arrived, and someone had taped off the house. The officer at the door stopped her entering.

"Sorry, ma'am. I can't let you in unless you suit up. I've already sent for the medical examiner and CSI."

"Is somebody dead?" Stella asked.

"Oh yes, very dead."

Chapter 6

In St Anne Street, they were happy with the overall outcome of the raids. No police injuries, and a decent haul of drugs for the chief constable to pose with on the news bulletins.

After the debrief, DCI David Griffiths took Jordan Carr to one side. "Let's grab a beer and have a chat."

This was not the way he'd hoped to start his new job. Of all the locations involved, the one in Kirkby had been the only failure. A couple of others had produced less than they would have hoped, but there was just one total flop, and it was one of his. He wasn't used to this. He didn't like this feeling of failure.

Griffiths got the beers in. "I bet you're feeling like shit, aren't you?"

"Yeah, pretty much."

"Don't. If anything I should be more brassed off than you. Till you came in I was liaising with Kirkby, so this is more my cock-up than yours."

"That's good of you, Dave, but we both know my name's going to be in the records."

"Yeah, and there's nothing I can do about it. I feel bad, to be honest, but I thought it was solid. I was sure everything was tied in. But look. It happens and there's no point dwelling on it. I suggest what you do, when you've had a good rant and possibly a few whiskies, is to concentrate on finding out what went wrong. It's important. It's pretty obvious they'd had a heads-up at the location. We need to know how. You might think it's moot because the moment has passed but if there's a bad apple somewhere out at Kirkby, we need to know about it. It could be it was just rotten luck, but I don't reckon so. Are you with me?"

"Yes, boss."

"Okay, so spend some time digging. See if you can fathom how this could have happened. Examine what goes on there."

"Are you transferring me to Kirkby, boss?"

"Shit, no. Listen, I know that at the moment this probably feels like a real big deal, but everyone knows you came in at the arse end of it. You were thrown in at the deep end with barely time to pick a desk so, if you can find out what happened, you can come out of this okay."

They both knew what he was being asked to do was uncomfortable and if he did find there had been deliberate sabotage then it would be unpleasant for everyone.

"If you're not up for this I can put someone else on it? We could even initiate an internal enquiry, but I'd rather wait until we have a better idea of what happened," Griffiths said.

"No, no. I'll find out. I hope I discover it was just bad luck but whatever it is, I will find out."

"Okay. We need to establish a way in first. With a situation like this we can't just catapult you on site because everyone will know what's going on. Go home now. Give your kid a cuddle and don't look so worried. I have faith in you, mate. It'll be fine."

Chapter 7

The squat was pretty foul. It was an end of terrace and had been a council house. Now, the garden was a mess. Mouldering leaves gathered under old rose bushes left to run wild. There was rubbish caught in the grass and a couple of car wheels, weeds growing through them, rusted in the middle of what had, at some time, been a lawn. The curtains in the filthy windows were ragged and sagging away from the rails. Inside smelled of pot and sweat and then the other stink, the one that caught in your throat and haunted you for days.

The weather hadn't been too hot now they were into September, but the windows were closed. The heating was turned on. Someone had managed to bypass the meter. The room was already filling with flies and the air was thick with the stench of death. Stella covered her mouth, partly to minimize the smell but also because her breakfast was threatening to do the unforgiveable and contaminate the crime scene.

She swallowed hard and peered into the dingy little space. There were old blankets, sleeping bags, and a few discarded clothes in heaps on the grubby flowered carpet. In the middle of the mess lay the body of a young man. His dark hair was short and shaved at the sides. He had probably been good-looking before someone had beaten him, bruising his face, breaking his nose, and then eventually finishing things with a chef's knife. The black handle still protruded from his flat belly.

Stella heard the arrival of the CSI team. She needed to get out of the way. With a final glance at the brutalized body, she left and went to join the officer who was guarding the door.

"That's pretty messy," he said.

"Aye, it is."

"Another low life stabbed in a drugged-up fight, I reckon."

"Hmm. Maybe," Stella said. "Who called it in?"

"A Mrs Kenny. Her lad was with some others. They noticed the house was empty and went peering through windows, not very nice for them but we've got a family support officer with them. They were here when I got here and to be honest, they struck me as more excited than shocked."

"I'll need to go and have a word. Can I take the address?"

She stayed for a couple of minutes until the medical examiner arrived, confirmed death and pretty much told her to go away and leave him to do his job.

"Any idea how long he's been here?" she asked

"I'll send you a report," James Jasper told her.

"Okay. Will you be doing the post-mortem exam?"

"Yeah, probably. Won't be today. Might be tomorrow. I'll let you know. Who are you?"

"DS Stella May."

"Right, DS Stella May, I'll send a message, but you might as well bugger off now. Leave us to get on with our jobs."

"Okay, I'll just go then, shall I?"

As she left, she ran through the things she needed to do. First of all, identify him. Make the dead call if he was local. She'd done them before when she was in uniform. Horrible experience but she'd cope. Then it was the three amigos: motive, means and opportunity. Actually, the means were obvious so that was one partly ticked off. The knife was evidence, however, they still had to trace where it came from. Motive. Could be drugs, could be something else entirely. The main thing was to keep an open mind. She took a deep breath. One step at a time.

In a house further down the street, three boys were squashed together on a settee. Two of them were overexcited, giggling and jostling. The other, the smaller one, sniffed constantly. There were dirty tear streaks marking his face.

Stella sat on the chair next to him.

"Hello. I'm sorry you're upset. What's your name?"

"George Kenny. That was a dead body, wasn't it? Will it be a ghost and come and haunt me?"

"No. Okay, George, I'm Stella May. I've got to find out what happened. I don't think there are such things as ghosts and anyway, he should be glad you found him. Now we can work out what happened. So, I don't reckon he would haunt you, not at all. Will you tell me what you did today?"

The boy nodded.

"I reckon you other lads should go with this lady." Stella indicated the support officer. "Maybe there's some juice in the kitchen and we can talk to you one at a time."

The other two had stopped pushing and shoving at each other and they stood now and went quietly into the kitchen.

"There's Coke in the fridge. They can have that." The woman positioned in front of the fireplace yelled after them.

"Can I have some?" George asked, glancing at his mother who was standing with her arms crossed and shoulders hunched, watching them.

She nodded at him and hissed breath in through her teeth. "You can when she's done with you." She cocked her head towards Stella. "I don't see why you should really. You never do what you're told. I said you should keep away from that shithole. Wait till your dad gets home. Bringing effin bizzies round here."

"Sorry, Mrs Kenny. I'll try not to be too long," Stella said.

It would be so much easier without the interference, but the child had to have a responsible adult there and bringing someone else in would take hours and antagonize the family.

Mrs Kenny sighed and slumped down into the other easy chair.

"Right, go on, George," Stella said.

"There's usually a load of people there, some real divvies, and scrubbers, prozzies, Stu says."

"George, I'll wash your dirty mouth out," Mrs Kenny snarled.

Stella glared at her. "Go on, George."

"There was none there this morning. Stu said we should go and see if we could get in. It wasn't my idea. I would never, so don't listen to him if he says it was me, he's a bloody liar."

"George!" This again from the mother.

"Well, he did, Mam, it wasn't me."

Stella sighed and rubbed a hand over her eyes. "Mrs Kenny, if we don't get this from the boys now, I think we might have to have you all come to the station and that'd be such a pain, wouldn't it?"

"George, tell her what she wants to know."

"George, carry on… please," Stella said.

"We just went to see what was happenin', we wasn't going to do nothin'. Not any damage, like. We just wanted to see. There are some crates at the side and we climbed on them and looked through the window. That's when we saw the dead bloke. We didn't know he was dead. But he was just lying still, like, not moving. Then Stu banged on the window, and he still didn't move and then he saw the blood, Stu did, and said we'd get the blame. We were scared so we came back here and told Mam."

Stella turned to the woman in the chair. "Did you go down there, Mrs Kenny?"

"Of course I did. I wasn't going to listen to these little sods and start an almighty hue and cry on their say-so. I've told 'em." She turned to the boy. "How many times have I said, don't go down there? Trails of women in and out, homeless, druggies, God knows what. It was horrible, what I saw. Horrible. Will I be able to get compensation? I might need therapy."

"Have a word with Constable Jackson, the support officer. She'll be able to help you."

Jesus, this was hard work.

"Anyway, George, is that all? You didn't go into the house or tell anyone else about it or see anyone there?"

The boy shook his head.

"Okay, we'll need to talk to the others. It's not because I don't believe you, it's because we need to make sure it's all written down from everyone. I'll get another police officer to come and do that, but you've been a real help. Afterwards you need to just try and forget about it if you can. It's horrible but we'll take care of everything now."

* * *

DI Dunn was waiting for her. He had his coat on and his briefcase was on the chair. "Right, quick rundown and then I'm off. It's been a swine of a day and I need a drink."

She told him the little she could. "A murder then, boss. A major case?" She couldn't quite keep the note of hope out of her voice.

"Don't get ahead of yourself. Chances are this is some sort of drug feud. It'll be connected to the debacle of earlier so when we've caught these pimps and dealers, we'll have the killer. One thing'll lead to the next. I can't see the DCI approving the funding for a specific enquiry. Not with what just happened. Anyway, when they get him out, might be tomorrow, but whenever, you can go to the post-mortem and write up a report. We'll do what's necessary but don't get yourself in a tizzy about major cases. This is all going to turn out to be the same thing. Come on, we might as well go. This takes us back to the beginning. If I find out who let them know we were coming, I'll throw the effing book at them. That DI from St Anne Street is coming in tomorrow. I'd rather have a root canal treatment.

"You can have a small task force," he continued. "As you know I have four more ongoing investigations, so you can have a detective constable and a couple of civilian clerks, and you report direct to me. Find out who he was

and what he was up to and what his link was to he other
lot. Westvale isn't very big, there has to be a cc nection.
You might as well get off home and come back in
tomorrow early. I want these lowlifes; I will have lem. So,
Stel, bring me something I can use. Soon as, yeah '

Chapter 8

She'd got her own investigation. She'd got a tear . Bloody
hell.

As she drove home through the early evenir crowds
Stella knew she was grinning. She couldn't help t. It was
wrong. Someone was dead. *But bloody hell, though!*

Parked cars lined the kerbs all the way along he road.
She glanced at the clock on her phone. It was wel past five
so, if he was on days, Keith from the flat upsta s would
already have taken the one space in the drive. Sh glanced
in as she passed and there was his clapped-out lini. She
carried on past vans and cars, and a great bi camper
taking up four spaces.

When she'd moved to Aintree her mother ha thought
it was 'out in the country'. After all it wa by the
racecourse. She'd been impressed with the flat. It ad a bay
window, a good-sized living room and even decent
kitchen. Next door was a doctor's surgery and tl cul-de-
sac ended at a hedge with the railway embankmei beyond
with some trees and shrubs greening up the p ce. 'Get
you,' Mam had said.

It didn't feel like 'out' of anywhere now. It was just
tarmac and bricks and cars. As she was about t try and
turn at the end of the road a white van which ad been
parked outside the house at the bottom indic ed. She
flashed her lights. Yes – result.

Mam was from Bootle. Now she lived in Kirkby, and it was okay. But she'd move back to the old streets if she could. She'd never be able to afford it, though. The council had moved her and even when Maggie Thatcher turned renting on its head Mam hadn't had the money to buy her place. She worried that now the family had grown up, they'd move her to a flat. But then Stella's brother had moved his girlfriend and baby in, taking up two of the spare bedrooms. They were getting away with it at the moment. Keeping their heads down.

She locked the car and walked the couple of metres down the road. Light shone through the bay window. Stella glanced at her watch. The timer wasn't supposed to come on for another hour. She sighed. Mam must be there. She'd struggled with the idea of giving her mother a spare key to hold. In the end she'd seen it made sense. In fairness she didn't often come round when she knew Stella wasn't at home. But she was here today. Oh well, it was okay, she could share her good news and they'd have a drink. She'd have to make it clear though that there was work to be done. It couldn't turn into a session, and she wasn't making the dinner.

She dumped her bags in the hall and called through to the living room. "Hiya, Mam. With you in a mo. I'm just going to get changed. I stink a bit." She knew she probably didn't but the smell from earlier was still in her nostrils. She needed a squirt of body spray. Really, she needed a shower, but it could wait until she was on her own. It would be a good idea to keep some perfume or something in her desk. In the bedroom she slipped a spare bottle into her bag ready for tomorrow.

Her mother tapped on the door. "Where've you been?"

"How d'ya mean? I've been at work."

"I thought you'd have been skiving off today."

"Why would I do that? Anyway, listen, I've got really brilliant news."

"Yeah, that's why I've come round. Now, I haven't told anybody. I promised I wouldn't, but I've been so excited all day."

For a moment Stella was puzzled. Then it came back. The lottery. Unbelievably she had forgotten all about it. It had filled her mind first thing but once she was plunged into the work stuff it had gone completely. Yet, here was her mum practically shaking with excitement. The air went out of her bubble. She had been dying to talk about the case, her team and now... For a moment, she thought she'd just give the ticket to her mum and let her have the money. It wouldn't do though. She'd in turn probably give it all to Peter and his girl and he'd buy a daft car, go on flash holidays, or something. Waste it and leave Liam with nothing.

She smiled. "Come on. This needs a glass of wine, eh?"

Chapter 9

It had turned into a session after all. Mam had been so wound up that she just couldn't understand Stella's stance. She couldn't grasp the misgivings.

"But, our Stel, of course you wouldn't change. You're lovely, you are. Why would you change? You're not going to suddenly turn into some sort of Lady Muck. I know you, queen."

"It's not that, Mam. It's other people."

"Oh come on, your mates would still be your mates, love. Okay, some of 'em might be a bit jealous but in that case they're not proper friends anyway. It wouldn't make any difference to family. Your dad would just be your dad, and granda – well, he wouldn't care at all. He thinks you can't do no wrong, no matter what. Okay, our Peter might be a bit envious, I'll give you that. But..." Here she had paused. "You'd treat him, though, wouldn't you? Give him something. Him with the baby and everything?"

Stella's heart sank. She would want to look after the family, but it would mean telling people and they wouldn't be able to keep it to themselves and soon everyone would know.

"It's not really all that much, Mam. I mean, yes, of course it's a lot, but with the cost of things now and well, it's just not so much."

"It's loads. It's millions, got to be."

"Well, I know. But, okay, think of it like this. How much is a house, just an ordinary sort of a house? Then a car, a medium-sized car."

"Yes, okay, I see what you're saying. But so what? Enjoy it. I don't know why you're not jumping up and down with excitement."

"I know I'm going to sound like a daft mare. I know you'll think so. But I'm not sure I want this. I'm not sure I want my life to change. I love what I'm doing. I love my job and everything. I wonder how people at work would treat me. They can be a bit brutal, you know? They have your back, but they are pretty harsh if anyone steps out of line. I feel a bit out of my depth just thinking about it. On top of that..." Then she told her mum as much about the case as she was able to without breaking any rules.

"I'm thrilled for you. I can see you're happy. But..." She gave an exaggerated shudder. "It's not nice. And it's dangerous, isn't it? You know I've tried to keep out of things. I've never interfered, have I?"

"No, Mam, you've been dead good. And honestly you shouldn't worry. It's not really dangerous. Okay, there are some nasty people involved but it's a big team. I'm not on my own and I'm just trying to find out who this person is and what happened. It's not much more than research. Anyway, what about when I was on the beat, walking about in the dark?"

"Yes, but it was different, wasn't it? I mean that was helping lost kiddies and telling people directions. I know there was some scallies, but they were just lads, weren't they? Misbehaving, skiving off, nicking pick 'n' mix."

Stella's mother really had no idea about the spaced-out, demented druggies, the knife gangs, the thugs shoplifting and throwing bottles. But then what was the point of telling her? She wasn't stupid but if this was the way she was handling the worry for her youngest child, so be it.

"Honest, Mam, there's nothing to worry about."

"Okay, if you say so. But look, what about the money? You have to have it. You could buy a nicer place." Here her mother glanced around the flat. It was cosy in the evening light. The table lamps had come on and Stella had switched off the harsher centre light.

"I thought you liked my flat?"

"I do, course I do. But just think, you could get something really posh."

Stella shook her head. "That's it, you see. It's not me. I'm not posh. I don't want to live with snooty people. I wouldn't feel comfortable. I just want to stay as I am."

"Well, alright then. Stay as you are and put the money in the bank. You never know what's going to happen, do you? There might come a time when you really need some money, and you'd have it," her mother said.

"And you promise you won't tell anyone?"

"No, I won't. Not if you don't want me to."

And that was how they left it.

* * *

When her mother had gone Stella logged onto the computer, opened the files, and started her notes. By two o'clock she was seeing double. But she'd got a good start. Everything she thought was relevant was noted and she'd planned the tasks for her 'team' in the morning. She emailed DC Rupert Moon – Jesus, what sort of a parent called their kid Rupert? – and told him to meet her at the squat early. Then they would go to the post-mortem exam. She hated them but it had to be done. She put a packet of extra strong mints in her bag.

Chapter 10

The tape on the fence and gate fluttered in the chilly breeze. A small group of young kids on scooters hung around, leaning against the garden wall. The uniformed constable on the door ignored them.

"Shouldn't you be in school?" Rupert said.

"Half term," one of them answered.

"Bloody isn't."

"Hey, you swore at me. I'm traumerred. I'm going to tell my da. He'll sue."

"Do me a favour. Anyway, get lost, there's nothing for you to see here. Nothing's going to happen."

"Is it true about that dead bloke in there, though? Was his head cut off and his guts hanging out?"

Stella signed the sheet on the clipboard and passed through the gate. She turned. "No, it's not. I wonder where you heard that. What do you reckon, DC Moon? Do you think they know something we don't? Do you think we should take them down the station?"

"Could be, boss."

As one, the little gang turned and scooted away up the street, a couple of them turning to give Stella the finger.

"Little sods," she said, "mind you, we will have to have a word with the neighbours. That's going to be one of the first tasks and I reckon we'll be pretty much on our own with it."

"Why's that? Surely, we'll have some help. It's a murder enquiry after all."

"Yes, but don't get your hopes up. I've been pretty much told to get on with identifying him just so we can show we tried. The DI has already decided it was a drugs thing and when he sweeps up the gang we missed the other day, he'll have his killer. Fair enough, to be honest, that's probably what it's going to be, but let's just do the best we can for the bloke. He's lost his life too soon, after all. Okay, maybe he has made some bad choices and mixed with the wrong people, but an unlawful killing is still wrong no matter what."

* * *

Dr Jasper was late. His assistant didn't seem fazed by it at all, he simply shrugged. "He'll be here in a bit. Well, the patient isn't going anywhere."

"No, true," Stella said. "But we have stuff to do. Do you think we should come back later?"

"Up to you. I'd hang on, to be honest. He'll not be long. I think he's been lecturing, and he gets involved, you know."

So, they waited. Stella made some notes on her tablet, recording the morning's events.

They'd been allowed into the squat. "Keep to the safe route and don't touch anything without asking first," the crime scene manager had warned. It was quiet in the filthy house. White-suited figures shuffled around picking bits from the carpet and measuring bloodstains. There were crates stuffed with evidence bags, labelled, and sealed. Little plastic tents with numbers on them littered the floor. They stepped carefully on the metal plates laid across the carpet.

The sergeant in charge of the SOC team didn't give them much attention. "There'll be a report. Nothing much to say right now. Body in the middle of the floor. Blood everywhere. Assorted belongings in every room but nothing really personal. The rooms upstairs were bedrooms. Girls in one of them by the look of it. It's the cleanest but they'd taken all their stuff with them. It was only the hair, some scrunchies, a bottle of nail varnish, empty wine bottles and the smell of body spray and hair product that made it obvious what the room had been used for. Six narrow mattresses on the floor. No bedding. I suppose they need it for wherever else they've gone. You can go and have a look if you like. But I thought you were more interested in the dead guy."

They went to look anyway. It didn't tell them much, but Stella took pictures with her phone. What had happened in the house would slowly be revealed. There was nothing yet to give them much help.

"Come on, Rupert, we need to get off to the hospital for the post. By the way, what would you prefer to be called?"

"Yeah, Rupert's fine."

"Okay. So, you don't use anything else. You know, a nickname, something like that?"

"No, not really. Well, at school they tried, but the options are a bit naff aren't they. Roop, for example. Never really accepted that."

She wanted to ask. What was it that had possessed his mum, was she a fan of the little bear, did she think it was upper class? Was she just really rather stupid or actually cruel? Maybe she hadn't wanted a baby.

Chapter 11

Stella knocked on the office door. She could see DI Dunn inside; DI Carr sat in one of the visitors' chairs, his long legs stretched across in front of the desk.

They glanced up and Dunn raised a hand. "Come in."

There were coffee cups and a pot on the table. She wasn't offered a drink.

It was mid-afternoon. She had sent Rupert into their corner of the open plan office with instructions to update the one whiteboard they'd been allocated. "Write small," she'd said. "From what we've just heard I reckon we might need space."

"Now, Stella. What can I do for you?" Dunn said.

"Just been to the hospital, boss. The post-mortem on the body from the squat."

"Yep. Who did that one?"

"Dr Jasper."

"Ha, was he late?"

"He was."

"Did he shout at the assistant for not having everything ready even though it all was?"

"Yeah."

Dunn grinned at the other man. "Have you worked with him?"

Carr shook his head.

"Oh right, well, most of us have had run-ins with him. It's good to see nothing changes. Right, any surprises, Stel?"

"Well, yes." Stella glanced at Carr.

"DI Carr is going to be involved with our case. As I've already told you we think there is a link with the drugs raid. Well, there has to be."

Dunn glanced at the other senior man, but Carr didn't respond. He was watching Stella, waiting to hear what she had to say.

"Go on," Dunn said.

"Okay, the bloods and fluids have gone off for screening, of course, and it'll be a while before it all comes back. The weapon is being examined by the lab. They'll need a while longer to check for DNA, but they said, given the situation, it could be covered in stuff or clean as a whistle. It all depends on whether or not this was preplanned or whoever did it knew how to clear the scene. The knife could have been brought to the squat or it could have already been there, in which case it'll be useless given the number of people in and out. However, the body – male, age early twenties – he was fit."

She pulled out her notebook and held it up. Dunn waved a permissive hand.

"The deceased was a white male, aged between twenty-five and thirty years," she read. "Muscle tone is good, he appears very healthy. No sign of disease, no obvious sign of drug use or excessive alcohol consumption. The last meal was chicken, salad, and some fruit. Evidence of a broken arm at some stage during childhood, well healed. Fingernails recently manicured, some skin residue removed and sent for DNA testing. The cause of death was the knife wound which hit the aorta. Dr Jasper said he would have died quickly and it'd been just unlucky, sorry, sir, I'm quoting. A slightly different angle and he could well have survived it."

Dunn looked at her, his head tipped to one side. "Hmm, not quite what you'd expect, eh?" Again, he addressed his comments to Jordan Carr who nodded this time.

Stella glanced back and forth between them. She spoke quietly. "Well, it doesn't look like it. Not a lowlife druggy at all. Clean, healthy, and well turned out, except for the chef's knife to the belly. There is another thing."

Carr spoke for the first time. "Carry on, Sergeant."

"Bruising to his knuckles. Probably caused immediately before or during the killing. The full report will explain it all, but it seems there was a punch-up before the stabbing or at least he fought back at some stage."

Carr spoke again. "What are your first thoughts?"

Stella turned to speak directly to him. "A bit muddled, to be honest. I just don't think he was part of the drug gang. I know whenever we net the big fish they're usually fit and well and living the high life on the misery of other people. But this bloke was quite young. So, may e he had connections, otherwise you'd expect him to be a oldier at the most. A mule even or simply an addict ru ning for them and being paid in stuff. But he was not ike that, not at all." She hesitated. "If I can…"

Carr nodded.

"It was a different address, so it's always po ible the two things are not as closely related as we recko ed," she said.

"Okay, so it looks as though you might have a harder job than we thought. What are your next steps?" arr said.

"I would like to do some posters, maybe pu it in the papers, a media appeal. House-to-house, o course. Anything that helps to identify him."

Dunn cleared his throat, taking control of the conversation again. "I'm not sure, Stel. Bear w h us on this. Just keep it a bit low key. We need to know ho he is, so keep on with that. Try the misper reports internet images, stuff like that. Leave the rest of it wi us for now."

"Okay, boss. If you think it's best."

"I know it's a pain, but we need to control the arrative on this. Drive the situation ourselves."

"Though I'm sure DI Dunn is making a go d point, Stella," Carr said, "try to keep an open mind. Tha 's always good. If you don't mind, I'd like to keep a watc ng brief here. Keep me informed. Keep me up to date ith your enquiries and if you need any input from us at St Anne Street, don't hesitate to ask. Is this all okay with y ı, Ian?"

Dunn had no choice but to agree. His smile ooked a little forced, but he nodded. "Of course, the ore the merrier and what have you."

* * *

Stella picked up a couple of drinks from the machine on the way back to the open plan office.

"Here, this said it was coffee, but I don't think I believe it. I won't be held responsible if it's soup or something."

"Cheers. So, what are we doing?" Rupert asked.

"We're controlling the narrative and sitting in the driving seat."

"Right."

"But the bloke from Serious and Organised, the new one, is showing an interest. Shit, we've got to get this right now, Rupert."

Chapter 12

Stella and Rupert were still at their desks long after shift change. They were scanning CCTV from nearby shops and traffic cams. No help. Scanning missing persons lists and internet appeals. No help.

Stella pushed back from the desk and eased her shoulders. "Ideas, Rupert?"

The DC scratched his head, ginger curls twining round his fingers. "Are we not doing a house-to-house?"

She screwed up her face for a second. "We're going to have to, aren't we?" She hadn't told him the details about her conversation in Dunn's office. In truth, she felt she had been handed a paperwork exercise and wasn't ready to let her DC know. "A lot of effort is still going into the 'not a drugs bust' drugs bust. I have the impression the brass are still trying to find a way to spin this so they don't take any blame. Everything's just a bit tense right now."

"What actually went wrong? Do we know?"

"I don't know much more than you. The up-to-date info was that the place was operating and then suddenly – zilch. They're being really tight-lipped about it all. That DI from Serious and Organised wasn't a happy camper and

Dunn had a face like a slapped arse so I'll be honest with you, I think they're working on the assumption that the problem could be here."

"Jesus. That's grim," Rupert said.

"It is but whatever happened, they knew we were coming, and they cleared out. All we can do is keep our heads down and work on this latest thing. I'd hate to think somebody here has cocked up, but it'll all come out in the wash."

"So, about this bloke. Our dead body. What's your honest feeling? Is he mixed up in it and the two buildings are being used by the same gang?" Rupert said.

"I reckon that's the thinking. But I'm not totally convinced. Not at all. He doesn't strike me as the sort of person to be mixed up with these bottom feeders."

"Maybe it's a whole different deal. What about the bedroom upstairs, the girls' one? What's that all about? If it was a brothel, it was a pretty grotty one. Someone like him, even if he was paying for it, you'd think he could do better than going there. Course, he could have followed one of the women home. Maybe had a session in his car and then followed her."

"No, I don't think that works. Have a look at the forensics. Where was he before that? Where did he have the fight? All the evidence suggests he was killed there in the squat. But how did he get there?"

Stella leaned forward and switched off her computer. "We should call it a day and then tomorrow we – all of us, the civilian clerks as well – just go through the CCTV again. I reckon we go back to the beginning. Assume he is nothing to do with the drugs bust and approach it as a completely separate case. Only…" She paused. "I don't think DI Dunn wants us to do that exactly, so…'

Rupert nodded. "Keep schtum as much as possible. I have to say I agree. It seems they are all so focussed on the other case they can't move away from it."

"Could backfire on us, though."

"Well, not really. If it is tied in with the other gang and we work it out, feather in our caps, innit. If it's not and we solve it, more feathers."

"How did he get to the house? Did he drive? If so, where is his car? Once we see how he arrived, then we can backtrack and find out where he was. I'm seeing double now, though. I need some kip. Tomorrow, Rupert."

Jeez, she wished he had a nickname.

* * *

There was no space for parking and Stella's car had to be left two streets away. It was quiet and dark. A drizzly rain was blown by a cold wind. She shivered scurrying through the deserted streets. A car pulled up alongside, crawling along the kerb. The three blokes inside peered at her through the glass. She turned to stare back at them. The one in the rear began to open his window. Stella reached into her bag and pulled out her warrant card and can of pepper spray. She stopped and turned directly towards them. She held up her ID and they gave up on any plan that had been forming. Flicking a V-sign at her, the back-seat passenger tossed out a half-empty lager can. The froth splashed across the pavement, and she jumped back before it hit her legs. She took out her phone and reported the incident to traffic. She grinned as the sound of a siren started up in the main road. Well, that was lucky.

She wasn't bothered about what might happen to the three numpties in the car. They had booze on board, maybe something else. Being stopped would piss them off. If necessary, she'd file a complaint, but it probably wouldn't go far. Still, maybe it would make them think twice before bothering a lone woman again. It was only one incident, though. One out of thousands and if she had been just a girl coming home from a mate's house, or from a late shift at the hospital, how scary would that have been?

She could move from this area. The money was there if she wanted it. More than enough for her to buy a flat at one of the new developments in the city. Somewhere out in the country, Aughton, Aigburth – whatever. Okay, it might make her safer, maybe. Great. But it wouldn't help all the other women. Anyway, she meant what she had said to her mother. She wanted to live where she felt she belonged. She didn't belong in Aughton with the riding and dog walking set; she belonged here, in the middle of things. She turned into her road. The lights were on in most of the houses. She could hear the sound of televisions drifting from the windows. It was home. She opened the front door and the smell of Keith's takeaway curry hit her full in the nose. She wondered if it would be possible to buy him out. She could have the whole house. A whole house and no curry stink. Hmm. A thought.

Chapter 13

Before she left home, Stella took the book from the bookshelf and shook out the lottery ticket. She laid it on the table beside her plate of toast. Once she made the phone call, that would be it. Life would change. Iam was wrong. She wouldn't be able to put it in the bank and carry on. She knew that. Look at last night. Twice, once after the confrontation with the prats in the car and then again when she walked into the fug of curry, her thoughts immediately went to changes she could make with the money.

So, she could throw the thing away, now, this morning. Or she could just get on with it and deal with whatever happened. *For God's sake, you moron. You've won the lottery. Grab it, grab it and change things.*

She made the phone call. They wanted to arrange for someone to come and see her. She told them she was too busy, and she'd get in touch when she had time. Strangely they didn't seem all that fazed. Then again, she probably wasn't the first to have doubts. No-one was unique. She should know that.

Driving to work in her ten-year-old clunker she thought about shiny new cars. Did she need one? Well, actually, yes, she probably did. This one had three owners before she bought it from a mate of her brother's. It was held together by rust and wishful thinking. Every time she left it for the MOT, she prepared herself for a call saying it had failed. Okay, so one thing that made sense. A new car. Probably a new new car, not one of Pete's mate's dodgy bangers. She could get an electric one or a hybrid. That way she could explain the extravagance. Protecting the environment. By the time she pulled into the car park she was quite excited about the idea. She filed it away for later. She didn't know how long it would be until she had her hands on the cash and there was no time right now for car shopping.

DC Moon was already in the office. A bottle of water, half empty on the desk, and an energy bar seemed to be breakfast.

"Do you want coffee, Rupert? I'm going down to the canteen for it. Shall I grab you some toast or…"

"No, you're alright. I've had this." He waved the biscuit at her.

Stella pushed the guilt back down where it belonged and went to find bacon and bread and caffeine. She patted her belly as she walked down the corridor. Flat and firm. There might come a time when she couldn't get away with comfort food but not yet. Not for a while anyway.

He was fit-looking, Rupert. Once you got past the fact he looked about twelve, and most of that was probably down to the freckles, he was actually built. He had the confident movement of someone who knew just what their body was doing. She must ask if he worked out, was keen on the whole health kick, or maybe he actually enjoyed eating nuts stuck together with dates or whatever. She ordered her coffee and see-sawed for a minute. She could just have a fat-free muffin. She shook her head. Nah. Anyway, there were seeds in the bap, and tomato sauce was good for you, wasn't it?

Chapter 14

"I was back at Kirkby yesterday." Jordan Carr was in the canteen with Dave Griffiths; they were eating eggs on toast.

"Right – and?"

"Far too early to say anything. I just had a word with DI Dunn, and he seemed to be as brassed off as us. I've requisitioned his files. Wasn't totally happy about it but he didn't actually object. I think he was more insured than worried. Anyway, I reckon I need to get to know a few of the people there a bit and as it turns out there may be a way in."

"Go on?"

"They picked up an unlawful killing yesterday. It's really near to where the raid was. Dunn reckons it's connected. He's put a young DS in charge and basically told her just to do the minimum until we can link the two cases. It could be he genuinely thinks that's the right way to go. Or…"

"Or it could be more sinister, and he doesn't want anyone digging too much."

"I think it's early to be making any judgement but I've asked to be kept informed and I thought I might keep in close contact with this Sergeant May."

"I don't want to put you in there. It would look bad on your record."

"That's thoughtful of you, Dave. I appreciate it."

"I recommended you come here because I believed you'd be a great asset. You weren't going to get very far working under Cross at Wavertree and we both knew that. This glitch is not your fault, it was just bad luck. So, can you work from here and keep an eye on Kirkby and this murder?"

"I'm sure I can. It might mean I'm there quite a bit, that's all."

"Fine by me."

Chapter 15

Back in the incident room the team were all together. The two civilians were women. One was young, about twenty, her badge read Melanie. Bright-eyed and blond-haired, she beamed at Stella as she joined them in their corner. The other was middle-aged, slim going on skinny, with short brown flecked grey hair. She gave a short nod but didn't bother to hide the expression of boredom. Probably miffed at being allocated to a secondary case when the place was buzzing about the drugs.

Jordan walked in and glanced around. Stella's stomach flipped as the hum of conversation quieted and he smiled at her from the doorway and raised his hand.

"Carry on, Sergeant. Okay if I just sit in?" He pulled up a spare chair and sat down tucking his long legs out of the way under the desk.

"Yes, sir. Of course. We're just getting started. Not been together very long, need to sort of, erm…" She knew she was gabbling.

"Yep. Great stuff," Jordan said.

Stella took a breath. "Okay. Our main aim right now is to identify this person and find out why he was here. It's been assumed it was the drug gang who are behind his death. Let's keep an open mind until we know for sure. We need to find out who he is and why he's dead. Once we know that, we'll find out who did it."

"And why nobody made any attempt to hide it." This from the blonde.

"Good point, Melanie. Yes, very good point."

"Thanks. Call me Mel if you like."

Stella nodded. She moved to the whiteboard and listed the questions then turned back to the others and waited for them to speak.

There was silence. "So, any more thoughts? Just anything that occurs to you, really?"

There was nothing. She looked in desperation at Rupert.

"Well, boss, we know he wasn't an addict."

Boss, he called her boss.

Stella bit back the grin. "We think that's the case. We haven't had the reports back from the lab. Ruth" – she turned to the older woman – "could you chase those up this morning?"

She was rewarded with a brief nod.

It was slow and awkward. This wasn't as easy as it looked. "Okay. Apart from the lab results, which will just help to fill in the gaps, everything we discover helps us to identify this bloke. Until we've done that, we can't even begin to work out the motive. So, I'm afraid it's CCTV this morning. Starting from – I'd say Sunday – we need to go through it all. DC Moon and I have already viewed it but haven't seen him arrive. Quite frankly we must have missed it."

"What about Facebook, Instagram and whatnot?" Mel asked.

"Yeah, I know what you mean but where do we start? If we could use facial recognition, it'd be brilliant but…" She shrugged. "It'll come, I'm sure. But it's a bit of a minefield at the moment. Anyway, that's irrelevant. Is there any way you think the social media sites could help?"

"Well, he seems to have been a bit posh. Doesn't the report say he's had a manicure? None of my mates have manicures. So, perhaps look into things like *Lancashire Life* and what have you. You know, the swanky parties and balls and so on."

"Waste of time, just an excuse to trawl the internet." This from Ruth soured the atmosphere and wiped the enthusiasm from Mel's face.

Stella floundered; how was she supposed to handle this?

"Well, I think anything is worth looking into. There's the evidence of the fight as well," Stella said. "That could be important."

Ruth sighed loudly, pushed back her chair, and stalked over to the desk where her handbag had been waiting, claiming the space. Stella glanced at Rupert who raised his eyebrows and pursed his lips.

Personnel issues, this was something new. Stella smiled at Mel who was collecting her backpack. She had to get this right straight away, a team was only a team when they played nice.

"Well done, Stella. You handled them really well. It takes a while to start working together properly but you'll get there," Jordan said.

"Thank you, sir."

"Call me Jordan. Right. I'll get out of your hair. I'm off to have a chat with your DI. Keep me updated."

Chapter 16

"Everything okay, there, Ruth?" Stella had joined the civilian at her desk. She offered her a bottle of water, but the other woman shook her head.

"Yes, fine thanks. I suppose I'll just get on with this. Any idea where we should begin viewing from, and exactly what we are hoping to see? Or is that going to be just left up to us as well?"

Okay. There was a criticism. This woman had been around for ages and obviously wasn't too chuffed at being seconded to a team led by a wet-behind-the ears DS. Fortunately, Stella had pored over the plans, the Google maps, and the images.

"CSI are still processing the place, but they are now in the rooms which were empty upstairs. So, we need to look for people on foot moving from parked cars in the streets around. There is a school across the corner from the squat. They have cameras – traffic ones for parking problems and then others for pedestrians in the grounds. That would be a start. There are flats opposite the house, and they have some because they've had problems with graffiti on the walls, I'd suggest they'd be other ones to look at. Why don't you give it a while and then we could go down and grab a coffee?"

"No, thanks. I bring a flask in with me. I don't like stuff from the machine and the canteen isn't clean." Ruth turned away and logged onto her machine.

"Okay. Well, good luck then." Stella walked away, tail well and truly between her legs.

It really was groping in the dark, she knew. But there wasn't any other way to tackle this. She didn't want to ask for help, not yet. DI Carr seemed lovely but it was up to her to impress him, if she could.

They stuck at it for a few hours. It wasn't possible to go much longer without a break because concentrating on nothing happening for a long time was soporific and very boring. Towards the end of the morning she popped out to the shops and came back with chocolate biscuits. She made sure they had drinks. Ruth took the water without comment but now the empty bottle was in the recycling bin. It was like befriending an angry puppy. She'd made a step forward.

"We'll grab a bite, Rupert, and then I reckon we can go back and speak to a few of the neighbours. We'll leave it till after four. The kids will be out of school then, so some of the parents and carers will be around, I reckon."

The DC nodded. "Can you just have a look at this, boss? It's tricky to see but it's just a bit odd."

"What've you got?" Anything would be welcome right now, even if it was just a car speeding.

She bent over the desk to see the screen as Rupert pointed with the end of his pen. "This is the footage from the school crossing. The one on the same corner as the house. You can just see over the garden fence. To be honest, you're probably not supposed to. People won't leave these things alone and they get shifted about."

They could see the tree in the corner of the space, the top of a ramshackle shed and then the edges of fences and the treetops in the rest of the terrace.

"Okay, watch this. It was in the early hours of Tuesday morning. The time stamp says one-thirty. Look, there behind the tree."

Stella peered at the shadowy movement. "Is that someone climbing over the fence?"

"Yeah. I'm sure it is. The house around the corner has a wide path running down the side which gives access. Unfortunately, the camera doesn't cover that bit. You see three women come down the road and it looks like they may go in the front. There is nobody out the back, it's in darkness. What if the bloke shinned over the back wall?"

"Yeah, but where did he come from?"

Rupert shrugged. "Dunno, boss."

Chapter 17

The crime scene was still taped off. A CSI van was in the parking space. Stella and Rupert signed the sheet, pulled on protective clothing and walked into the hall.

"Where's your boss?" Stella asked the white-suited figure kneeling in front of a cupboard, removing old newspapers, and sliding them into evidence bags.

"Kitchen, I reckon." He or maybe she waved a hand in the direction of the back of the house. Stella stood in the kitchen doorway.

"Sorry." She really must stop apologizing. "Sergeant Flowers?"

A short wiry figure backed out of a pantry. "Yep. That's me."

"DS May. Can I have a word?"

"I'll be sending my report through by about dinner time tomorrow. Apart from the stuff you've already been told, according to my people, there's not much else. The place is dirty, grotty and damp. Only a couple of rooms have been used and not for long, I don't think. No functioning cooker; water's cut off, so they've had to use bottles. I don't recommend you go in the bogs, to be honest."

"Okay, great. Thanks. There is just one thing."

"Oh." He cocked his head to one side, but it was impossible to read his expression behind the mask. His eyes crinkled at the corners; it could be a friendly smile or something else entirely.

"I just wondered if you'd done the back garden?"

"By done, I assume you mean processed?"

"Well, yes."

"Not yet. We didn't think it was a priority, seeing as the body was inside along with all the other evidence. We will, of course. Would have done it already if I had enough staff. Haven't, so didn't." He shrugged.

"Okay. Well, could you look at this?"

She held out her phone and he leaned to peer at it. He held his hands out to the sides and it was obvious he wasn't going to contaminate his gloves if he didn't have to.

"Ah, interesting. Okay. Fortunately, there hasn't been any rain. If there were imprints or anything out there, they should still be there. Stevie, talk to the DS and then go and make a start on outside."

The back end of someone half inside the cupboard under the sink shifted.

"Right, boss. Just about done here." It was a female voice, and the figure emerging was small, slender, feminine even inside all the protective gear. She turned to Stella and nodded. Blue eyes sparkled between the hood and mask. Stevie Rowlands. "You the DS?"

"I am. Can I just show you this?" Again, Stella ran the video.

"Okay. On it." The woman moved smoothly past, stripping off her gloves as she went.

"Thanks so much," Stella said to the back of the DS who had returned to the pantry.

"No probs," Flowers said. "We'll let you know if there's anything."

"Okay. We'll be talking to the neighbours. A bit of a house-to-house. Me and… DC Moon."

"Ha, good luck with that then." He gave a short huff of a laugh and she felt herself dismissed.

They left the house, threw their suits into a box by the door and walked down the path.

"Rupert?"

"Boss."

"Have you worked with DS Flowers before?"

"Once. A case with DI Dunn before he was promoted."

"Was he treated the same way?"

"How do you mean?"

"I dunno. I just have the feeling I'm not being taken seriously."

"No. He's like that with everybody. A bit up imself, I reckon, but he's good at his job."

"Fair enough."

"Of course, everybody knows this is your first case. On your own, like."

"Yeah, but it should make them want to help me."

The young detective turned, looked her in the eye and raised his thin eyebrows.

"Hmm. Okay," she said. "Come on then, let's get on with this. I want you to chase him, though. For the report on the back garden. That's important."

"Yeah, I'll liaise with Stevie." He grinned and walked on.

Chapter 18

They knew there were people in some of the houses. They weren't answering the knock. Curtains shifted, dogs barked, and in one a child was dragged away from the door. They saw through the frosted glass and knocked again. Stella lifted the letter box flap and called out.

"Hello. Police. DS May. We'd like a word."

There was no reaction.

The people who did answer had little to tell them. They'd seen and heard nothing. They thought the house at the end was empty and, *'wasn't it time the council did something about the state of it, anyway?'*

It was tempting to throw in the towel. They split up to get the depressing work over more quickly. Stella reached the end of the row and pretty much decided it was a lost cause. She opened a wooden gate held on by one hinge and a piece of rope. The path was swept but the garden was weedy and neglected. Neat net curtains covered the windows. The frames were rotting and the paint on the front door had lost its gloss. The doorbell didn't work and there was no knocker. She banged with the side of her fist on the wood.

The door opened but only to the width allowed by a security chain. A wrinkled face surrounded by a fuzz of grey hair filled the space. Sharp grey eyes peered through the gap. Stella held up her warrant card and introduced herself.

"Sorry to bother you. I wondered if I could have a word about the house at the end there. The one on the corner."

"Aye, the one with the dead bloke inside."

Of course, everyone knew. "That's right."

"Just a minute."

The door closed and there was the rattle of metal and then it was pulled back. The woman was tiny, dressed in a pair of baggy, black sweatpants and a striped sweater, tartan slippers on her feet.

"Come on then." She turned and walked down the narrow hallway leaving Stella to enter and close the door behind her.

There was the faint odour of something floral in the background. The sitting room was bright and tidy, no sign of the dust and neglect which was so often the case in houses belonging to old people. A three-piece suite covered in red fabric was positioned around a heavy-looking wooden coffee table with just one large candle in a saucer on it. Apart from that, the only other furniture was a bookshelf built into the alcove beside the chimney breast. It was stuffed with books, which overflowed onto the carpet. They were mostly hard-backed and some of them were very thick. Stella tried to read the titles but she was too far away. Any idea they were just for show or left over from when younger people lived in the house was scotched when she noticed a couple on the floor beside the chair nearest to the fire. One was open and the other had slips of paper serving as bookmarks.

Stella held out her warrant card again. "DS Stella May."

"Aye, you said."

"We're investigating a major crime. You've obviously heard about it?"

"Don't hear much of anything these days. But the window cleaner was blathering on about it. All conjecture and hearsay."

This woman didn't sound like a Scouser. There was no discernible accent apart from a definite Northern twang.

"Right. Well, we're just trying to find out if anyone saw anything. Tuesday night or maybe very early Wednesday morning. Or if they know anything about what was going on in that house."

"He came over the back fence. Came down Mrs Roberts' side passageway and climbed up. You'll find his footprints in the flower border, such as it is. He was angry."

"You saw him?"

"Don't sleep much anymore. I sit by the window and watch. Cats are out. Now and then there's a fox, not often."

"And when you saw this man, was he on his own?"

"Yes, leastways he came on his own. There were people in the house, some in the front garden, I could hear them."

"You could hear them? It's quite a long way away."

"All you need to do is listen. People don't listen."

"Is there anything else you can tell me that might be helpful?"

"He didn't want to be there. He was angry but he had no choice. The one who came after him. That's the one you should be looking for."

"How do you mean?"

"There was another one. After him. Look for him."

This was getting a bit weird now and Stella thought it was probably time to call an end to it. She had a little bit more information, but it only served to confirm what they already knew. The old woman was probably enjoying the attention and wanting to keep her talking, but it was time to leave. She stood and gathered her things together.

"Your nana is happy about the money."

"What?" Stella stared into the wrinkled old face.

"She knows you'll make good use of it. She's happy for you. She's so proud."

"My nana's dead." There was a clock ticking somewhere. She hadn't noticed that before.

"Yes. But she's near. She wants you to take care. There is danger around you."

Chapter 19

"You alright?" Rupert was waiting near the car and frowned as Stella walked up, plipped the key and threw her bag onto the rear seat.

"Fine, why wouldn't I be?"

"No reason, only you look a bit–"

"A bit what?"

"I dunno, boss, a bit shocked."

"Don't be daft. Come on. Let's get back, it's been a long day. We need to compare our notes and then get off home. I want an early start tomorrow. I haven't heard anything from the CSI people, have you?"

"No. It's getting dark now so I don't suppose we will. Oh, by the way, the camera in the flats wasn't working. Vandalism."

"Okay. We need to hassle the CSI team a bit about this. His footprints must be there by the fence."

"But, boss, what's it going to tell us in all fairness? We know he came over there. We even know what shoes he was wearing."

Stella huffed a sigh. "Yeah, you're right. But it'll be proof for later, won't it, and there might be something else. When you saw him, jumping over the fence did you carry on watching?"

They were in the car now and pulling out into the main road.

"I saw him move down the garden and then he wasn't visible any longer. He was hidden by the wall."

"Did you see anyone come after him?" The old woman's words were influencing her thinking. It was ridiculous.

"After him, boss?"

"Yes. Someone else behind him."

"No, I went over the footage a couple of times, but to be honest, once he disappeared, I just marked the spot on the vid."

"Right. That's the first thing we have to do tomorrow. Watch for a while longer."

She drove back to the station with her mind in turmoil. With a little distance between herself and the old crone she realized she should have asked more questions. She'd been freaked out. Her nana had been dead for three years. She still missed her, but this sudden comment about the money – how could that old woman have known anything about it? Nobody knew.

She didn't believe in spirits and fortune tellers and all that woo-woo stuff. But it had shocked her, and she'd taken her eye off the ball. She'd need to go back and find out just what the woman had seen of this other person who had come later. Maybe if she viewed the CCTV footage tonight there would be enough on there so she wouldn't need to. She hoped so.

The civilians had already left. There was a note from Mel to say she was still trawling the missing persons reports but she had nothing yet. It was very long and what was she to do next?

Stella had texted Ruth, told her about the sighting and redirected her attention to the side road and the house on the corner. It didn't seem however, that there was anything much to report. Her desk was empty, the chair pushed underneath as if she had never been there.

After Rupert left, Stella spent an hour peering at the screen. Over and over, she watched the victim climb the fence and drop into the garden on his way to be murdered. Nobody else followed the same route. She watched until the night had gone, the screen showed a sky beginning to lighten. Still there were no other figures in the side passageway. No visible sighting of someone else on the fence. Maybe the CSI team would have something for her later.

She was going to have to go back to the old woman, wasn't she?

She wondered how much Carr wanted to be informed. There wasn't much to tell him. She sent a quick message through and then felt embarrassed. He probably didn't want blow by blow. How much would she have told Dunn? She would just have mentioned it when she saw him. This could all become a bit difficult. She didn't need it on top of everything else. She'd have a word and agree some sort of procedure with DI Carr. He seemed approachable.

Chapter 20

It was very late, and Stella called at the chippy on the way home. The grease from the fish sat heavily in her stomach and she wished she'd managed with a sandwich. After a shower and a glass of Andrews – her mam's cure all for stomach problems – she went to bed.

Sleep wouldn't come, and the early hours found her standing in the bay window watching dark clouds scudding across the sky. The old woman had unnerved her and she really didn't want to see her again, but the mention of another person who came afterwards couldn't be dismissed.

The best thing was to get it out of the way and so, just before seven, she walked out into the damp chill and drove to Westvale.

A lone uniformed officer huddled under the concrete overhang shielding the front door of the squat. He looked cold, miserable, and bored and she left him alone. She should have thought about it and brought him a hot drink. It was too late so she glanced to see all was as it should be and then turned to the house at the end of the terrace.

The door swung open quickly after her gentle knock and the old woman turned and went down the hallway without a word.

"I'm sorry to bother you again, Mrs... erm?"

"Minoghue, Betsy Minoghue and it's not Mrs. Don't be bothering with all that Ms and Miss nonsense either. Just call me Betsy. It's what people do."

"Okay. Thanks, Betsy."

"I've been puzzling about what you said yesterday. You said there was another person. Someone who came after?"

"Aye."

"Well, we looked at our film of the house and to be honest, there isn't anyone, not as far as I can see."

"And yet here you are."

"Yes, here I am."

"You need to stop being blinkered. You need to stop thinking you know what happened and see what really did."

"So, was there someone else, afterwards?"

"That's what I told you."

"But—"

"Just because he came after doesn't mean he came behind."

Stella frowned and thought for a minute. "Oh. So, he came to the house later but not the same way."

Betsy tipped her head to the side and gave what might have been a small smile. She raised a bony hand in a mock victory salute.

"Where did he come from then? If you saw someone else, where did he come from? Was he on foot, in a car?"

"I didn't say I saw him."

"What?"

Now there was a definite cackle. "I'm playing with you, girl. You need to calm down. You need to start thinking logically. Yes, I saw him. He came from the side road. Turned in at the entrance to the garage."

"Okay. We can't see that area on the video."

The old woman shrugged. "I don't know about films and videos. You'll have to handle that. But you'll find him."

"Can you describe him?"

"It was dark. He was dark. Black clothes, a hat."

"Okay, but how tall was he? Did he seem young, old?"

Betsy sighed. "You'll need to be giving me your wages if I do all your work for you."

Stella felt irritation building. She shifted on the seat, moved her bag.

"Don't be getting niggled with me. He was about six feet. He was not old but not a kid neither. He carried a bag. After he left, they all left. All out like rats from the ship, running and scurrying. Filth. The girls came after, huddled and scared, and they took them away in a van."

"Why didn't you tell me all this before?"

"You didn't ask. You thought you knew it all. You thought I was a daft old biddy."

"I didn't."

"Ha. I'm going to make my breakfast. Let yourself out."

With that she pushed herself from the chair, eased her back and walked out of the room. Stella heard water running in the kitchen and the metallic scrape of a kettle on the hob.

"You couldn't make a cuppa for the bobby down there, could you?" she said.

"Took him one earlier. When you come back bring me some cake."

"I don't think I'll need to bother you again."

"Battenberg."

Chapter 21

"This is bloody frustrating." Stella was back in their corner of the big office and peering at her screen. "You'd think someone had deliberately angled these cameras so we couldn't see what we need to."

Rupert glanced up and opened his mouth to speak.

"Oh, I know they didn't. I realize we are happy to have anything at all, but it seems as if all the bits that would help us are just out of view."

"How long are we supposed to keep doing this?" Ruth said. She had turned away from her desk and was pouring pale coffee from a thermos.

Stella bit back the retort she wanted to give. "I think until we see those kids in the garden. We all know what happened after that. Are you viewing the front street? As I told you before, according to the house-to-house there may have been someone turning up on his own. A dark figure carrying a bag. I have no timing, but it was after our victim arrived. It's a bit vague but it's all we've got. I do think it's important."

"Yes, vague is right. Anyway, I've seen the scum all streaming out."

"Why didn't you say?"

"I've written it in my report. It shows it around about five in the morning."

"Tell you what, Ruth. I see you're having a bit of a break. Why don't you let me take over that view and you do the traffic cameras from the main road? See if you can find out where the van came from that transported the girls."

"How do you know about that? If you've already seen this stuff, why are we wasting our time?"

Shit.

"I made an informed guess. If they hadn't moved them all together then they would have been wandering the streets. They are a commodity for these evil bastards, they wouldn't just let them go off on their own."

The older woman shook her head and snorted. She took her cup and went to stand looking out of the window. Her shoulders exuded ill temper and Rupert screwed up his face. Melanie giggled but quickly covered the sound with a cough. Stella closed her eyes and bit back a sigh. It was like working in a kindergarten.

"Right, so I'm doing the front of the house, as much as we can see and I'm going back to the beginning. I suppose it's too much to hope there'll be any private security cameras in any of the houses and I certainly didn see any. So, Melanie, you carry on with the ones at the r r of the school. Rupert, can you leave it for now and cha e up the lab. We need to know about the knife."

"I did give them a shout earlier and all they ould tell me was it is a pretty ordinary kitchen knife. The s rt plenty of people have nowadays. German make. C ered in prints, all different. It'll take ages to sort ther all and check if any of them are on our database b they're working on it."

"Right. Have you had any luck with the mi er lists? Anyone who could be our victim?"

"Not yet, boss."

"Why not try again. Maybe there's something w."

Stella knew it felt muddled and hit and mis and she really needed to show she was in control. Troubl was, she didn't really feel she was. She had to do this and o it well. Her first case on her own, she couldn't fail, specially given the extra attention she was getting from th city. All she needed was a break to show her the way.

The internal phone rang, DI Dunn wanted r in his office. Immediately. Her stomach clenched, sh had so little to tell him and the bulk of it was from a eird old woman who spoke in riddles.

Chapter 22

DI Dunn was standing with his back to the of ce door, gazing out of the window.

"You wanted to see me, sir?"

"Just need an update on that unlawful killing. 've got a meeting about the drugs raid carve-up later an I'd like something a bit positive to say. Tell me you've had some progress."

"Well..." She paused, and Dunn turned to look at her.

He crossed his arms and frowned with something approaching disappointment.

"We've done a house-to-house. That led to a couple of things I'm looking into. We've made a big move forward. We now know how the victim arrived at the squat. It seems he came of his own accord. He climbed the back fence and entered the premises voluntarily. But in fairness the CCTV coverage is a bit dodgy." As she spoke, she realized she had made an assumption and stated it as fact. Her face heated and sweat gathered under her armpits. She took a breath.

"We're looking for another man." It was too late, the words were out, she wanted them back but now she had said them, and the DI was looking interested and a bit hopeful. "We have reason to believe there was another man who arrived at the house sometime after our victim. Not much later, everyone left. We have seen that on the CCTV and then – erm, then they took the girls away."

"Reason to believe?"

"Yes. As a result of our house-to-house enquiries."

"A witness?"

He was looking really interested now and even more hopeful.

"A witness." She hadn't actually lied. All she had done was repeat what the DI said. That was all.

"Well, you seem to be moving along with this. Well done. Have you found the link yet with the other case? There has to be one, I really need you to find it as a matter of urgency. But, anyway, carry on. Well done, Stella."

"I did send a sort of report to DI Carr, just a short precis."

"Did you? Well, I don't know how much he'll want to be bothered with the nuts and bolts. Why not wait until you have something interesting to tell him? Run it past me as well." He paused and pursed his lips. "I wouldn't have thought I'd have to say that, Stella."

"No, boss. Sorry."

On the way back to the big room she replayed the conversation. Apart from the cock-up at the end, she'd done okay. Everything she'd told him was in her reports. Maybe she'd made it out to be a bit more positive, just a bit more sound than it was, but none of it was untrue. There was also the other problem. His insistence that the drug dealing and other criminal activity in the failed raid were connected with her case. The DI was convinced and yet, really, was it so impossible there could be two such houses? They knew hers hadn't been occupied for long. The CSI sergeant had said as much. How long could you use a blocked-up toilet anyway? She didn't really want to think about it, but it was relevant. The other place had been under surveillance for weeks. Weeks of watching and waiting until everything was in place so the big raid could be coordinated. There had been no mention of a secondary location.

Maybe there was no connection. Maybe this was a temporary gathering of bottom feeders and their victims. Her throat dried with the thought of going to see the DI and telling him what she had found was of no value in relation to the major case that was embarrassing him. That was not what he wanted, and she really did need to try and give him what he wanted, especially as she'd just irritated him by mentioning DI Carr. What a bloody rat's nest.

Chapter 23

Immediately Stella stepped back into the room, Rupert sprang from his chair and strode across to the whiteboards. She could see the excitement in the set of his shoulders. He lifted a hand in greeting.

"Mel found the van, boss. It has to be the one. Five o'clock in the morning and it's the only thing moving. It drove past the school playground towards the front of the squat where we lost it. It wasn't visible on any of the other cameras leaving the areas. Then about twenty minutes later it came back the same way. We tracked it down onto the A506. They joined the M57 at Junction 6 going south. After that it was onto the M62 onward to the M6. We've been able to follow them all the way to London. They parked up in a car park in Hounslow."

"Okay. Did they go straight there or did they make a comfort stop?" Stella stuck her hands into her pockets. They didn't need to know she'd crossed her fingers.

"Short stop on the M1 at Watford Gap."

"Have we contacted the Northamptonshire force? I want the camera footage. Anything from the car park showing the people carrier and anything inside that shows the passengers."

"That's going to be a hell of a lot of footage with crowds." Ruth grumbled.

"Yep. So, soon as we can, Rupert."

"I've put a call in," he said.

"Excellent. We need to shout out to the Met, see if they can get someone round to the car park. We need that vehicle."

"Why?" Ruth said. "Your victim wasn't in it. We've seen now, he came on his own."

"Anything that can give us prints and DNA from people who were in the squat will help to trace them. It could help us to eliminate those who had nothing to do with the killing. It's information, Ruth, and the more we have the better. You know this."

Mel said, "I've been on the blower to them, already. They sent a car round right away, but the van was empty. They are going to impound it. They asked if somebody was going down there. They'll send us what CCT[something] they've got and reports when they've processed the vehi[cl]e. Mind you, they did say it'll be a while. They did ask if w[e']d rather have it back here and do it ourselves. I said I'd g[o] back to them."

"Great stuff, Mel, well done," Stella said.

The young woman beamed at her.

"Put all this on the boards. This is excellent s[tu]ff, guys, I'm chuffed to bits. So, soon as you have some [pi]ctures, I need copies and me and you, Rupert, are going b[ac]k to the squat. We'll talk to those boys if we can. Se[e] if they recognize any of the girls and" – she paused – '[it] might be worthwhile checking with other neighbours. I know they're not keen to talk but they're not all blind a[n]d deaf. I reckon we might as well have the van back here a[n]d let our own forensic department deal with it. It's possib[ly] quicker than having the Met do it and at least it'll be eas[i]er for us to have a look. Can you get on to that, Ruth?"

"But what does it matter?" Ruth said. "I mea[n], do you think one of the girls killed him?"

"We just don't know at this stage, do we? W[e] have to trace as many of the people who were there as [w]e can. If we can find these girls in London, then they may [b]e able to help us. If we can gather some names, w[e] can do meaningful checks on the databases."

"Ha. Good luck with that then. I mean, Lo[n]don, it's impossible."

"Yeah, thanks, Ruth, way to be positive."

Stella turned away. She wasn't going to let th[e] negative vibes get to her.

She wondered where you could buy a Batten[b]erg cake now without going all the way down to the Tesco [E]xpress.

Chapter 24

Stella paced back and forth, she tried to review her files but all she wanted was the stills from the CCTV and she couldn't settle. They'd all seen it now and were waiting for enhanced shots of the driver and all the girls who had travelled down to London.

They already knew some of the pictures would more than likely be useless. The driver had pulled up his hood before he left the vehicle and kept his head down as he walked through the services. He sent one of the girls to buy him a burger from McDonald's and they all used the toilets. One of the women who perhaps was more switched on than the others and more aware of the dangers in their immediate future had turned deliberately to show her face to one of the cameras. They watched as she tried to encourage the others to do the same but instead, they lowered their heads and pulled scarves up to their chins. Although most law-abiding citizens had accepted the safety aspect of universal surveillance, these people didn't want to show their faces and the reasons would be manifold. They could be runaways, illegal immigrants, no-shows for probation checks. Until they were found, Stella could only guess. That they were almost certainly working as prostitutes added an extra layer of danger for them. They had already been in close contact with a violent murder and the risk to each and every one of them scared her.

At shift change she had to accept they wouldn't be getting anything from the digital technology department. They'd asked if anyone in the Met working with retrospective facial technology could help but the technology was still only being tested and Merseyside hadn't been one of the forces involved in the trials, so really it was obvious they needed to rely on stills taken from the surveillance cameras. They could go through the databases and misper images, comparing. It was tedious work but it might unearth something. Once they had a name, they could put out an alert and the image. There was the very remote possibility that one of the girls would be picked up for shoplifting, prostitution, buying or selling drugs. They were part of a dirty and desperate world that surely would drop one of them into the hands of the police. Unless of course they had already been shipped out of the country. It wasn't impossible. They were the only link with the squat, everyone else was in the wind. Just one of them would be a major leap forward.

"I reckon we might as well get off home," Stella said. "I want to make an early start tomorrow and if we haven't had anything back then I'm going to try and download something myself."

"I can probably get something useable," Mo said. "I love working with all that stuff. I've got an application in to go and work in the digital technology department." She raised her hand, the fingers crossed.

"You should have said," Stella told her.

"I didn't like to. You know I haven't really had any training. Well, not specific, I did my degree in photography and digital content creation but…"

"Why haven't they snapped you up already?" Rupert said.

"To be honest, I've been trying to decide what I wanted to do so it's not long since I put in the application."

"Okay. Well, first thing tomorrow, can you get onto that?" Stella said.

"Tell you what, I could do it tonight and send over to you if you can make it okay for me to download the footage onto my own computer."

Stella glanced at her watch. She shook her head. "I don't think it's going to work. The DI will have gone off home now and I don't think I can give you the go-ahead with you being ancillary staff. We can't do anything which might screw up a prosecution down the line. Great idea, mind you, and if you can give it a go tomorrow it'd be brilliant. I know we could all have a go and just cut and zoom and brighten and stuff, but if you can do a better job, then go for it."

Chapter 25

She was pinning so much on finding at least one of the girls. She ought to widen her horizons. Stella was worn out and dispirited. They still hadn't identified the victim and she made a note to speak to DI Dunn in the morning. They should go to the media with it. Okay, he was dead, but they could produce a recognizable picture of him for the news bulletins, the *Echo* and maybe even a few noticeboards.

If he had been a down-and-out rough sleeper then it would have made sense that they couldn't find who he was. There were so many, either deliberately hiding from friends, family or debtors, and then the others who had nobody looking for them at all. No-one who gave much thought to where they were sleeping and how they were coping. But this bloke wasn't like that. His body had been clean, his hair well styled. Everything else had gone. No wallet or watch, no jewellery. Surely, someone was missing him. But they hadn't been able to find him on any reports. The social media searches had come to nothing. Ruth had smirked when Stella told them to give it a break for now.

She was failing. She felt it, they were getting nowhere, and she was running out of ideas.

There was a knock on the door. She groaned, slipped her book back into her briefcase and closed her laptop. It could just be Keith from upstairs wanting to borrow some milk. She listened with an ear to the wood and heard the tell-tale rattle of metal. Her mother, with her habit of jangling the keyring while she was waiting. Stella sighed and closed her eyes. But then she opened the door.

"Hiya, Mam. What are you doing here? It's a bit late."

"It's only just after eight and I thought I'd give you time to get your tea."

"I haven't been in long."

"Oh God, girl, you'll be wearing yourself to a frazzle. Have you had something to eat? Look at you – you've lost weight. You look skinny."

"I haven't lost weight. You always say that. I'm the same as I was when I left school. Anyway, I had a sandwich at work. I don't want anything."

"I brought this." Her mother waved a bottle of red wine in the air.

"Oh, well that's nice, but honest, Mam, I'm pretty whacked. Could we not have it tomorrow?"

"Oh, come on. It'll buck you up, lovely, and you look like you need to unwind anyway. I need to have a word, to be honest."

"Come on, come in. But I want an early night. I'm dead busy in work and I have to get in before seven in the morning."

"We'll just have the one glass then. We can have a quick natter and you get off to bed."

Stella brought the glasses from the kitchen and once they were settled with their wine, she curled her feet under her on the settee and nodded at her mother. "Go on then. What's to do?"

Lydia May coughed. She put down her drink and turned so she was facing her daughter directly.

"Look, love. I hope you won't take this the wrong way. Please don't. I struggled with myself not knowing whether to say anything but anyway here I am. So, first of all – have you claimed that money?"

Stella's heart gave a jink. "No. Well, I did ring them, but they have to come round and talk to me and – honest, Mam, I just haven't got the time right now. It's alright, the money's mine. That's not a problem but I want to just wait a bit and then, well, when I've got time to sort it out properly…"

"When do you think it'll be?"

"I don't know, do I? This case I'm working on, it's taking time. It's not easy, there's a lot of stuff that needs going through."

"But it's been a couple of days. You must have sorted it out by now."

"You're kidding me. Sorted it out? You've no idea, have you?"

"No, of course I haven't, but surely it doesn't have to be the only thing you do. I mean there are other people there. You're not doing it on your own, are you?"

"No, I'm not, but it's my case. That means I have to make all the decisions and plan what we do next. I haven't any room for thinking about other stuff."

"Oh. So, when do you think then?"

Stella felt her nerves start to jangle. She was too tired and too worried to deal with this. "Look, Mam, I really am whacked. I'll let you know when I'm going to sort out the money. I will, but right now it's pretty low on my list of priorities."

"It must be nice to be you."

"What's that supposed to mean?"

"Well, just that most people would be itching to get their hands on it. Dying to have hold of that sort of cash. Course if you're so well off you don't need it – it must be lovely."

"Don't be ridiculous. You know I'm not. It's just – oh Jesus, I wish I'd never told you about it."

"Fine, fine then. Maybe you shouldn't have. Maybe you should have kept quiet and then you could have it all to yourself. No need to share, no need to help out your relatives."

"Mam, where's all this coming from? What's going on?"

Lydia had snatched up her bag and stood from the chair, looking down at her daughter. "Oh, never mind. You've changed. There was a time when you used to put your family first, but not anymore. Now you've got your oh so special job and you're in charge of your care, you've no time for us. Well, sorry I bothered you. Enjoy the wine."

She turned and stomped from the room and down the hall, and the glasses in the kitchen jingled as she slammed the door. Stella heard the front gate rattle back on its hinges. She peered through the curtains and watched as her mother made a call on her phone. She should go and speak to her. She should call her back inside. She should find out what had been on her mother's mind. But she didn't. After ten minutes a taxi drew up and whisked her away into the night. They never rowed. They'd always been close, good mates. They'd had many a laugh together. Now look. She didn't have the money and already it was changing things.

Her eyes filled with tears, she bent and picked up her wine glass, swigged back the mouthful still in the bottom. She took everything through to the kitchen and poured the leftovers down the drain. She walked through the hallway turning off the lights. She stripped off and fell into bed. She'd have a shower in the morning. Right now all she wanted was sleep.

Chapter 26

DI Dunn usually spent a couple of hours in the office on a Saturday morning. It was a chance to catch up on paperwork. It was a good time to have a word with him but this morning he was cranky and short-tempered.

"So, we don't have an identification, and we don't have any witnesses and in fact we don't have anything?"

At first Stella felt he was being helpful, understanding her situation. She began to relax. Now, there was the chance for her to use his experience and advice. But he was shaking his head.

"You haven't really got very far with this, have you? I was hoping for a bit more by now. You have been keeping up with developments on that bloody abortive raid, haven't you? There are reports from the other stations, information gathered and so on. You need to do that so you can get a bead on the connections."

"Yes, boss." She hadn't but it didn't seem the right time to tell him. "As much as I can and if there are connections, we'll find them." She paused. "Of course, there's always the chance the two things are not connected, isn't there?"

"Highly unlikely, I'd say. Anyway, keep me informed and let's try and get some traction on this. It might be that I should hand it over to DI Lawler, he's still working on the drugs thing, trying to salvage what we can. It might dovetail very well. Good man, Lawler."

With that he pulled a pile of paperwork towards him and took the top from his pen. She was dismissed and not only that, she was on notice that the case was slipping through her fingers.

It was only as she walked away from his office that she realized she hadn't had the chance to discuss the media appeal for her victim. She turned and looked back at the closed door. She'd leave it until tomorrow.

In her mind, Nana tutted and told her she was being a doormat.

Maybe DI Carr could help her. She dismissed the idea almost before it was fully formed. That surely would put the cat among the pigeons. This felt like a case of too many chiefs and not enough Indians as her dad used to say. She'd never really understood what he meant until now.

Mel had come up trumps. The young woman had been in the office since five o'clock and had done a great job with three images of the prostitutes. She was going to be a great asset to the forensic imaging team.

That was where the good news ended, because the van had been stolen three weeks previously in Warrington. Another dead end.

"Right. Back to Westvale with these piccies." She tried to sound positive and keen. "Rupert, are you ready? Girls, do another scan of the misper lists. It's three days now, the alarm could have been raised. Ruth, could you do social media as well? Mel, anything else you can do with the pictures of the women, and could you send your enhancements down to the bloke we're dealing with at the Met? They might be still in London, and they might even be working. We've got to have a break soon."

As they walked from the room they heard Ruth, it was a quiet mutter. "'Girls', for God's sake."

She'd meant to be friendly and upbeat and ended up brassing off the political correctness police.

"I need to pop into the Tesco on the way, Rupert. Is that okay?"

"No probs, boss."

Chapter 27

The door in the house at the end of the terrace was ajar. Stella pushed at it gently.

"Hello, Betsy. It's DS May."

"I'm in the kitchen. Did you bring my cake?"

When she reached the end of the hallway and held out her hand the cake was snatched away. Betsy Minoghue peeled back the cellophane and sniffed at the marzipan.

"Huh, Tesco. Not the best but it's what I expected. You won't be wanting any, will you?"

"No, no it's fine. You go ahead."

"I'm not eating cake at this time in the morning. I'm not a child. Come through, I need to sit down."

The old woman pushed past and stomped down to the living room carrying a large mug of strong tea. Stella was glad she wasn't offered one, it was dark enough to strip the skin off your tonsils.

"So, what do you want? Stuck, are you?"

"No, not stuck," Stella said.

"We'll do better if you tell the truth. You don't have to impress me, I'm not your boss."

The lie she had told about keeping up with developments reared its head for a moment. Stella pushed it aside. The woman was odd and a bit spooky, but she wasn't superhuman.

"I just wondered if you recognized any of these women and if you could tell me anything about them?"

Betsy held out a thin knobbly hand. She slid the images through her fingers as if they were playing cards. "This one's Ceecee. She's a hard bitch but so would anybody be given the things she had to put up with." She wagged the second picture in the air. "Fee, short for Fiona. Poor thing. She's didn't have long. This one is Pat. Don't know what her proper name is. She likes a bit of chocolate, does Pat. They aren't bad women. They've had bad lives. Leave 'em alone if you can. Do you know where they are? They scuttled out of that place in a panic and off and away in the van. You must have found it if you have these."

"Yes, we have."

"Taken 'em to London, have they?"

"Yes, but how did you know?"

"Don't be daft. Look at the picture. That one, Fee. You really are going to have to improve. You don't look, you don't listen, and you don't think."

Stella snatched the picture back and lifted it towards the window for more light. Bugger it, how had she missed that. In the background was a sign advertising long-term parking for Heathrow Airport.

"How well do you know them?"

"They used to come to me when they were scared. When the blokes were on the rampage, and they'd had enough. When they just needed to breathe and forget what they were and what life was doing to them. We'd sit quiet and now and then I'd read 'em. Mostly I just gave 'em time and peace. I'm sorry they've gone. London's a hard place. But then, everywhere is a hard place when you've gone into that life."

"Can you tell me anything else about them?"

Betsy shook her head. "It's not my job to nose into people's lives. They tell me what they want to, and I tell them anything that might be to their advantage. Women like them, they don't give away much. You know that."

The old woman leaned forward and grabbed Stella by the arm. "You find them girls, you be nice to 'em, do you hear me? There's only good luck kept any of us ending up like that. A couple of bad turns of fortune and who knows how you'd end up. Ha, not you now. Not with all your money. Now bugger off. It's time for my bath."

She stood and left the room and minutes later the sound of running water rattled in the air. The smell of hot steam drifted down the stairs and Stella had no other choice but to leave, pulling the door closed behind her.

Chapter 28

DC Moon had gone to speak to the boys. George Kenny was at home but the other two were off playing football. He didn't want to make a big deal out of it and pull them out of the game on the off chance they knew the women. The family liaison officer had left but Rupert was worried about George.

"I know he was trying to look tough last time we spoke to him, but at the end of the day he's just a little kid. No child should have to see things like that. His mother said he's been having nightmares. I suggested she take him to the doctor, but I don't know if she will."

"Hmm. I wonder if a victim support worker could help," Stella said.

"I gave his mum the telephone number to call them. Anyway, he didn't seem to know anything about the women. If he did, he was too scared to say much. He just shook his head. Did you get anything from Mrs Minoghue?"

"Yes, she knew the girls quite well from the sound of things. She gave me their names but didn't admit to knowing much else about them."

"Didn't admit to it? Do you think she knows more?"

"I'm sure of it. She's a funny old biddy and a bit spooky. I reckon she's one of those seers or mediums or something. She knows things without being told. I've never really gone for all that stuff, but she's shocked me a couple of times with what she said."

"Like what?"

Stella hesitated. "Oh, you know, just stuff. Let's get back and see what's what. We need to re-group. We're fishing about in the dark, aren't we? We need to identify our dead bloke because until we do we're going nowhere. I wonder if the DNA results are back. Mind you, that'll only help if he's on the system, and he doesn't look the type."

As they pulled into the car park, Stella's phone chimed.

"Mel, we're back, just parking up. Problem?"

"Yes, boss, afraid so. I called DS Watt in London. I sent him the images we had. He rang back pretty much straight away. One of the women has been found in a back alley."

"How do you mean, found in an alley? Was she working?"

"No, boss, she was dead."

"Oh, shit. Overdosed?"

"No. Maybe best if I tell you in the office. We're waiting for an email with pictures to confirm it."

* * *

The pictures were nasty and upsetting. The woman Betsy had identified as Fee lay in the filth in a narrow lane behind a restaurant. Livid bruises stood out against the pale skin and her hair was matted and thick with blood.

"Poor thing," Stella said. She was chilled not only by the pictures of the body but by the memory of a throwaway comment in the overheated living room of Betsy Minoghue's house. *That's Fee, poor thing, she didn't have long.*

Just what did that mean?

Chapter 29

DI Dunn was on his way home when Stella called.

"You can liaise closely with the Met but I really don't think there is any reason at all for you to be rushing off down there. They're more than capable of solving their own crimes."

"But, boss, she was in the squat with the body. Probably there when he was killed."

"Yes, and unfortunately she won't be able to give us any information because she has now been killed miles away. I mean, Stella, obviously you'll need to keep in touch with them, but she was a prostitute. It's a dangerous game. She was away from her usual beat, away from her usual protection. Chances are she's crossed a local pimp and he's used her to send a warning out to anyone else thinking of straying into his patch. It's brutal and awful, I'll give you that, but really when you've been doing the job as long as I have, you'll learn that this stuff happens. You need to look at the big picture. You just carry on trying to find out who the bloke in the squat was. He was well turned out and not known to us. With a bit of luck he'll have some sort of connection to the big cheese in our own case and we'll be able to claw back a bit of respect. You mark my words, that should be where you're looking."

"But, boss, what about the other girls?"

"What other girls?"

"Well, yes, women. The ones who were taken down to London in the van. Don't you think they might be in danger? I mean if this Fee has been killed."

"She was in the wrong place at the wrong time. Leave it to the Met."

Stella put down her phone. How could he do that? On the one hand he held this absolute conviction that her dead bloke was connected with the drug gang they had failed to round up. Then on the other hand he was just as convinced the poor dead woman in London was nothing to do with it at all. And what about the reference to 'our case'? One case, one enquiry. He only saw all this work as an aside.

She respected the DI, you had to, he was senior, he'd been around longer. He'd been where she was now, wet behind the ears. So, he must be right, mustn't he? And yet, there was Nana again, telling her to speak up for what she believed in.

The job didn't leave you much wiggle room. If you screwed up early in your career it followed you for years. The small mistakes everyone made as a uniformed copper usually ended up with a sarcastic nickname or tedious and annoying ragging, a silly noise when you walked into a room or whatever. It wasn't too hard to cope with if you kept your sense of humour. If she screwed up now, if she failed, if this case was taken away and given to Lawler, it would dog her for years. It would hold her back, a black mark when she put in for promotion. She looked across the room to where Rupert Moon was examining the pictures from London. He was the closest thing to a partner she had. They hadn't known each other long but he seemed a decent bloke.

"Rupert, have you a few minutes?"

He nodded at her and raised his eyebrows.

"Let's grab a coffee, I want to run something past you."

Chapter 30

They walked up to McDonald's. The coffee there was better than the stuff from the vending machines in the station and they didn't want to sit in the canteen.

"Do you want a burger or anything?" Stella asked.

"No, you're alright, boss. I try not to eat too much of that stuff."

"It shows, don't take this wrong but you look pretty buff."

Rupert blushed as he glanced away.

"Honest, I wasn't being weird or anything, it's just that you do look good. You work out, don't you?"

"Yeah. I do. I've done it ever since school. I'm a ginger, called Rupert. It was tough at times and I either hid myself away and snivelled about it or made sure I couldn't be thought of as a wimp."

"And did it work?" Stella said.

"Pretty much and it's a bit addictive you know. Working out. I really enjoy it now. Anyway, that's not why we're here, is it?"

"No, sorry, of course not. Look, keep this to yourself." And she went through her worry about the way she was being directed. The feeling she had that linking the two cases was short-sighted and a mistake and the fear that she was being disloyal thinking that way.

"I guess you just have to do what you think is right, boss. It's your case. I get what you're saying but I reckon just do what your gut tells you. If you come unstuck at least you'll know it was because you were doing what you believed in."

Stella didn't speak for a minute and then she nodded and smiled. "Thanks. Okay. Let's get back. I'll make a call to the bloke at the Met. I wonder if they can do a hook-up so I can see the post-mortem exam."

"They must be able to, surely. That's a good idea actually," Rupert said.

"Okay. The old woman, Betsy Minoghue, she said we should be looking for the man who came after. Did I tell you?"

"No. She has intrigued you, hasn't she? Do you think she knows more than she's said?"

"Well, let's just say she seems to have a really good idea of what's going on."

"It's back to the CCTV then, I suppose. But we must have seen all of it a dozen times."

"You're right. Tell you what. Let's come at it from a different angle. Let's go and have a talk to the girls down in town. We'll take pictures of the women who have been taken to London and see what we can find out about them. If this is nothing to do with the other drugs case, then we need to find out what it is about. With what's happened to Fee, I'm thinking it's more about the prossies than the bits of drugs they were dealing from the squat. Go on home for a couple of hours and then I'll meet you at the station later. Nineish. Okay?"

"Yes, sounds like a plan, boss."

* * *

Stella felt a buzz of excitement. She was taking control, breaking loose from the constraints put on her by the DI.

She'd call in and see her mam. Make peace. Lydia hadn't been in touch since the silly row, and needed sorting. She hated being at odds with her mother. Her spirits lifted as she walked back to the station, made a couple of calls, and picked up her rattletrap car.

Chapter 31

"Hiya, Mam." As Stella let herself into her mother's house and walked through to the kitchen she caught the smell of roast chicken and hot apple slightly overlaid with dirty nappy and the highly scented bags they were screwed into. She'd not been here since Peter and Shelley had moved in and the place had been given over to child-rearing.

"I'm in the back room," Lydia called through. "Just sorting some stuff. Actually, now you're here you can take some of this lot with you."

The small room at the back, once the dining room, was cluttered with boxes and plastic bags.

"What's all this?"

"I need to get rid. Our Peter and Shelley can't share a room with the babs all the time. It's not right. So, we're planning on turning the front room into his nursery."

The front room. That had been her room. Okay, she hadn't slept in it for four years, but still. It was her room. One of the bags held rolled-up posters of pop stars. Another had fluffy toys in. Her mother saw her looking at that one.

"We kept Floofball and Pigsy." She referred to two old favourites. "I said we'd let little Jamie have them. But these need to be got rid. They're full of dust and some of them are matted and the eyes are missing."

"Well, they could be washed and repaired, couldn't they?"

"Nah, it's not worth the bother. Nobody wants 'em now. You can't put them in the charity shop, not with all the new regulations and stuff." Lydia paused for a moment to look at her daughter. "Course, they were yours. You can have them. Take 'em with you and do what you like with 'em."

"I haven't got room in my place. I was leaving them here until I decided what to do with them. Are those my books?"

"Yes, just your kids' books and some of the stuff from school. I thought I'd stick those in the shed."

"But they'll get damp; what about mice?"

Lydia looked up. She tipped a head to one side and smiled. "Aw, look at you. You're all upset about your teddies. Where's the tough detective now, eh?"

"I'm not. It's just, well… they are mine and I think I should have had some choice about what happens to them, that's all."

"Well, here you are, choose. You take 'em with you or I stick 'em in the bin and the shed. We've no room. The baby's stuff takes up every bit of space. They need so much more now than we did back when you were born. He's my little grandson so I want to do the best for him."

"How long are they staying then?"

Lydia just shrugged. "What did you want, anyway? There's some chicken left from dinner time. I can make you a sandwich."

Stella shook her head. "No, you're alright. I'll come back in a couple of days." She turned to leave but before she did, she ran up the stairs, grabbed the two teddies from the small front room and stuffed them into her laptop bag.

Chapter 32

Stella called Jordan Carr. She hovered for a while wondering whether to speak to Dunn first, but Carr had asked to be kept informed. He turned up on Sunday morning as they were preparing to watch body-worn-camera footage from the Met.

"I'll sit in," he said as he pulled up one of the chairs.

She felt better with him there. That wasn't good, she had to be self-reliant, but it was a fact. He sat with his arms folded quietly watching the big screen with them.

The alleyway was gloomy and dingy. It was narrow and damp with big wheely bins pushed up against the walls. Blown litter collected in corners and decaying bits of food were squashed into the cobbles.

The image was clear, but movement made it difficult to watch until the uniformed officer, wearing his body camera, slowed his approach to the pale form splayed in the corner against the dark brick wall.

He bent to the woman just long enough to check that life was extinct. It was obvious, but he still had to go through the motions. Her long blond hair was matted with blood, her eyes stared out at the grim surroundings and the stiff, pale limbs were crooked and awkward.

Stella wanted him to cover her, she wanted him to close her eyes and lay a blanket over her. But she knew he couldn't and what he did was absolutely correct. He called in the report, gave his name and the situation in calm, unhurried words. Then he turned back and crouched beside the woman, he put out his hand as if to touch her face. They heard him, quietly, hardly above a whisper, saying a Hail Mary, telling her he was sorry, and they would take care of her now. He stood, turned, and faced the alley, securing the scene and waiting for the circus to begin. It was those quiet words spoken beside the body which brought tears to her eyes. She brushed them away under cover of rearranging her fringe and scratching her nose.

Stella knew they would view the footage many more times and the shock would eventually dissipate, but for now they sat in silence and watched the place become a hive of activity. Tape was stretched across the entrance. Floodlights turned the space into a horror show of stark images, and white-suited figures moved carefully through the alley. A while later they heard the bobby greeting the medical examiner.

"Do we know when they are going to perform the examination?" Carr asked.

"Tomorrow morning, they're setting up a live feed for us."

"Brilliant. I'll join you. It won't be as good as going down there but it's better than nothing. I don't suppose there are any results on the fingerprints they took?"

"They are certainly a match from some at the squat and in the van. But there are so many on the knife they haven't been able to say definitively," Stella said.

"I'm assuming you're going to have a natter with DS Watt now and get their thinking. I don't believe there's no connection with our case, that would be ridiculous. But we need to concentrate on that and then the two things will join up at some point. They have to, nothing else makes sense."

She had noted the possessive he had used. She had backup, proper support. It felt good.

Mel looked up from her screen. "Boss, I might have something interesting here. A missing person report. The description sounds as though it could be our bloke. Been missing since last week. He works in the city centre, a bank, in the investment department apparently. Anyway, nobody missed him because he was supposed to be on holiday, but he was due to attend a wedding yesterday. He never turned up, didn't contact anyone, and his mates haven't been able to reach him."

"Do we have his name?" Stella asked.

"Phillip Harwood. Age twenty-seven. Lives in the city. I have a list here of his friends. One of them lives near to him, Douglas Jewell."

"Send his address to my phone."

"Things coming together, Sergeant," Carr said. "I'll let you get on. I'll pop in tomorrow for a catch-up."

"Sir."

They watched him leave and then Stella grabbed her coat.

"Come on, Rupert, let's go and see Mr Jewell."

Chapter 33

"Albert Dock. I haven't been there for years. Do you remember the weatherman who used to jump about on a floating map? Idiot." Stella had pulled out onto the A506. The A59 took them past the Black Bull and its rows of small shops with dingy flats above. Red brick and tile everywhere.

"Don't you live round here?" Rupert asked.

"Over nearer to the racecourse, but it's not far. Not the best area, is it? Still, I like it and it's handy for the train into town. Where are you?"

"Oh." He paused for a minute. "We're in Skem." He glanced at her but there was no overt negative reaction. He still felt obliged to continue with his usual clarification. "We're in old Skelmersdale. It's not bad. It was nice before the new town and all the problems. My granda had the house and then my mam and dad, and now it's just Da and me. It's boring, I'll be honest. There's nowhere much to go and not much to do. But I'm sort of used to it. I would have moved ages ago, but I don't like leaving Da on his own and it's the house he grew up in, so, can't even think of leaving. I mean, he's fit and well and still goes out to work but…" He shrugged. "Anyway, who can afford to move now. I don't see any point paying out rent when I've got a perfectly good home and there's no way I can get a deposit together yet. Do you rent?"

"No, I own my flat. It's just in a converted house but it's quite big. I had some money left in a will from an old aunty. Actually, she wasn't really an aunty, just somebody my gran knew from when they were in the munitions factory in the war. She married a rich bloke – well, rich to us – and then they had no kids. I don't remember ever meeting her. She died when I was really young but apparently, she liked me, or I suppose she liked the idea of me, so."

"Jesus, that was lucky," Rupert said.

"Yes, it was only enough for the deposit. I've got a big mortgage, but I know I'm lucky."

As she spoke there was a little niggle of guilt. She was pretending to be the same as him, she knew she wasn't any longer. Unless of course she chose to be. She wished, not for the first time, that she hadn't bought the ticket. Who could have imagined winning the lottery could make you so confused and miserable. She should just throw it away.

She knew she wouldn't.

* * *

They parked in Gower Street. As they walked towards the corner, the cold whipped Stella's hair around her face. She pulled it together into a bunch and stuffed it inside the collar of her leather jacket. She stuck her hands into her pocket. The satnav on her phone took them past the Holiday Inn Express and along the waterfront.

Before they went into the apartment building, Rupert turned to look out across the water towards Birkenhead. They heard the slap of wavelets against the river wall and there were a couple of big boats in the distance sailing down towards New Brighton and Liverpool Bay. One was an unglamorous container ship, but there was a cruise boat, lights reflecting off the little swells and the churning wake as it made for the Irish Sea.

Rupert sighed. "I love this. Always did. When I was a little kid my granda used to take me across on the ferry. We didn't get off, just went for the ride."

"Ha, that's a while ago, then."

"It was, but I still remember it. We've got some pictures as well."

"Aye well, you can tell me all about it sometime but right now we need to talk to this Jewell bloke."

"Sorry, boss, it's just that this always seems to me what Liverpool is about. The waterfront, the ships, the Graces of course. I know it's a lot different from the way it was but it's still brilliant, isn't it?"

"Yeah, course it is. Well, we're here for a start. Come on." Stella nudged his arm, turned, and pushed open the glazed door.

Chapter 34

The entrance was spacious, clean, and well kept. "It's like a posh hotel," Rupert muttered as they walked towards the lifts.

"Nice place, don't you think?" Stella said.

"Brilliant, yes."

The concierge behind his desk looked up and smiled. "Can I help you?"

Stella flashed her ID. All credit to him, the smile stayed in place.

"DS May and DC Moon. We need to speak to one of your residents." She gave him the apartment number. "Mr Douglas Jewell."

"Is he expecting you?"

She caught the start of a smirk, quickly wiped.

"No," Rupert said, "but this is police business. We'll just go up, eh?" He made a move toward the lifts.

"Hold on. I'll give him a call."

They waited until they were inevitably given the nod.

"Little Hitler. Give a bloke a uniform and that's the sort of thing that happens," Rupert grumbled as they stepped inside, and the doors closed quietly behind them.

"In all fairness he was probably just doing his job. I bet the punters living here pay through the nose for their support service."

"I suppose."

By the time they reached the third floor Jewell was standing in the hallway. He was tall and fit-looking. Blond hair styled, dark-rimmed glasses. He wore soft, navy training trousers and the hoody top sported a designer logo. Either knock-off or expensive. Stella reckoned expensive judging by the way they fitted his behind.

"Is this about Phil? Well of course it is. Have you found him, the wanker? Charmayne and Tony are well pissed off. They paid out good money for his meal and everything."

"Do you think we could come inside, Mr Jewell?" Stella said.

"Yeah, sorry. Come in." He looked down at their feet and seemed about to speak, thought better of it, but made a show of slipping off his French-style espadrilles before he walked down the wooden floor and into the living room.

It was a struggle not to stare. The view from the window was magical. Boats bobbed at their moorings and lights had come on all around the area.

"Lovely view," Stella said.

"It's cool, isn't it. Makes you feel as though you live in Venice or somewhere. Phil's view is even better. He's one floor up so he can see a bit further. His place is smaller though."

"He lives here?"

"Yeah." A flash of doubt and just a hint of worry showed in the bloke's eyes. "Is he okay? I mean he's not been in an accident, has he? Shit, if he's been in hospital and we were pulling him to pieces all this time he'll be properly brassed off. Is he hurt?"

"When did you last see him?"

"Last week, Monday. He came in for a few hours to finish off some stuff. He should have been on holiday but it was typical of Phil. Then he left. I spoke to him Tuesday morning, just to talk about the wedding and where we were going to go for a bevvy first, and that was it."

"Did you try and contact him again?" Rupert asked.

"When he didn't turn up at the pub on Saturday, yes. But he didn't answer. I left a message and then I called again later, but there was nothing. Shit, is he okay?"

Stella had moved to stand in front of a narrow table under the window. "Is this him, with you in the picture?"

"Yes. The two of us at a golf tournament. Corporate bonding and what have you. Actually, it was okay. We both like a game. I taught him – well at first, you know, until he got lessons from the club pro."

Stella lifted the framed image and showed it to Rupert. He nodded.

"Could you have a look at this picture on my phone please, Mr Jewell?"

His face had lost all colour and as he held out his hand the fingers shook.

"Is that Phillip Harwood?" Stella said.

"Oh, Christ, what happened to him? He's been beaten up. Is he in a coma?"

"I'm sorry, Mr Jewell, but Mr Harwood is dead."

Chapter 35

Doug Jewell filled them in about his friend. The worked for the same bank – himself for more than six years, Phil for about two. "I sort of took him under my wing a bit. He wasn't used to living in a city. Without being rude, he was a bit of a country bumpkin. Oh, he wouldn't mind me saying so. We used to laugh. I called him a yokel and he said I was a spiv."

He paused for a moment, rubbed a hand across his eyes and then continued, "Yes, he lived upstairs and had done since he got his job at the bank. He had family. His mum and dad lived somewhere 'down south' but they weren't in touch very much at all. There was a sister. There was some sort of story there. She was younger and he occasionally mentioned things that had happened when they were children. What about his mum and dad? Who's going to tell them?"

"We'll get in touch. Actually, you might be able to help us out. Us and them. If you were to come and identify the body, officially, it would save them the horrible journey. I expect they'll come but it will be easier if you've already done that. One of the things relatives find hard to accept is that there's been no mistake. People hang on to hope even when they've been told there's no point. If we can reassure them – that's probably the wrong word. What I mean is, I would like to tell them there is no doubt," Stella said.

"Okay. I guess I could. I mean where is he? Is he badly, erm, damaged? From the picture, I see his face is bashed about but what about the rest of him? Was it a bad crash? He was a nutcase on the road. His car might have been a classic, not like mine, but he wasn't sodding Stirling Moss, was he? I was always telling him he'd end up killing himself. Oh shit. I didn't mean that. It just came out."

"Tell you what, Mr Jewell, why don't you sit down. Let's get you a drink, water maybe, or would you like something stronger?" Stella waved a hand in the direction of the seating area.

"Okay. Actually, yes, can you pour me a whisky?" He glanced at his watch. "I was going out, meeting some mates, but I can't now. Can't face it. When do you want me to do it – see his body?"

"Tomorrow will be fine. I'll tell them to expect you at the morgue." Stella sat on the edge of one of the big soft settees as Rupert rattled bottles in the kitchen. "Mr Jewell, I'm afraid your friend, Phil, wasn't in a road accident."

They gave him as much information as they could, which wasn't very much. He was horrified, insistent that his friend was 'a lovely guy. Kind, generous. Didn't have any enemies. Not really.'

"How do you mean, not really?" Stella asked.

"Well, we deal with a lot of money, it's a high-pressure job, sometimes it gets stressful, and people lose their rag. It doesn't mean anything. It's just release of tension."

"And was there anyone recently who 'lost their rag' with Phil?"

"One of the supervisors. He cocked up, nearly lost a big account, and tried to blame Phil. There was a row. But honestly it wasn't major, and they sorted it. There was no real harm done. I mean, Chas – he wouldn't – no way could he be involved in something like this. Stabbing Phil. Christ, no."

"We'll have to ask you for his address. We'll have to have a word with Chas."

"No, honestly. I wish I hadn't said anything. It was nothing. You won't mention me, will you? Really, everybody gets on well. We've got a great gang of mates. We get together a lot and I wouldn't want to upset anyone."

"We'll be discreet but if you could just write own his address, please," Stella said.

"We'll need to have a look at Phil's flat. Do you know if the concierge would have a key?"

"No. I've got one. We had one each in case we went away or forgot them. You know the sort of t ing. We collected the mail for each other, watered plants."

"Yet, you didn't go up there, didn't give hin a knock when you couldn't contact him? You know, just i case he was there ill or something," Rupert said.

"No. I didn't. Wish I had now, but we tried r t to live in each other's pockets, you know. Respect bou daries. I just assumed he was away, and he'd be back soon.

"Okay. I'm sorry to have to ask this but do yo know if Phil ever took drugs?" Stella asked.

"Nah."

The response was too quick, the denial too a tomatic. Stella just waited. Jewell took a big gulp of the w isky and then held the glass in his hand swivelling it back nd forth between his palms. Stella just waited.

"Okay. I suppose it can't hurt him now. He lid now and then have a bit of coke. Mostly if we were g ing out, just to get in the mood, you know. Everybody d es, don't they? But he wasn't an addict or anything like th t. To be honest he was a bit straight laced. Well, compare to some of the guys. Some of them overdo it at times but not him." He paused for a minute, colour rising in his face. "Not me either. I don't."

"No, of course not, Mr Jewell," Stella said.

"Can we call someone for you? Ask a friend a family member to come and sit with you?" Rupert asked

"No. No, really, I'd rather be on my own. need to think about this. Will you let the bank know? Do have to do that?"

"No, not at all. Just leave it all to us. Now, if u could just get us the key."

"It's there in the dish on the table. The one with a plastic whale key ring."

Rupert fished it out. "We'll come back and let you know when we've finished. We'd like to keep this key. You can't go into his flat. Under the circumstances."

"Right. Okay. What about his plants?"

"We'll take care of everything," Stella told him.

* * *

As soon as they walked into the bright living room, they knew the plants were beyond needing water. They were scattered across the pale green carpet, the soil spread over the books and broken pottery which was dumped on the floor. It was rubbed into the seats of overturned chairs.

"So much for Little Hitler downstairs and paying through the nose for security," Rupert said.

Stella took out her phone to report the break-in and organize a crime scene team.

Chapter 36

Rupert and Stella had put on their gloves before they opened the door, but the suits and bootees were in the car.

Stella leaned forward to peer further into the flat. Everywhere was a mess. She could see through to the kitchen where doors hung open and broken crockery littered the floor.

"No point going in really, not right now. We haven't a clue what we might be looking for and we'll do more harm than good. We'll tell the crime scene manager there could be drugs. To be honest, I'll be surprised if there is. I'll bet he was just a user and bought stuff when he wanted it. There is no chance he was killed here, but we need it processed as soon as possible. It's a mess, but w have so little information about this bloke and this migl at least give us something more to work with. I ca 't see a computer but there's a monitor and keyboard on he floor under the table by the window. That's probably /here he had his workspace. Damn."

They handed the scene over to a crime scene nanager. Gave him a rundown of what they had so far an left him and the CSI team to start their work.

"I wouldn't even stay too late, to be ho :st. The bloke's dead already and we're going to be reall lucky if there's anything here," Stella said as they left th wrecked apartment.

As they stepped into the chilly evening, Stella ulled up her hood and stuffed her hands into her p kets for warmth.

"We might as well get off home I reckon, R pert. We need to get in early in the morning for the pos mortem exam. We need to arrange for someone to go ar l inform Phil's family. First thing tomorrow we need to find out where his parents live. It's possible the bank wil have an address. If not, we'll pass it over to Mel and R h. They need to scour his social media accounts in case here are friends from when he was a kid and try to disc er more about this sister. You can get onto the bank. Prol bly best if you go in person – here." She handed over a business card. "Doug gave me this while you were in th kitchen. It's his but it gives you the address. We will need ccess to his bank accounts as well."

"Have you got something on, boss?"

"Yes. I'm going back to the squat."

He waited for her to say more, explain her lan, but they were back at the car, and she slid into the dri ng seat.

"Is there a Tesco or a Waitrose round here?" s e asked.

"Hang on, I'll google it."

As Rupert clicked and scrolled, Stella pulled it of the car park.

"Which way?"

"Go left, there's one down there. It says it's still open."

"Perfect."

"Don't think you can park here, boss. It's a bus stop."

"Look, you sit in the driver's seat and if anyone comes along just flash your warrant card. I won't be a minute. I just need a cake."

"You've got a real sweet tooth, haven't you? Doesn't show, mind you. Sorry, that was out of order. All I mean was you look nice and slim. Oh shit…"

"Rupert, shut up."

"Shutting up, boss."

She didn't buy a plastic bag and when she stuffed the ginger cake and the Battenberg onto the shelf under the glove box, Rupert simply raised his eyebrows.

"They're not for me."

"Totally shut up, boss."

Stella laughed as she pulled away from the stop and out into the light Sunday evening traffic.

Chapter 37

Jordan sat in the dining room, a glass of rum on the table in front of him with a slice of chocolate cake. He'd spent the afternoon in the kitchen, cooking and baking. It was his way of unwinding and clearing his mind. By the time he had portioned out the curry and burgers and stowed them in the freezer he'd made a decision.

He ran it past Penny and she smiled at him.

"I knew this would happen. I knew you wouldn't be able to do a half job. It's not you, is it? I'm glad."

He picked up his phone and clicked the speed dial for Dave Griffiths.

"Sorry to bother you on a Sunday."

"You're alright. I was just sitting here with some beers and old reruns of the World Cup. As if I wasn't depressed enough as it is."

"You know if ever you feel like company, we'd be happy to see you, mate."

"That's nice of you. I might take you up on it one of these days but don't take any notice of me. I'm like a pig in muck really, nobody to make me have a shave or change my top. Mind you, I wouldn't mind some of your grub now and then. I do get a bit cheesed off with ready meals."

"Come round next week. Sunday. I'll do a roast."

"You're on. But that's not why you rang, is it?"

"No. I want to talk to you about Kirkby."

"Ha. I knew it wouldn't be long. You want to go out there, don't you? You want to get your mitts on his case, and you want me to clear it with their DI Dunn."

"Er, well, yes. As it happens, I do. They've had a pretty important development. That sergeant is doing a good job, I reckon, but I think she's perhaps not getting quite the support she needs. Hope I'm not speaking out of turn here."

"No, not if it's truly what you believe. I can't comment without more information and right now I've got enough on my plate. Actually, that brings me to another point." The next few minutes were taken up with the future plans which now would need to be changed, and Jordan's place in them.

"Are we clear, mate? We need your commitment for the next couple of days and then you can concentrate totally on the body in the squat."

"Yes. It's all great," Jordan said.

"Okay, in that case, give me a chance to speak to them in the morning and then relocate tomorrow afternoon. Oh and, Jordan…"

"Boss?"

"I'll make sure it looks good in the reports. Dedicated officer and what have you."

"Cheers, Dave."

Jordan put the phone down. This was all good, but did it mean he'd made a mistake? Was Serious and Organised not the place for him? The thought was a bit depressing, but he had to be honest with himself. There was a fizz in his gut that he hadn't had before, while he was on the sidelines of this case. Maybe when it was all over, he would need to reconsider.

Chapter 38

For the first time since she had moved in, Stella looked around her flat and found it wanting. It was cosy and the furniture was new, most of it was from Ikea but still smart-looking. Her floor was reclaimed-wood boards like the ones in the Albert Dock, but they didn't have the deep gleam of those, and the joints weren't as perfect. The paint on the frames around the windows was flaking here and there. The cracks in the ceiling were still waiting for her to get around to filling and painting.

There was no doubt the apartments down there on the waterfront were amazing and her place here on the outskirts of the city wasn't. She knew what was behind this, of course. It was the same as the idea of a new car – the money was there, and it was feeding into a greed which she didn't know she possessed.

She pulled her computer from the bag, poured a big glass of red wine, and sat down at the kitchen table. She needed to update her book and make a to-do list. They had uncovered a lot of information today and when she reported to the DI tomorrow, she had proper stuff to tell him. Things were now more complicated. Who had ransacked Phil's flat? When, and why? How had they managed when there was twenty-four-hour security? Did that mean her instincts about Douglas Jewell were wrong?

She closed her eyes for a minute and took a deep breath. It was too late to do anything much more. She was aware that Phillip Harwood's family needed to be informed as a matter of urgency. She couldn't reasonably do that until tomorrow after the formal identification. Best to be absolutely sure. Everything was stalling. It was like treading water. Frustrating. Scary. She couldn't fail and right now it was hard to believe she was getting anywhere at all.

She put away her work and shuffled back on the settee tucking her feet under her. It was quiet in the street except for the constant hum of the traffic on the main road. She didn't normally hear that unless the wind was blowing in a certain direction. The strobe of light from car headlights arced across the curtains. There was the thrum of a car engine outside for a while and shortly afterwards she heard the front gate rattle. Keith, coming home, either from a late shift at work or a night out. She'd soon know. The car drew away, a taxi then. He slammed the door and thundered up the stairs – a night out. At least he was alone, there were no loud mates thundering up the stairs and jostling on the landing.

A few minutes later she heard him in his bathroom. It was unmistakable. She tried not to listen, but it was too late now. When the flat had been converted, no enough thought or expense had been given to sound insulation. She felt irritated with herself and sad and hated the fact that her thoughts were being distracted when she needed all her mental energy to be focused on the victims and justice.

She put her work bag and the two cakes on the table in the hall. She had a shower and went to bed with her hair still damp. She knew she'd pay for it in the morning when it was knotted and frizzy.

Chapter 39

As she pulled away from the kerb Stella glanced at her watch. She'd slept surprisingly well and was much more upbeat this morning. The case was moving slowly, but it was moving. It was just after seven. Was it too early? Old people didn't sleep much, did they? Betsy had told her she didn't sleep.

The squat was still taped off. The CSI team would be a while longer although there surely couldn't be much more left to discover. The place hadn't been a proper home. But they would keep going until they were sure they had found anything there was to be found.

The uniformed officer had been stood down. Maybe the local youths would try and break in. It was a risk but up to now, that hadn't happened. There was such a staff shortage they probably couldn't even spare a special constable to stand there for hours on the off chance.

The lights were on in the front room of Betsy's house. Stella knocked gently on the door.

"It's open, come in."

It was overwarm inside and there was the smell of toast and still a hint of something a bit floral. In the front room a candle, the source of the scent, burned in the saucer on the table. Cards were laid in a pattern in front of it. They weren't Tarot, which wouldn't have surprised her, and Stella assumed the old woman was passing time playing some form of patience.

"Are you winning?"

"None of us are winning, but some of us play better." Betsy looked up and smiled. "Just looking to see what's happening with you. I thought you might come last night."

Stella looked back at the display. "Is it not patience?"

Betsy didn't answer but continued to lay out the cards. "You need to up your game. Your mind is in a tangle."

She couldn't argue and now she understood the woman was using cartomancy for fortune telling. It was all nonsense of course.

"Put the kettle on. We'll have tea."

"Do you want cake? I brought two." Stella held out the two blocks one in each hand, like an offering.

"Ginger. Well, you can give that to the birds. Put the other one in the tin. I'll have toast. You should have some as well."

There was no arguing with her. After all, Stella had gone there to talk to the woman, and it was obvious that was going to happen on Betsy's timetable. As Stella left the room the cards were gathered up and the candle extinguished, pinched between Betsy's fingertips.

The kitchen was old-fashioned. Orange tiles and green doors seating it firmly in the seventies. It was spotless and the fridge held fresh salad, eggs, cheese, some cold chicken. She might be old, but she had all her chairs at home, Stella thought.

"What do you want on your toast, Betsy?"

"Marmalade, it's in the brown jar."

"Is this home-made?"

"Don't be so daft, of course it is."

She couldn't find the tray, so Stella carried the breakfast in one piece at a time. Betsy had wrapped her cards in a black silk cloth and the candle had been moved to the side table near the fire.

"Right," the old woman said as Stella lowered herself to the settee, the plate of toast on her knee.

"First off, you need to clear your mind. You'll never get anywhere with all the clutter stopping up your thinking."

"Okay. But how do I do that?"

"By dealing with things. Get your money. Make peace with your mother and talk to your brother. Then you can start to sort things out for other people. Do it today. There's no time to waste. I don't want another of my girls crossing over. It's not their time. Come on now. Oh yes, and your nana wants you to watch out for someone you're working with. Someone with a secret. They're not on your side."

"Who? Who is it?"

"Ha, what do you think I am, some sort of magician? I just pass on the messages. Work it out for yourself. You're supposed to be a bright spark."

"So, the money?" Stella said. "I'm scared of the money. I'm scared of what it might do, how it might change everything. I haven't even got it yet and already my mam's in a huff with me and I'm getting dissatisfied with stuff I used to be content with. My flat, my car."

"Oh, for heaven's sake, girl. You're focusing on the wrong things. There's nothing to be ashamed of in wanting to live somewhere nice. A car, well that's just stuff and you would have been wanting a new one next time you had a rise at your work or something. It's all just wrapping. What you should be looking at is all the things you could do to help."

"How do you mean, help?"

"Stop being so vague. You know full well what I mean. This world runs on money. All of it. Oh, I know we sometimes pretend it doesn't. There's little that can't be improved if you've got plenty of it and it's not about cars and houses. It's about ease and comfort and health and joy."

"I thought money couldn't buy happiness?" Stella was uncomfortable with the way the conversation had gone. She was being lectured by this nowty old crone and she'd been hoping for help and advice.

"Nor can it. But it can certainly ease some of the misery. I've had enough of you now and I'm waiting for a visitor. Go on to your work and take care of business. The big boss's coming today. About time as well. That'll help."

Stella gathered up her things in silence and turned to leave.

"Estella." The old woman used her baptismal name. Nobody used it. "You've got a lot to do. It'll work out but it's up to you how well that is. Be careful. When you come back next time bring me some pickled onions. I haven't had a decent pickled onion in months. I don't get supermarket ones."

"I can't go trolling round the shops for some onions."

"Oh, you will."

As she left, another woman wearing a jacket with the hood pulled over her head was walking up the narrow path and they stepped onto the grass to avoid each other. It was only after she got into the car that Stella realized she had just seen George Kenny's mum.

Chapter 40

Rupert was already in the incident room. He'd booted up the computer and the big screen was lit. "I've been on to London, boss. They're starting the PM in about half an hour. I was going to record it for you."

"Excellent. Carry on with that anyway. It'll be good for us to have our own copy."

Mel joined them.

"You probably don't want to hang around here. Why don't you just carry on with trawling the net for stuff about Phil Harwood?" Stella said.

She turned to Rupert. "This isn't right. Let's find somewhere quiet to watch. I should have thought about it last night. We can't have this going on in an open office. They should have let us go down there. This is a pain in the arse."

"There's the room by the bogs, the one that had the leak in the roof," Rupert said.

"Yeah. That'll do."

The small office was in darkness, there was the smell of damp and the furniture had been relocated leaving just a desk in the corner. The top was warped, and the drawers were stuck.

"Sorry, Rupert, this is a bit grim," Stella said.

"It's okay, boss. You're right, we can't have this playing in front of the civilians. I'll get it set up."

"Great. Do you want coffee? I could do with one. I'll go to the canteen. We don't want machine sludge."

On her way back with the two drinks Stella glanced into the larger incident room. Mel had her head down focused in on her screen and Ruth had arrived. Betsy's words were rolling around in her head. Who was she supposed to be careful of? Not Rupert, surely. She liked him, she had been impressed by his work and his friendship. Not Mel, the young woman was keen and hard-working. So, one of the other officers, maybe even the DI — she worked with them all, didn't she? There were the civilians, the cleaners even, they were all colleagues one way or the other.

It was all rubbish, all this stuff about messages from her nan, but it had focused her mind. They could all cause problems if they decided to. But why? She'd never done anything to annoy people, not deliberately anyway. It was the money again, wasn't it? As soon as they found out about it, things would change. Some of them, a few, would just be happy for her. More would wonder if they could blag something for themselves. Then there'd be the jealousy, people who just couldn't be pleased about someone else's good fortune. It happened when there were promotions, when somebody's kids did well at something. Even weddings and babies. There was always someone who'd be dog in the manger about it.

She shook her head. She really had to stop thinking about this stuff. The old woman was just a nutter and if it wasn't for the fact that she was convinced she still knew more than she was saying then Stella wouldn't be going back again.

Would she?

Jordan Carr was walking down the corridor towards her.

"Morning, sir."

"Morning, Stella. Are you busy?"

"Well, we're just waiting to see the post-mortem from the Met."

"I'll sit in if that's okay and then we need to have a chat. Have you heard from DI Dunn?"

"Not this morning."

"Oh, okay. Awkward. Never mind, one thing at a time. Where are we?"

She pointed along the corridor. "Sorry. This isn't very good."

They arrived in the smelly, dark office just as Rupert finished the set-up. The screen was live and showed the interior of the morgue in London. The body of the in the middle of the room was covered by a sheet. A trolley of instruments was pulled up beside the table and in the background was the sound of someone clattering about out of shot.

Rupert had brought their chairs in from the large room and when he saw Jordan, he strode out to come back with another one. They sat in a small semi-circle around the scarred old desk just as the medical examiner walked into view and uncovered the poor murdered woman.

Chapter 41

"Good morning. I'm Dr Lewis." The woman glanced directly at the camera. "I believe we have remote viewers. I hope you can see okay from this angle. We have sound so any questions, please feel free to ask."

Stella leaned forward. "Thank you, Dr Lewis. I'm DS May and I have DC Moon with me and DI Carr. We're grateful to you for arranging this."

"Oh, I didn't arrange it, the tech guys did some stuff with cameras and wires. I think it's a good idea actually. It could save a lot of time and money spent on travel. You'll have to let us know how it is from your end. There's no reason this couldn't become a regular thing."

She turned to the body on the table where an assistant had removed the cover and Fee lay exposed apart from a small cloth preserving what dignity she had left.

Stella and Rupert had attended posts before, but this with no smell was just as if they were watching a television programme. The commentary was like those that crime programme fans had become so used to.

"A young woman, white, early to mid-twenties." And so it went on. Fee's height and weight, her general health from the external viewing. The scraping of residue from under her fingernails, the removal of tufts of hair, swabs, and the excision of a small tattoo of a bird from the left hip.

"We'll send you images, of course. The tattoo isn't very old so you may be able to find out where it was done. If that's of any help in your investigations. I think it's a swallow. We'll have tests run on the ink," Dr Lewis said.

Then there was the more intimate examination. Stella was aware Rupert turned away as the modesty cloth was removed. She liked him for that.

"There is no sign of violence here. No tearing or bruising. No indication of sodomy. We will, of course, send off samples, but I don't think we are going to get any sperm. We have examined her with the black light and though there was plenty of blood around the stab wound, her thighs and genitals appeared clean. So, she had washed herself after any sex act or someone else washed her. Given that, I would expect the other person or persons probably used a condom. Maybe we'll get residue from the outside of it. Of limited help really but we'll keep you informed."

Then there was the examination and excision of the stab wound, and the damaged internal organs. Nothing unexpected showed up. The cause of death was the dramatic damage to the heart. But they had all known that anyway.

"The weapon was probably a knife, not serrated. Blade one hundred and thirty millimetres round about, and at its widest about thirty millimetres. Very common shape, a chef's knife. Most kitchen sets have one like it. It's all very well refusing sales of knives to people but when every home has one, how can you possibly hope to police it?" She shook her head.

"Thank you so much, Dr Lewis," Stella said as the pathologist stepped away from the table and peeled off her gloves leaving the assistant to replace the organs they had finished with and sew the poor woman back together.

"We don't have a next of kin yet, do we?" the doctor asked.

"No, we only have the name Fee from someone who knew her up here. We are still searching for more information."

"Well, she'll stay with us for now then. I'll arrange for you to have some close-ups, and as soon as the report's ready I'll ensure you have a copy. Any questions, just email my assistant and I'll do what I can."

They turned off the screen and Stella sipped at the coffee which was now stone cold. "Aw, she was dead nice, wasn't she? No shouting, no telling her assistants off, and she was on time and everything."

"Yeah, but not as exciting as Jasper. She didn't even throw anything," Rupert said.

"True. We didn't learn much really, did we?"

"There's the tattoo."

"Yeah. There is that. If we can find where she had it done, we might at least find someone who had spoken to her recently. It'd be a start."

"Have they not found her anywhere on the CCTV from the city centre?" Jordan said.

"Not yet," Stella said. "I had a word with the uniform sergeant, and his patrols in Sheil Road had pictures of her. Nobody knows her. Not that they're saying, anyway. I wonder if maybe they weren't working the streets as such. Just using the squat and maybe the punters are brought by car or, you know, just told where to go. It seems to me more likely they weren't even having sex there, or not in the horrible bedroom anyway. You know they could be more like escorts, taken off in the people carrier. Parties, stag nights, those sorts of thing. With no clothes in the place we really don't know how well they presented themselves. There was perfume, and hair products. Not much but at least they were taking care of their appearances. Maybe we should broaden our thinking. You know Phil Harwood was a rich bloke. Not the type to trawl the streets looking for business. Maybe this is a different sort of operation altogether."

"That's a good thought, boss. It's always seemed a bit odd," Rupert said, "a posh guy like Harwood in a dirty, smelly squat."

"Maybe he wasn't looking for a quickie. Maybe this is something else entirely."

"Like what?" Rupert said.

"Shit, I don't know. I'm just saying, let's try and, you know, think outside the box. But also, let's find out where she had her tattoo done."

"I've got an appointment at the bank in about an hour. If we get the image by then I could troll some of the tattoo parlours in town afterwards. These guys often know each other's work, don't they?"

"Great idea." Stella was going to suggest they go together but she had given the task to Rupert, and it would probably put him out if she took over now.

"Okay, Rupert. You'd better get off. Good luck with that. Keep in touch."

Jordan hadn't joined in the conversation but as they collected their belongings and returned the chairs to the incident room, he asked Stella who the witness was who had given them the name and if he could see the statement. He made a point of scrolling through the notes on his tablet.

"Oh, right. It was just some old woman who lived out there, near the squat. I'm sorry we didn't actually get a statement."

"Ah. Perhaps it would be an idea to do so."

He was right, of course he was, now he'd mentioned it. She'd cocked up. Was this the problem Betsy had warned her about? Not a trouble causer as such but just someone who would show up her weaknesses? She was shocked to feel the prickle of tears at the back of her eyes. She had wanted to impress, and it wasn't going well.

She wasn't sure what she was supposed to do now. Was he going to speak to DI Dunn, or did he want her to stay and talk?

"We need to have a chat later," he said, glancing at his watch. "In the meantime I'm going to speak to Dunn. Time's getting on."

Her phone burbled. "Sorry, sir." She held up the handset.

"It's fine. Carry on."

"Boss, it's Mel."

"Yeah, what can I do for you? I'm just on the way out."

"Sorry. It's just that they've rung from the morgue. They've been waiting for Doug Jewell to go and identify the body of Phillip Harwood."

"Yes, and what's happened?"

"Well, nothing, boss. Nothing at all. He hasn't turned up."

Chapter 42

"Okay. You carry on, Stella," Jordan said. "I'll still be here when you get back."

Stella messaged Rupert.

> *Change of plan. Meet me at the Albert Dock flats. Doug Jewell has gone AWOL.*

She could be worrying unnecessarily, of course, but she had a bad feeling about this. When they'd interviewed Jewell, he seemed genuinely upset and wanting to help. So, no message, no call, and no show was a bit odd. It could be that he'd bottled it and couldn't face the idea of seeing his friend dead. There was only one way to find out.

She was able to park in Gower Street again and as she walked from the car park Rupert ran to catch up.

"What's going on, boss?"

"Not sure yet. He didn't turn up. I've tried calling but there's nothing, not even a voicemail response. That's odd, and I rang the bank. He hasn't turned in for work. How did you get on down there?"

"Yeah, not bad. Pulled rank a bit with their HR but I've got the contact details for Phil's parents. I was going to give their local nick a call and ask them to arrange the visit. Cornwall it is. Truro. I spoke to his boss as well. Not much to tell, no problems with his work. He was actually well thought of and progressing in the company."

"What about that Chas bloke?"

"I had a word with him. I think it was a bit of nothing, to be honest. He said he barely remembered the incident and him and Phil had played squash since then, been to a few gatherings. He seemed surprised it had been mentioned at all. He was pretty cut up about what had happened, and I believed him. He wasn't so keen on Jewell, though. Said he kept him at arm's length. Wouldn't give me much info. Just said he wasn't the sort of bloke he spent time with. Told me he was more a beer and footie bloke. I tried to draw him out but that was as much as he'd give me. Of course, if you want to interview him yourself, boss…"

"No, that's excellent work, Rupert. Really good. We'll put him on the back burner unless something else comes up."

The concierge recognized them. "Oh, not you two again."

"What happened to being helpful to the authorities?"

"Aye right. You've no idea the turmoil you've caused. CSI everywhere and newspaper reporters out the front and upsetting the tenants. It's been a real pain in the arse."

"Yes, well it wasn't much fun for Phil Harwood either," Stella snapped.

The bloke blushed and looked away.

"Fair play, I suppose. I'm probably going to lose my job over this mess. There's to be an enquiry into how come there was a break-in and it's gonna come down on my head. Me and my mucka."

"I assume you've given your statement?" Stella said.

"Yeah, I would have thought you'd read it by now. There wasn't much I could say. I knew nothing, saw nothing, and can't explain any of it. The cameras were working all the time I was on shift, and nothing happened."

"So, how come your head's on the block?"

"I hadn't done all my rounds when I should. To be honest, we're short-staffed, pulling double shifts all the time, and I had a kip in the storeroom. It's all in the statement. I know I was out of order, but we've got a new baby at home, and I was absolutely knackered. Sod's law, isn't it? We've reviewed the CCTV and there was nothing on it that I should have seen but they reckon if I'd been doing my patrols, I might have heard something." He sighed and rubbed his hands over his face.

"Well, I'm sorry. Anyway, what we need now is information about Douglas Jewell."

"Yeah, what about him?"

"Have you seen him? When did you last speak to him and, basically, is he here now? If not have you any idea where he is?"

"Oh him. He was down here yesterday asking me what I knew. I told him nothin'. He looked a mess, a wreck to be honest. I haven't seen him since then. Yesterday about lunch time."

"We're going up there. If he's not in, we need access to his apartment. Can you help us there?"

"I don't have keys if that's what you're asking."

"What about in the other apartment, boss?" Rupert said. "He said they held keys for each other, didn't he?"

"Let's go up and give him a knock and if he's not there, which I reckon is the way this is going to be, get on to CSI. See if they've found a key."

"Do you want me to ring up?" the concierge asked.

"No, we've tried ringing him. We're just going up. We'll need the CCTV for the last two days. If you could start downloading it, it'd be a help."

He wasn't there. They had known he wouldn't be.

"CSI have bagged a key, boss. I've asked them to bring it back. It's got the flat number on it."

They spent the time roaming the corridors and pushing against closed doors.

"Did they find out how the original intruders gained access?" Stella said.

"There's a report just come through. I'm reading it now. They haven't found anything definite and it's driving Sergeant Flowers batty."

"Well, maybe there were no intruders."

"But, boss, you saw the state of the flat. You're not thinking Phil did it to his own place, are you?"

"I'm keeping an open mind at the moment and just letting some thoughts percolate. Going with the flow."

Chapter 43

After the devastation found in Harwood's flat Stella anticipated a similar situation. It wasn't so, the place was clean and tidy. Blinds had been partly lowered at the windows. The kitchen was spotless. No dishes on the drainer and the washing-up brush was propped in a plastic tub to dry. Back in the living room, there were big leafy plants on the wall opposite the window and the area looked like an intensive care ward.

"Have you seen this?" Rupert said. "The plants are all standing in bowls of water, they weren't like that last time."

"Is it relevant?" Stella asked.

"My gran used to do it when we went on holiday, so they didn't dry out. I think we can assume he planned to leave."

Stella turned and walked along the short hallway to the bedroom. The bed was made. The linen basket was empty except for a pair of boxers and a T-shirt. She slid open the huge, mirrored doors on the wardrobe.

The space wasn't empty, there were suits, business shirts, ties rolled and stowed in separate compartments in a couple of drawers. Dark socks were neatly folded together. Shoes and trainers, black, brown, leather, suede, all lined neatly on racks, some of them in clear plastic boxes. The second door revealed shelves stacked with laundered shirts in plastic bags, running gear and shorts. Casual trousers hung next to lounging wear. Everything was neat and well organised and the empty spaces very obvious. Stella ran her gloved hands along the empty hangers. On the top shelf were a couple of travel bags but again gaps showed where objects had been taken out.

"Yeah, he's done a runner. Rupert, get on down to that bloke in reception and find out about his car. Then get a BOLO call out. This plonker has just become a person of interest."

"On the way, boss."

* * *

By the time they arrived at the nick the call had gone out nationwide for sightings of a black BMW and Douglas Jewell. DI Dunn was in the incident room, pacing.

"Hmm, pacing's not good, is it?" Rupert muttered.

"Not so much," Stella said. "Something up, boss?"

"My office, if you would," Dunn said.

He stormed off and, with a quick glance at the rest of her little team, Stella followed. She would not scurry, but she picked up the pace as he turned and glared at her.

"Okay. There's been a change of circumstances. As you know I've got a lot on my plate at the moment."

"Yes, sir."

"So, it's been decided that oversight of your case will be handed over to someone else. Because DI Carr has been showing such an interest, we've decided he would be the best person for the task."

"Sorry, sir, I don't quite understand."

"For God's sake, Sergeant, it's not rocket science. To put it plainly, you now answer to DI Carr."

"But he's at St Anne Street."

"Not for the moment. He's been redeployed. He'll be based here and will be the SIO on the murder case. You can go. I'm up to my eyes here."

Heading back to the incident room Stella tried to make sense of what had just happened. Was this because of the cock-up at the drugs raid? Was it really just that Dunn was overwhelmed? It was always possible given the staffing problems. Had Carr screwed up somehow and this was a parking place for him? It was impossible to say. But no matter what, she couldn't help feeling it was going to work out better for her. Dunn had been difficult since the drugs raid. On the other hand, she had just messed up with Carr and the stuff about Betsy Minoghue. Her mind was in turmoil. The only thing she could do was calm down and carry on.

Carr met her outside the incident room. "Okay, you up to speed, Sergeant?"

"Yes, sir."

"I'm looking forward to working with you. Have you got a few minutes now to get me right up to date and tell me your next planned moves?"

"Yes. Do you want to do it here?" She pointed into the room.

"I reckon so."

"Okay, I'll organize a desk."

"No, I'll do that. There's no rush. In the meantime what's all this about a black BMW?"

She went through the events at Albert Dock. "I reckon I've got it all under control. In fact, boss, I reckon this is a big leap forward. This bloke's done a runner. I don't know yet how it all fits together but it's definitely dodgy, isn't it?"

"Yes. You're right. Of course you are. But how? If he's involved with the drugs gang, which still has to be a possibility, this is going to put the cat among the pigeons."

"Really I'm still not convinced the two things are so closely connected. I know it's two addresses in Kirkby but the two are very different. The original place we raided was big time, heavy hitters, teams of runners, county lines kids, and loads of product moving through. My case was little more than a minor crack den with a few hookers, and the dead bloke, of course. They could be completely unconnected."

"If there is a connection it will become obvious, but I think linking the two has been muddying the water."

At last. Stella felt some of the tension ease. He was on her side. He agreed with her. So, Betsy, is that it now? Was it Dunn who was causing the problem? She pushed the thought away. What did that daft old woman know?

"I would like a warrant to have a team search the flat down at Albert Dock," she said. "And a good look at Jewell's bank statements and anything else we can find on him. Where he was born, what his background is."

"We can do that. In the meantime, shall we go and let everyone know what's going on?"

Chapter 44

There was no report of the black BMW. For a while they thought it had been spotted on the M6 heading south. It was raining heavily, and the visibility was affected but, in the end, it was just an innocent driver who never knew he had been the subject of police interest.

"We can't do much more now," Stella told the team. "Ruth, anything new from the Met?"

"I think I would have said."

"Yeah, of course you would."

She glanced at Jordan who raised his eyebrows. It was time to have a word with Ruth and sort out whatever the woman's problem was.

"What are we doing about identification of the first victim, boss?" Rupert said. "Now Doug Jewell has gone, we still need to do that. His family haven't been informed. It could come back on us."

"Yes, good point, Rupert. Leave it with me, have an idea."

Jordan didn't stand up, he didn't tap on the desk with a pen, nothing like that. He waited for a lull in the conversation and just began to speak. His voice was low but clear and they all turned to him to listen.

"You've all been doing a great job. DS May has been outstanding but this is obviously a major case. There are now two unlawful killings probably connected and it's been decided it might be good to have more experienced help on the ground. DI Dunn is in the middle of something else which I can't comment on at the moment, so I have come in to assist. DS May is still running the show. The only change is that she will be reporting to me and if I can be of any help at all for any of you, I'm here. It's not a permanent transfer for me so I'm just going to sit in here with you. I think there'll be a spare desk somewhere we can forage." They laughed. "So, any questions?"

There was nothing.

"Okay then. Back to you, Stella."

"Thank you, sir."

"Jordan, call me Jordan, all of you."

"Well, I reckon we might as well just carry on. It's nearly end of shift so wind up and then everyone get off. Briefing at seven-thirty in the morning. Thanks."

It was too late to go into town now and supermarket pickles had already been vetoed. Stella searched for delicatessens on the way back to the area where the squat was. There was a butcher and deli with pictures of well stocked shelves. Worth a try, but honestly, why? She was a police officer. If she had a question, then all she was supposed to do was ask. There was no need, in fact it was a bad idea, to ply a possible witness with food and favours. On top of that she was going to have to formalize this if it went on any longer or DI Carr would have serious questions about her working practices.

She thought about Betsy and headed to the butchers. He had pickles, some of them were familiar but on the shelves behind his counter were jars with the magic word 'artisan' on them. They were three times the price of the others. She bought two jars.

The door to the old woman's house was unlocked but closed. Stella knocked.

"Betsy, it's me. Can I come in?"

"That's what you're here for, I suppose. Shut the door, you're letting the draft in. I'm in the kitchen."

The house was filled with the smell of fried fish and chips. Stella's mouth began to water.

The little table was laid with two places, two plates were warming on the cooker and there was a dish in the oven covered with foil.

"Sorry, are you expecting visitors?" Stella said.

"You're here. Take your coat off. Are those my onions? You get the tea out of the oven. Here, let me have them."

Betsy reached and took one of the jars, twisting the top easily and then dipping her thumb and finger into the vinegar to scoop out one of the little onions. She chewed and smacked her lips.

"Aye, that's alright. Well come on, are we going to eat those before they get cold? I suppose you'll want tomato sauce."

"I'm sorry, I didn't come to eat with you."

"But you're here and you have to be fed. Sit down, girl. You want to talk, and I want to eat. Let's get on."

Chapter 45

Betsy didn't speak much during the meal. A request for bread and butter, a couple of comments about the weather. It was later when the dishes were washed and put away and they sat in the living room, a glass of whisky each, that she turned to Stella, took her hand, and spoke in a low voice, almost a whisper.

"You need to get yourself together, girl. The women, down in London, they need you to sort yourself out. We can't have any more death. It's up to you."

The words brought out the prickle of gooseflesh on Stella's arms.

"I know, Betsy, but it's all complicated. I can't get any further forward. Now one of my witnesses has gone missing. We can't find him. I'm no nearer to ever working out the motive for the first killing. Shit, I haven't even been able to have the man from the squat properly identified."

"You know who he is," the old woman said.

"Yes. But legally we have to confirm it. His parents live in the south, and I didn't want to bring them up here before we had him officially named."

"Do you think it'll help? Honestly. They've got the rest of their lives without him, a few hours driving to Liverpool is nothing compared to that."

"But it would be awful for them. Hoping all the way that we'd made a mistake. I don't want to send a picture or anything. It's so horrible."

"Aw, bless you, child. Yes, they'll talk about it afterwards. They'll tell people that all along they convinced themselves you were wrong. But they'll know. His mother will know already there's something happened. She'll feel his absence even if she doesn't recognize it. You know who he is. Honour his memory. Tell his mam and dad."

"Okay. You're right," Stella said. "The bloke who's gone missing is his friend. We thought he was, at any rate. Now, I don't really know. It looks as though maybe he was the one who killed him. I mean, why would he run away, if not?"

Betsy just shrugged and sipped her drink.

"Okay, I came really to ask you seriously, what do you know about Fee? All we have so far is that she was stabbed to death. She wasn't raped, she wasn't beaten. We don't know where she stayed for the bit of time she was in London. I know she worked on the streets and it's dangerous, but this doesn't feel like a sex crime to me. What do you know about her? Tell me everything."

"She used to come and talk. They all used to come and talk. I didn't ask them questions. They told me what they wanted me to know."

"That's all? But what did she tell you?" Stella leaned forward forcing Betsy to look her in the eye. "You don't know anything about her except her name? You don't know where she came from or whether she had family?"

"Aye. She had a mother, no father that she knew about. She didn't speak to her mam. She was ashamed."

"Ashamed?"

"Yes, of what she'd become. She was planning to get some money put aside and go to college. She wanted to be a nurse. She had plans. But she owed money."

"Who did she owe money to?"

"I can't name no names. I'm just an old woman. Vulnerable. You'll get there in the end."

"No, you can't leave it at that. I can take you to the station. I can question you as a hostile witness. You have to tell me anything at all you know."

"Aye you could, but you won't."

"Bloody hell, Betsy, you're impossible."

"Pass that bottle and I think it's time you went. You've still got a lot of work to do and not long to do it. Those girls need you to fix this. Let yourself out. And go and see your mam."

It was too late. She'd ring her. Tomorrow. It had been ages since they had gone so long without talking. When she was training, she'd asked the family not to ring too often, and they'd respected that. But usually she spoke almost every day to her parents and her granddad. She was tired. Tomorrow would do.

Chapter 46

There was a message on Stella's landline. Friendly, perky, and upbeat. The lottery people wondering if she had any idea when it would be convenient for them to visit.

She had to make a decision about that. She had to call her mum, and to sort out the food which was beginning to smell in the fridge, and she had to make an appointment with the garage because the sinister rattle at the rear end of the car was getting worse.

She had a quick shower, turned out the lights and crawled into bed. She sniffed at her pillow. Yes and she needed to do some laundry.

* * *

It was still dark when the team gathered for the briefing. Cleaning staff were pushing vacuum cleaners about in the corridor outside. The incident room smelled of coffee.

Jordan Carr was already there. He'd brought in a box of doughnuts.

He sat quietly until the team had their drinks and cakes. "Okay, this is by way of a heads-up. Today when you were all tucked up in your beds there was a major drugs raid at an address in Northwood," he said. "It was handled from St Anne Street acting on information from people arrested in the previous exercise."

There was a hush and a definite rise in the tension. "At this time it is still ongoing. Clearing up by now but soon you'll be more aware of it. There will be repercussions for this station. St Anne Street are in charge but your station will be part of the backup and some of the suspects will be brought back here for processing. This was a direct result of the botched raid in Westvale and I'm pleased to be able to tell you that this time, we have been much more successful. I'm sorry if you think I should have said something, but the major thing was that this had to be kept quiet, and it was."

"Is this why you were here then, sir?" Melanie asked.

"No, not directly. I am here as I said yesterday to help in your murder investigation."

"Does this mean our case is definitely connected with the drugs gang then?" Rupert said, glancing at Stella.

"Not necessarily," Jordan said. "DS May remains in charge of the murder enquiry. I am still here to assist where I can and act as SIO, but this is another thing. It's just more stuff to deal with and we all have to get on with it. So, for the moment I think we should just carry on with what we were doing and, if you have a moment, Stella, I'd like a quick word." He moved out into the corridor.

Stella was furious. She could barely breathe. Her hands shook and she thrust them into her pockets as she stood in front of Jordan her head lowered, teeth clenched and unable to speak through the fury.

"Stella," he began. "Calm down."

"So, this is it then is it, sir? Just a way to wrap things up quickly. I realize it'll be really convenient for everything to be lumped together but was there any need for this." She swept an arm back towards the incident room. "This pantomime. Why not just tell me it had been decided? Nobody ever believed it was a separate inquiry. I actually thought you believed in it, in keeping an open mind. Why wasn't I told, why wasn't I part of this raid? This stinks, it really does. Jesus, Northwood – it's just down the road. We should have been a part of that."

Jordan didn't interrupt. He waited until she calmed down and stopped glancing back and forth along the corridor and shaking her head.

"I'm sorry," he said. "It was eyes only. We still don't know what went wrong last time. We had to move quickly, and it had to be kept between the smallest number of people. But it's done now. We've been successful. I was there this morning. I saw the results of the raid. And it was great."

"Yeah, and that's it, isn't it? St Anne Street, Serious and Organised. Clear-up rates are important, aren't they? And, oh look, one of their officers is in charge of my murder."

"No, you've got it wrong."

"Really? Sorry, sir, but I don't think so."

"What do you think then?"

"What?"

"How do you see what has happened this morning, a successful raid, as interfering with your killings?"

"I reckon it's obvious, isn't it? My victim will just be lumped in with all the rest and it'll be accepted they were just drugged-up nobodies. Fee was a prostitute, so she won't matter. All just part and parcel of the mess. What is it you're going to do now, just take what we've done and put it with the rest of the reports? Big clear-up. Well done, everyone."

"Stella, you've got it wrong. But I don't think we should debate it here. Why don't you go and get yourself a drink? I'm heading downstairs to help out. I'll speak to you later."

He walked off leaving her leaning against the wall. She was still shaking with anger but it was just beginning to dawn on her that she had been way out of line the way she had spoken to him.

Way to go, Stel. How was that, Nana? Not too much of a doormat then, was I?

Rupert had his head down over his computer. She didn't know how much he might have heard. He gave her a few minutes before he spoke.

"We've got Phillip Harwood's parents coming in later," he said. "Shall I arrange for a family liaison officer to look after them or do you want to do it yourself?"

"Er, yes. Least I can do, and I have questions," Stella said.

"They've refused to stay up here. They're going back home straight away afterwards and arranging things from down there. Doesn't seem they're a close family."

"No, but I still need to speak to them. I need to know more about him."

She hadn't wanted this battle and she especially didn't want a face-off with Jordan Carr. She liked him. She had thought he was straight. Now it seemed maybe she'd been wrong. Was he just a plant to take over her case? Well, it wasn't happening. She would stand her ground. It would be easier not to. Easier to just let it go. She didn't join the police because it was easy, though. Fee in London, the other girls and Phil Harwood weren't going to be sacrificed to the clear-up rates for St Anne Street. This might just be a point when she refused to back down even at the risk to her career. The idea made her feel sick.

Chapter 47

Reports began to filter through about the raid. It had been mayhem for a short while. There had been reports of a gunshot. It had turned out to be nothing more than the back door collapsing under the combined weight of several thugs who forgot there was a brick wall around the backyard, and the gate had been nailed closed years ago.

The officers involved had been spat at, sworn at, and some of the girls and the younger kids cried and begged for understanding, for a favour, for a chance. It was in some part sad, some part harrowing, and it was dangerous, but it was the job. They went through the routines. Identification, arrest, and rights, and just now and then a word of comfort and reassurance.

Paddy wagons scooped up the detritus apart from the broken and bleeding, a couple of whom were whisked away in ambulances. Within the hour calm had been restored and the windows were being boarded, much to the disgust of small boys armed with rocks and ill intent.

Simultaneously in Aughton, two large, detached houses received surprise visits from detectives quietly escorted by armed officers. They had warrants. Before the teams had moved in to search the spacious rooms, solicitors in flash cars had screeched down the driveways with briefcases, mobile phones, smart suits, threats, and questions.

DI Dunn paced through the sordid spaces in Northwood, while the detectives from St Anne street sat in the warm and comfortable lounges of Aughton.

The raid was a success. The cells and interview rooms were filled with dealers, addicts, and hangers on. The station was overcrowded, the noise excessive. They brought in people from child services for some of the very youngest. At least they were safe for now, for a little while. Maybe one or two of them could be reclaimed. Just maybe. As for the rest they would be processed, not for the first time for the majority.

"It's like a cattle market down in the cells," Rupert said as they leaned against the wall taking a break.

"It's worse, at least at a cattle market there's a point to it. With most of these there's just no point at all. Even if they go down for a bit they'll come out and get straight back into it again. Sometimes it all feels hopeless," Stella said.

In the city centre nick, the drug bosses spent little time in cells and most of them were out before it was dark. In Kirkby, it was a day of unanswered questions and requests for bacon baps and cans of Coke and '*Please anything to stop the jonesing.*'

For them it was rough and unpleasant and many of the suspects were physically unable to help much. The medics sent some to the hospital in too poor a state to be questioned.

It was a long, hard day with short breaks for coffee and no time for food and by the end of it, with reams of notes to write up, everyone was exhausted.

Just before the end of shift, Jordan came back to the incident room. He flopped down on the creaky chair they'd found for him and put his head in his hands.

"You alright, sir?" Rupert asked him.

"Yep. Just a bit knackered, to be honest."

Stella appeared at the side of his desk with a cup of coffee and a doughnut. "This is one of the leftovers, I'm afraid, but..." – she shrugged – "sugar, it might help."

Jordan nodded and smiled at her. "It's probably all good news for you, Stella. From what I've heard up to now anyway. We'll speak first thing in the morning. Right now, I think most of us just want to get out of here."

Chapter 48

There wasn't much discussion. They were going to the pub. End of.

It wasn't a noisy group at first, but they were mostly satisfied with what they'd achieved. Their reputation recovered by a successful operation. DI Dunn was smiling again. He stood them all a drink even though so many of his own officers hadn't been directly involved, and once they'd been served their burgers and chips, their soup and sandwiches, the tiredness began to ease and the noise level rose.

In the corner, Stella and Rupert sat with Mel who had been seconded part way through the morning to help with administration. Ruth was conspicuous by her absence.

"I haven't seen her since about eleven this morning. She was in first thing and then I just noticed her bag had gone and her machine was turned off. Perhaps she had the doctor or something," Melanie said.

"She didn't say anything to me. Mind you, you guys are on flexitime, aren't you? Odd to take today off, isn't it? With all that was happening. What do you know about her?"

"Not much really. I've never worked with her before, and she told me 'she doesn't *choose* to discuss her home life with colleagues'. I thought, well, sod you, and didn't ask again."

"Okay. I'll remember that," Stella said. "I expect she'll be in tomorrow. How much have you seen, Mel? You've been typing up reports all day."

"Yeah. Nothing very exciting, to be honest. Just what you'd expect. Possession, supplying, a couple of GBH which pleased DI Dunn. Been looking for them for a while. But mostly it was a bit ordinary after all the fuss early on."

"Nothing about the squat? No mention of our body?"

"No – not that I've seen. It was raised quite a few times, but nobody is admitting anything."

"You heard anything, Rupert?"

"Nothing from the people I've spoken to," he said. "Seems like most of them were only too happy to be dropping other people in it and pointing fingers. If they'd seen the chance of a deal, they'd have had your hand off."

"Yeah, that's what I've heard." Stella couldn't keep the grin from her face.

"You were right, weren't you, boss?" Mel said.

"It's beginning to look like it."

"Aces. In that case I'll get another round in, yeah?" Rupert said.

"No. I can't. I have to go and see my mam and I'm driving anyway, thanks though. You and Mel carry on. I'll see you tomorrow. Oh yeah, just before I go, there's nothing about Doug Jewell, is there? I've had nothing."

"Nope. I'll go through the reports before I go home and let you know if there's anything," Rupert said.

"Brilliant. Thanks for that."

* * *

She could go home and have a shower, get changed, but it would just delay things so Stella drove straight to her mum's house. The door was opened by Shelley with the baby clamped on her hip.

"Oh, it's you. It's a bit late. We've had our tea."

"I didn't come for tea. I just came round to see Mam."

"She's gone out. Gone down the bingo. She's had the baby all day and needed a break."

"How come she had Jamie?"

"I'm back at work now so we're having to share the minding till we get somewhere sorted."

"Is that a problem then?"

"Yes, it's a problem." As she spoke Shelley waggled her head back and forth in a 'you know nothing and understand less' attitude. "It's money. Have youse any idea how much childcare costs? Well, no, of course you haven't. Youse don't need to bother about that, do you?"

"Well – no." Stella couldn't work out how that put her in the wrong. Just because she hadn't had a kid before she could afford it and had somewhere to live. "Anyway, I'll just say hello to Granda."

"He's in bed."

"Is he badly?"

"Poor thing. Yes, it's his hip. The doctor had to up his pills to help with the pain and they've knocked him out."

"I didn't know," said Stella.

"How would you? You never come round, you've never even rung your mam."

She wasn't going to make excuses. It had been mam who stormed out of the flat. "Still no idea when he'll get his hip replacement?"

"You're joking. No chance for months yet. Not unless he can pay. I don't suppose you've got a few thousand quid spare, have you? He'd get it done quick then alright. Private hossie. No wait. It's not fair."

"Is Peter at work then?"

"Aye he is. Won't be back till late and me on me own with this one. You can come in for a bevvy if you like."

Stella looked at the little boy who was grizzling and drooling, sucking on a piece of soggy breadcrust.

"No, you're all right. Tell Mam I came, will you? I'll see her at the weekend. Ask her to give me a ring."

"Right."

So there it was again. Money. This time there was no question. Granda needed money. He was going to get it. She'd put in the call first thing next morning and take an hour off to get it all out of the way.

Chapter 49

In the end, the visit from the lottery people didn't take long at all. She'd asked them to come early telling them she would be pushed for time. If they were put out, they didn't let it show.

Three million pounds. It didn't sound like money. She couldn't imagine it. What would that even look like? They told her she needed to open a special bank account for it, and she let them help her. They gave her advice about giving any of it away and the tax repercussions for other people if she wasn't careful. They had a bit of a try at getting her to have a splash in the paper. They all knew before they even asked that she wasn't going to be up for it, but they were obliged to try. In the end she just told them it wouldn't work with her being in the police and they had no choice but to accept her decision. They had brought champagne and orange juice and she felt mean turning down the Bucks Fizz, but she couldn't go into work smelling of booze. They left it for her for later.

She waved them off at the door just as Keith clattered down the stairs. "Morning, Stell. Bit early for a party, or was it the tally man come to check on your lodgers?"

"Oh, ha ha. No, just a business thing."

"Oh, get you with your business thing." He gave her a quick hug and pushed past and out into the damp morning.

She wondered again what his reaction would be if she offered to buy his flat. Would he be able to afford somewhere else? She could have the place made back into a house. Then again, there were those lovely places down in Albert Dock.

No, she couldn't live there. It would just feel too odd. For now she was determined she wouldn't do anything sudden. She'd give Granda the money for his operation, that was certain. As soon as she could. Then she might think about helping Peter and Shelley with money for a place of their own. Get them out from under Mam's feet. Of course maybe she wouldn't want that. Maybe she liked looking after her baby grandson. This was supposed to be a good thing but if she started throwing money about and making decisions for people, she could see how it could all go wrong. She could, however, help Granda. That thought was lovely.

Tonight after work she'd go and see them again.

Back in the house she collected her things together as the mobile burbled. "Rupert, what's up?"

"I've been checking the overnight reports, boss. I did look last night and there was nothing about Doug Jewell but there's a report I spotted this morning about a car. Burned out. It was a BMW. Parked on some spare ground beside the M57. Fire brigades reckon it was torched."

"Is it his?"

"We've got on to the DVLA – I've asked them to expedite it. Should hear back pretty soon."

"I'm on my way in. Oh. There wasn't anybody in it, was there?" She knew as she asked that he would have told her up front.

"No. It's not completely destroyed. I've sent the co-ordinates to your phone. I could meet you there if you like."

"Brilliant idea. See you in a bit."

"Do you want me to let DI Carr know?"

"Right, good point. No, tell you what, I'll do it."

Chapter 50

By the time Stella arrived Rupert had already had the burned-out car taped off. He stood beside DI Carr watching as a low-loader negotiated the narrow roadway leading into the field.

"They were going to shift it," Jordan said. "But we wanted you to see it first."

"Thanks. Actually, they might as well come back later. It'll be a while before this can be moved."

Jordan held up his phone. "I gave the Crime Scene people the heads-up. They can come down once we have confirmation it's Jewell's car."

As he spoke, Rupert's phone vibrated and he glanced at the screen and nodded.

"Yep, it's his. I'll give Sergeant Flowers the news, shall I?"

Jordan nodded. "Yes, thanks, Rupert."

The DC moved away to find somewhere quieter to make the call.

"So, this is a development," Jordan said.

"It is." Stella paused. "Sir, I want to apologize for yesterday. I was out of line and behaved badly."

"I totally understand, Stella. Most of us have been there. You get a case you're passionate about, you get possessive. Don't worry about it. But honestly, you don't need to worry. I'm on your side and all I want to do is help. I've got a bit more experience and I hate to say it but a bit more clout, so let's work together and find the bastard who killed your bloke and possibly the woman – Fee, isn't it?"

"Yes, sir, Fee." She held her breath for a moment wondering if he'd mention the witness, but he moved away towards the car.

They walked around the blackened hulk. Most of the damage had been to the inside. The paintwork was bubbled, and the glass shattered. Inside was a mess of melted plastic and twisted metal. It wasn't likely they'd get much to help them from there. It was a relief that there was no body inside, but where was he? What had happened to Doug Jewell? She peered down at the tufty grass, blackened all around the scene but untouched where it spread towards a little copse of trees just in front of the motorway embankment. She walked away, stepping carefully across the field.

The ground was soggy underfoot and churned up by many feet. It was probably going to be impossible to find any evidence there. It was nobody's fault really but if the fire brigade had been aware of the hunt for the car maybe this would be a different story.

While she waited, she walked nearer to the trees looking for anything that might be of use. The further she got from the car the less it was disturbed. Rupert finished his call and strode across to join her. She held out an arm.

"Hang on." She bent and pulled aside a low-hanging branch. "Look at this. Try not to walk on this bit." She pointed to a patch of ground, churned up, the grass flattened and above it broken twigs and torn leaves. "Look, this goes up the slope towards the road." She pointed at the faint trail in the grass and soil. "Looks to me as if something has clambered up here, what do you reckon?"

"Could be. Or been dragged, or maybe something has come down from the hard shoulder. I wonder if there have been any accidents recently. Or maybe fly-tipping."

"What? Fly-tipping that somebody has bothered to clear away? Oh, look out, there's a pig flying past." Stella raised her eyebrows. "We should find out who this place belongs to. There are some piles of gravel over there. They look as though they've been put there deliberately, and there are some pallets and sacks near the gate. It must belong to someone. Find out."

"Okay."

Stella turned to Jordan. "What do you reckon, sir? I think we need to get more people on this. We have to view the motorway CCTV. See if there was anything going on up there." She pointed to the road and the flashing traffic. Did the brigade have any idea how long this had been here?"

"Not today, they said. The wreck was cold, no need for any damping down."

"I don't think Mel and Ruth are going to be able to handle this on their own."

"I agree. Let me deal with that. Rupert, will you take some pictures and contact the owner of this site? How about we meet back at the station at about half eleven? In the meantime requisition the CCTV from the motorway and get Mel and Ruth on it straight away. Is everybody okay with all that?"

"Yeah, no probs. This is totally our case now, boss, isn't it? No more trying to make it part of the drugs thing," Stella said.

"Absolutely!"

"Thanks." Stella's phone rang, a private number. "Oh, hang on, what's this?"

It was the bank, they wanted to make an appointment to discuss investment options and her advantages being a premium account holder and to reassure her they were there to answer all her needs.

"I need you to get off my phone. If I want to talk to you, I will do." She clicked it off and thrust it back into her pocket.

"I hope that wasn't your boyfriend," Rupert said.

"No bloody way."

"Oh, sorry – that was a bit out of line." He blushed and glanced at Jordan who was studying a piece of wood intently.

"You're alright, Rupert, it was just some business I haven't got time for just now. Come on – let's get moving with this."

Chapter 51

Back at the station they gathered the small team together. Jordan didn't stand in front of the whiteboard, he sat beside his desk. He spoke conversationally but they all listened.

"Things have moved on in the last twenty-four hours. First of all let's just get this out of the way. DS May was right. Credit where it's due, she stuck to her guns. Well done, Stella. I don't think we have lost much time or traction because it seems very much that the case has turned out to have no connection to the drug dens we've been clearing out. It's down to her. I want to acknowledge that."

Stella knew enough not to speak, she could gloat a bit later when she was on her own, but for now she nodded and managed a slight frown.

"So, we need to move along with this now and I'm going to arrange for more bods to join the team."

"Thank you, sir." Stella looked around the group. "With the discovery of this burned-out car" – she pointed to the picture in her file – "you will all have copies of this and it's on the screens. I would appreciate some more help with the CCTV. It's possible Doug Jewell, who was a close connection to our male victim, may have been taken away by force, or he may have just done a runner, and I think it's vital we find him quickly."

"What's your instinct? Do you think he was involved in the killing?" Jordan said.

"I'm not sure whether he was or whether the two of them were involved in something together. I have to say that is my main worry. If they were and it was enough to get Phillip Harwood killed, then Jewell could be in grave danger. We need more about both men."

Jordan nodded. "Okay, what do you think we need?"

She didn't know. How was she supposed to know what she needed and what she could have? Stella thought back to the few major cases she had been involved with. Was he testing her? Surely, he knew what they needed and more importantly what they could reasonably expect. Well, okay, if it was a test, she was up for it.

"I need some more civilians to help with the CCTV and I would like to put out an appeal for sightings of him so there'll be telephone and email answering to do. I spoke briefly with Harwood's parents yesterday, but they were only here for a short while. They came and identified the body and then wanted to leave. I got the idea there was a lot of regret there because they'd sort of lost touch. They refused to stay in the area. Just wanted to get home. Something about dogs with the neighbours. Seemed odd to me. They were looking at the body of their son, but dogs seemed more important."

"I suppose if, as you say, they were no longer close, it's sort of understandable. Very sad really. Did you ask them about the daughter?" Jordan said.

"I did and they have completely lost touch and haven't seen her for several years. They wouldn't be drawn on that, just kept saying they didn't know where she was. I asked for a picture and I'm hoping they'll send something through by email. I've arranged a Zoom with them for later."

"Okay, I'll sit in. What else is going on?"

"I'm liaising with the Met about Fee, and I really need a catch-up with them. It's a lot, boss."

"It is but you seem to have it all under control."

"Thanks, sir. I'm grateful for your help."

"We'll work it all out. You've got the start of a great crew here. Now what we want are results."

"Mel, Ruth, and Rupert have been brilliant, but I think at the moment, we just need more people."

"I'm on it." Jordan grinned at her.

* * *

It didn't take long. A couple of phone calls and Jordan pushed back his chair as he put down the phone. He had been surprised how much difference it had made moving to the organised crime section. He hadn't expected to have so much more clout. He came to stand beside Stella. "Right, we've got some more admins and a couple of uniforms as well. You've got quite a team now, Stella."

"We have, boss. Thanks. Actually, while we're on the subject, there is just one thing. I do worry about Ruth Cowgill."

"Why's that?"

"She's never actually seemed really happy to be on the team. I thought maybe it was because of me. You know, she's been here a long time and I haven't. Hopefully now you're on board she'll be happier."

"Maybe. But I don't know why she should have felt like that. I'm impressed with how well you've done, speaking truth to power as they say; it's never easy and you stuck with it. She should have been proud to work with you."

Okay, now Stella would gloat. Just a bit, quietly.

Chapter 52

By the afternoon more clerical staff had arrived and Stella had spoken with the press liaison department to arrange appeals on the local television, and a splash in the *Echo*. They'd been granted a warrant to access Jewell's bank account and search his flat and work computer.

"Okay, everybody, listen up." *Oh shit, had she really just said that?* She coughed. "After the appeals go out, we'll very likely have a lot of calls – well I hope so at least. So, for now, as soon as you've organized desks for yourselves, get onto viewing the CCTV on the motorway. Last time Douglas Jewell was seen was at his home just after lunch time last Sunday. Mel, you and erm…" Stella pointed at a young man who had already plugged in his computer and was busy typing notes. "You, sorry, I don't know your names yet."

"Charlie, boss. Charlie Corkhill."

"Okay, Charlie, work with Mel to see if he can be traced from the city out to Kirkby. Where did he go? Was he with anyone? Did he choose to go to the piece of spare ground, or did someone force him? There must be loads of cameras. Start with the obvious route first and if that doesn't work look at more obscure ones."

"How about we try it the other way, boss?" Mel said. "We have him at the dump site, and we can just work backwards?"

Stella grinned and glanced at Jordan. He smiled back at her.

"Or you could work backwards from the dumpsite," she said. "Just testing!"

There was a ripple of laughter.

"Now, he may have clambered up the embankment himself and tried to get a lift. He may have been taken up there against his will. Of course, he may not have gone up to the road at all. My instinct from viewing the scene is that he did. Did he flag down a car – what? Is everybody happy with that?" There was a quiet murmur. "If anyone has any questions, there's me, DC Moon, Mel, and Ruth who have been involved from the start and, of course, there is DI Carr."

Stella pointed to the desks by the window. Mel was grinning and blushing slightly. It didn't take much to give people a boost. It felt nice.

A couple of uniformed officers arrived mid-afternoon, a young woman, and an older man. Stella didn't have much for them apart from answering the phones.

"I've usually done a fair bit of collating, ma'am," the bloke said. "If you like I could do the management job."

"Cheers, Robert. That'd be great. Oh and could you follow up Douglas Jewell's bank accounts. Anything that seems odd." She was stumbling forward. The older staff probably knew it, but they were all being brilliant.

"Call me Bob, ma'am."

"Thanks, and I'm boss or Stella, up to you really."

She sat at the desk listening to the hubbub around her and saw the whiteboards filling with information and for a moment she was overwhelmed, but then she had a memory of Nana. '*You're clever, you are, our Stella. Don't be a doormat.*'

After a while Mel swivelled her chair and called across the room. "We've followed his car, boss. He was on his own leaving the flats. Went straight to where we found the wreck, no detours or stops. It gets very interesting after that."

Stella had joined the others at the desk and leaned in to see the screen.

"He's driven straight from his flat. He turns off the engine and lights. It seems he's waiting for someone." Mel moved the cursor along the toolbar. After what registered as almost thirty minutes there was movement from off screen. "Here they are."

"Can we get a clearer view of that bloke?" Stella said.

"It's so dark by then and they are quite a long way off. I think we'll need specialist help with it."

They all huddled closer but it made no difference to the picture, which was indistinct. They watched tiny figures around the dark bulk of the BMW. The car door was opened but it was impossible to say who had control. Jewell emerged and there was a scurry of movement and then they moved off, quickly out of shot.

"Okay, that's bloody frustrating," Stella said. "Bob, can you get on to forensic imaging and have them give us a hand with this?"

"I will, it's a bit late for today and I'll have to call in some favours to get it done quickly."

Favours! It was great to have some older staff, ones who had enough time in the job to have built up 'favours'.

Stella glanced at her watch. "Put the time up, will you, Mel." She walked to the middle of the group of desks and waved an arm in the direction of the boards. "Everyone, he left the car around this time. Eight-fifteen. He was with another person. We can't see where they went but it gives you a narrower timescale. We are going to try and get better pictures but for now, it's about end of shift and I want you all in early tomorrow. Have we got a couple of volunteers to man the phones after the *Echo* comes out?" She didn't wait for long. "Brilliant, thanks, I reckon three of you will be enough. The rest of us, in early tomorrow. Seven. It could be a busy day."

"Do you fancy a bevvy, boss?" Rupert had caught her in the corridor on the way to the car park. "Bit of a celebration like. Now we've got a proper team, and backup."

"I'd love to, but honest to God, Rupert, I've got to get home. I've got my notes to update and if I don't get down to Tesco I'll be eating Sugar Puffs for my dinner."

"After another Battenberg, are you?" He laughed as she raised her eyebrows at him. "Maybe tomorrow then, eh?"

"Aye. Tomorrow."

Chapter 55

It was late. No point checking. Keith from upstairs would be home and hogging the parking. The road outside her flat looked chock-a-block, but there was a space in the next street. That wasn't bad. It was raining now and bloody cold for September, but she had her puffa jacket. Stella gathered her things together and hid the satnav under the seat. Nothing left lying about to tempt a chancer.

It was a wet Wednesday and there was nobody about. In the houses along the road the curtains and blinds were closed, keeping out the miserable evening. Stella ploughed forward, head lowered against the wet, her hood up. She slung the laptop bag across her body and held the two bags for life from the supermarket, one in each hand. A couple of cars swooshed by flinging up cold, dirty water.

It didn't take long to reach the corner and she glanced up in the light from the street lamp. The rain slanting sideways in the wind glittered orange in the glow. It would be good to get inside. She had intended going to see Granda, but she was tired. She'd ring tomorrow. She'd tell him to contact his doctor and start getting things in motion for his private operation. She hadn't decided yet how much to let them know, but was it realistic to believe Mam hadn't told her own father about the lottery win? Of course not. She smiled to herself. They were probably working just as hard not to mention it as she was. It would be a relief to get it all out in the open. Then she could make peace with Mam, and all would be well.

She would buy Peter and his girlfriend a house, something small just to get them going. Mam could choose whether she moved or not. She could put some money into an account for the baby. Then the rest of it could go into savings. That was enough for now and she could stop thinking about it. No money worries ever again. No need to fear the leccy bill. No need to think about whether she'd be able to afford a holiday. Actually, it was pretty bloody fantastic, wasn't it? She was getting used to the idea and was convinced she could handle it, she could even enjoy it and later, when there was time, she would think about charities. Some of it had to do some good.

She was nearly home. Keith's car wasn't there. She cursed under her breath. She could have parked in the drive after all. Typical.

Her mind was full of so much stuff, the rain, the swish of tyres in the puddles, all the things she had allowed to distract her. All the things that meant she didn't hear the approach of footsteps, rapid in the darkness. She wasn't aware of the change in the air as someone rushed up behind her. At the last moment she heard the rustle of clothes, the huff of breath beside her ear and the quiet click as the knife opened. By then it was too late, far too late. She spun on her heel, lifted her arms in reflex as the shopping flew from her hands and the shoulder bag shifted across her stomach. Blessed shoulder bag. The knife hit the soft nylon and then there was a clink as the blade struck the plastic cover of her laptop. The power of the blow knocked her backward. She screamed and twisted away, her self-defence training surfacing from where it sat mostly ignored somewhere in the back of her brain.

The bloke's hand struck downwards slicing through the thin polyester of her jacket sleeve. There was no pain. On some level she knew she was cut. She screamed again and heard a car, a horn, a yell, and registered it was Keith. She was punching now, and scratching and kicking, aiming her knee at his groin. Keith came up behind and dragged the assailant away. He was strong, worked out in the gym at the hospital, and he was enraged.

The thug was fighting back, fists, elbows, feet, but two against one, he knew he had failed. He pushed Stella away, so she fell backwards on her behind in the dirty water. He took one last swing at Keith's head, missed, and then bent to scoop up the knife he'd dropped. He sprinted away into the night.

Stella was already on her phone calling it in. Keith was gathering the debris. He kicked his takeaway curry carton into the gutter. Doors were flung open, and the crowd gathered around them. There were sirens in the distance. It would be too late. The bloke had vaulted the fence at the end of the road, crossed the railway line and was away.

A couple of the neighbours helped to gather the spilled shopping. Stella clambered to her feet with the help of the bloke from the corner house. With a murmur of thanks for all the help, Keith wrapped his arms around her, and they staggered down the front path to then have a bit of a problem both squeezing through the door. By now blood was running down her arm and dripping from her finger ends.

"Hold it up, Stel. Keep it elevated and we'll sort it out just now."

He pushed her onto the settee and peeled off the jacket.

Chapter 54

"Honestly, I'll file a report in the morning."

The uniformed constable looked unsure, but Stella was senior to him. He didn't know what to do.

"I've called for an ambulance." At least that was action.

"Oh, shit. You need to cancel it. Really."

Keith tutted loudly. "Hold your soddin' arm up, will you."

"Sorry, sorry, Keith. Bloody hell, that hurts."

"Yes, well I've got to put pressure on it. Look, you need to have this stitched. Can you move all your fingers?"

"Yes, look." She wiggled her hand.

"Any numbness, pins and needles?"

"No, just your effin fingers. Christ, do you have to press so hard?"

"Well, unless you want to bleed to death!"

"Don't be daft."

"Look, Stell. It needs stitches. It does, honestly. I'll take you in. If I do that, you won't have to sit in the corridor for hours, okay?"

"Okay." Suddenly she felt very, very tired and cold, and she couldn't be bothered to argue anymore. "Do what you like, but no ambulance."

"Leave it with me, will you?" Keith said to the bobby who was already on his Airwaves set calling off the paramedics.

"You'll file a report tomorrow for sure?"

"I promise."

Keith was as good as his word. He took her in the staff entrance and left her in his office in the physiotherapy department with a hot sweet drink for the shock. When he came back, he had an exhausted junior doctor in tow who carried an armful of sterilized packages. He was sweet and efficient and kind, and she fell for him until on the way out he gave Keith's bum a squeeze and she had to rethink the situation.

"Friend of yours?"

"Yeah, Paul. We have a bit of a thing now and then. Anyway, he's done a good job on your arm. I've got a prescription here for your painkillers and some antibiotics just in case. What are you going to do about reporting this?"

"I'll do it in the morning. I just want to go home now and have a big, strong drink."

One drink turned into several and Stella insisted on replacing the takeaway curry with a pizza, which was all they could have delivered so late.

"Filthy muggers," said Keith.

"Yeah, I know." But she didn't know. Why had she been targeted? Why had he made no attempt to grab her shopping, her laptop bag? Okay she had managed to hold the thug off and Keith had done the rest, but it didn't feel like a mugging. The knife had been drawn and ready not to threaten, but to strike. There had been no attempt to grab her bags, just the thrust to her belly which made her feel sick when she thought about it.

"I suppose they might take some notice of you, if you report it."

"We do try, you know, Keith. We really do. But it's like trying to empty a bath with a thimble and the thimble's getting smaller all the time."

"I know. I wasn't getting at you. I'm upset, I hate to see you hurt."

"Aw, thanks. It might have been much worse if you hadn't swept in like Superman."

"I'm just glad I was there."

"Do you like living here, Keith?"

"Oh yeah. I do. I mean, okay this has just happened to you and that's grim, but generally it's not a bad area and it's handy for work, and the shops, and transport."

"Would you move?"

"Possibly. Sometime. When I can afford it but that won't be for ages yet and to be honest, I'm not really bothered. I like living upstairs from you. You're a great neighbour and the flat's not bad. Okay a bit of it was done on the cheap, but it's okay. Actually that's probably what I'd be more likely to do. I've got one bedroom I don't use because it needs doing up, the window leaks, and I'd like to smarten it all up really."

"So you wouldn't sell it now?"

"No. I can't afford anything better so why bother. Why? Don't tell me you're moving. Don't let what just happened drive you away."

"No, it's not that. Just talking really."

"Right. Look, I'll let you get to bed. Are you okay?"

"I'm fine. My arm's starting to throb but that's no surprise. Thanks again for saving me, you were brilliant. I don't suppose you got enough of a look at him to give us a description?"

"Nah, I was more bothered about you. It was a bloke, about my height, white, wearing jeans and a leather jacket over a hoody. Fair hair, I think, but it was only a glimpse when I pulled his hood off. I will if you think it might help, but it's not much is it."

"No, but it's something. I didn't really get a look at all. I'll have my friend take a statement tomorrow. If that's okay?"

"Yes. No probs. Take your painkillers and try to sleep."

Chapter 55

The doctor had put her arm in a sling, but Stella couldn't go into work so obviously injured. She'd just try and keep it still and elevated. The throbbing would remind her anyway.

"You alright, boss?" Rupert hadn't even let her sit down before he came over to the desk frowning.

"Yeah, why?"

"You look a bit off this morning. Pale, tired."

Stella jerked her head towards the corridor. "Outside?" she said.

She checked they couldn't be overheard before she told Rupert about the attack.

"Shit, boss. What are you going to do?"

"Obviously, I have to make a report, but I don't particularly want it becoming common knowledge, not yet. In the meantime could you go and get a statement from my neighbour? He's on late shift today so he's expecting you at the flat. At least then I can tell the DI I'm doing something, and it keeps it all sort of official."

"That's really nasty, maybe you shouldn't have come in."

"No, I had to. So, seeing as I am here, is there anything happening?"

"There is. Sort of. Steve was the first to see the vehicle on the hard shoulder of the motorway on the CCTV review. It was just up from where Jewell's car was torched. It was pulled in for just a few minutes. A white van, newish. A VW. It stopped and two men came up the bank, over the fence and onto the road. I've had a look myself and one of them is Jewell. Once they are over, they climb into the van and off they go. I've got the forensic imaging department working on it. I've asked them to send us stills to see if it helps. We've looked at it in slow motion, but I can't really tell. I've requested footage from the ANPR from the motorway. We should have that in the next hour and then I'll get on to the DVLA. It'll be nicked though, won't it?"

"Good chance, I should think. Okay, I'll have a look at it. Not because I think I'll be able to judge it any better, but because I need to see it, so I know what we're talking about."

"I'll get you a coffee, boss. You look like you could use one."

"Would you? I really appreciate that, Rupert. Hey, is there any sign of Ruth? I see her desk is still vacant."

"No, I hadn't thought about it. We've been busy with reports from the *Echo* appeal, but they're moot now we know he went off in a van and we can get a trace on it."

"I'll get on to HR. If she's sick, they should have let us know. We need to have someone stand in."

* * *

Jordan was horrified. "Good grief. You shouldn't even be here. Why didn't you report this last night? You should be signed off."

He wasn't listening. He was so outraged by what had happened to her that he couldn't hear what she was telling him. Stella took a step closer to his desk, bent slightly at the waist. She didn't want to look threatening, but she needed him to hear her.

"Boss. I'm fine. Honest to God, I am. I got stitched up, I have painkillers and I feel fine."

"You should go and see the nurse."

"I saw a doctor last night. He didn't want to sign me off." She hadn't asked, it hadn't come up, but it was true. Paul had never mentioned work.

Jordan stopped ranting and looked at her. "For Christ's sake, sit down."

"Yeah." She sank onto the chair. "I wasn't badly hurt. If it hadn't been for the knife. I've got a couple of bruises and that's about all."

"But there was the knife. There'll be delayed shock. We don't want you with PTSD."

"I'm fine. I really am and I don't want to sit at home wondering what's happening with my case. That'll drive me mad."

He paused, then nodded. "Alright. I understand, I do. You should still go see the nurse. Promise me you'll go home if you don't feel right. We'll keep you informed if anything happens."

"Deal." Maybe he would listen now. "So, as I was saying. I'm writing my report about it and Rupert is getting a statement from my neighbour. But I'm not convinced this was a mugging."

"Right. What was it, then?"

"It was an attack. Unprovoked and I think planned. It was a cold wet night, where I stay is quiet even during the day. The shops are not very near, so there was no reason for a mugger to be lurking about there."

"He was waiting for you?"

"I think so."

"Are there any cameras?"

"There's one in the car park of the Indian restaurant but it's too far away to be of any use. He could have been recorded, but I didn't get a good enough look at him to be able to recognize him anyway."

"What about your neighbours? Do any of them have security systems?"

"I don't think so. It's not that sort of area."

"Is it worth asking?"

"Rupert is going down there. I'll have him look around. The doctor's surgery might be a possibility."

"Get on that. If it's true you were targeted, we need to stomp on that, make some sort of statement. Was it because you are on the force? Or could it be to do with this case specifically?"

Not only had he been listening, but Jordan's mind had gone down the same road as hers. Stella had been hiding from the idea that she was in real danger. She couldn't do that anymore.

Chapter 56

She needed to focus. Stella tried to push away the shock and fear that the attack had caused. That feeling had to be channelled into anger.

Rupert was out for a couple of hours. Time to review the report and the CCTV coverage of the VW which had taken away Douglas Jewell. The view was from a camera covering the big roundabout on the road beside the motorway. They could make out the bottom of the van and the figures running across and scrambling up the slope. One they believed to be Douglas Jewell. Certainly at one stage the man behind reached out to push him upwards. It was impossible to tell whether it was to help or because he was being forced to go up to the motorway. The clearer film of the van was from the signage gantry just beyond the junction and it was too far away to be decisive. It had, however, given them the make, colour, and number plate as the vehicle pulled into the carriageway.

Dashcam footage from passing motorists would be great now. They would need to look at as many as possible to get an idea of what had happened. It could work. There was something else. It wasn't possible to shake it loose yet, but her brain was showing her something her mind couldn't quite grasp. Jordan came and sat beside her, and they replayed the grainy film over and over. After a while Stella leaned away from the desk and stretched her shoulders, wincing at the referred pain in her arm.

"I'll get us some coffee, shall I?"

"No, let me go. You look a bit done in," Jordan said.

"I'm okay, but I reckon it's time for a couple of painkillers… Could you make it three coffees?" Stella said to Jordan as Rupert came back into the room. It was a bit cheeky, but the DI wasn't the least bit put out and came back from the canteen with coffees and buns.

"He's nice, your neighbour," Rupert said. "He was dead worried about you. It was lucky he went out for his curry last night otherwise…" He paused and shook his head. "Under the circumstances, the description he's given us isn't bad. Also, I've spoken to the doctor from the surgery next door to your place. He's given us the card from his security camera. I dropped it in to the video imaging guys. They rolled their eyes a bit but they're going to have a look."

"Did the people at the doctor's see anything?"

"No. The surgery was closed, of course, and they don't bother viewing the video unless something happens, and your attack was way past their hours."

"Fair enough. Okay, since you've been gone, we've arranged a shout-out for dashcam footage from the motorway. It means we'll probably have to put in a late night. We need to help the digital department out. We can't just send them everything. Can you give the others a heads-up?"

"No probs. I hope you're not planning on staying, yourself."

"Jeez, what is it with you blokes? I'm fine really. Get on to HR, would you? We'll have to have a replacement for Ruth. She's still not shown and it's no good Jordan getting us new bods and then losing one straight away. I wonder what's going on with her."

Rupert shrugged. "Haven't got a scooby."

Stella took a moment to drink her coffee. She wasn't going to let them know but her arm was screaming at her. Perhaps she should use the sling after all. Everyone knew about the attack now so what difference did it make?

Rupert swung round from his desk. "That's done. Replacement as soon as possible. No way they were going to tell me anything about Ruth. I did try but I didn't get anywhere."

"To be honest, I don't think we ever really got on so maybe it's for the best. Right. I've got a little errand to run. I'll be back in about an hour." She stopped at Jordan's desk. "Just heading out for a bit, boss. I thought I'd go back to the squat. See how things are going there."

"Can you leave it for half an hour?" he said. "I could do with heading down there. I've been meaning to visit."

"I've got Jewell's parents' Zoom call." It wasn't until later, but she didn't want company. Not right now.

"Okay. We'll make a point of getting down there. Soon as we can fit it in. I know we've got all the video but there's nothing like a look round in person."

She grabbed her coat before he could change his mind and headed for the car park. When the mobile rang her first instinct was to let it go to voicemail, but the name on the screen was DS Watt from the Met.

She should bring him up to date with the change in staffing and give him Jordan's number. She would. In a while.

"We've got some news for you, Stella. The other girls who were in the car with Fee."

"Yes?"

"We found their digs. A shared house, not too bad actually. Known to us already. We keep an eye on it because of the girls they bring in from Europe, but it's been a bit quiet lately. Then yesterday there was a barney and we hoiked in a couple of the women."

"Was it our women?"

"No, but in questioning a couple of them admitted to knowing Fee. They were pretty freaked about what happened to her. Obviously. Anyway, seems the others who came down with her have made a run for it. Middle of the night job. There in the evening, then everybody goes out to work for the night and then nothing by the morning. Caused a fuss as you'd imagine, and that was the main reason for the row which had us involved. Some of the blokes there were heavy-handed when they realized two of their 'ladies' had vanished. Anyway, top and bottom of it is we've seen them in Victoria Coach Station. They were heading north. They got the Birmingham coach, but my thinking is that they might be heading back to Liverpool. They just hopped on the first bus out. They must have bought tickets on board. You can do it with cash. We're waiting for the driver to come in so we can have a word. We're trying to trace them after they left the bus at Mill Lane depot in Brum but nothing yet. They're good at dodging cameras, I guess they have to be given their night lives. The new station in the city centre is huge so it's taking some looking at. Anyway, I thought you could give your patrols the word and have them keep their eyes open. They haven't done anything we can have them for. We know they were on the game, but we never had the chance to pick them up working. We need to have a word with them about Fee – we're getting nowhere finding out what happened to her. We've dragged in the toerags who were the minders. I'll keep you informed if it leads to anything."

"Thanks for all that. Leave it with me."

She climbed into her car. This made no difference to where she was headed. In fact it was all the more reason to go back to Kirkby.

Chapter 57

Stella parked in the road outside the squat. The crime scene tape was still there but the bobby had gone from the front door. She slipped on gloves and shoe covers and stepped into the kitchen. It was quieter than the last time she'd been in: just two technicians on their knees in the front room, one of them scraping something from the floorboards.

"Is Sergeant Flowers around?"

"No, he's gone off to a burned-out car. Left us here to finish off. We're getting there. Should all be finished in the next couple of days. Nothing new to tell you, ma'am."

"What's that?" Stella pointed to the evidence container.

"Dried semen, I think."

"Oh, yuk. Glad I asked."

She heard them still chuckling as she closed the door behind her.

A group of boys were sitting on a low wall opposite. She raised a hand in greeting and George Kenny nodded. The others were too cool to do anything more than stare, though the one called Stu flipped a middle finger at her. She crossed the road.

"Don't do that, Stu. How come you lads are here? Shouldn't you be in school?"

"How old are you, missus? It's after school. We have to spend long enough in there anyway," Stu said.

"Well, shouldn't you be at home doing homework, or at footie training or something?"

"None of your beeswax, is it? We can do what we like. You're not the boss of us." Stu twitched his shoulders and lifted his chin.

She held up her hand in submission. "Alright. Seeing as you're here. Have you seen any of the people who used to stay here? Any of the women?"

"The prossies, you mean?" George sniggered as he spoke, and Stu nudged him in the ribs.

"The women, yes. Or the blokes?"

"Nah. Nothin'. A couple of druggies came and tried to get in last night but they couldn't open the doors."

"Had you seen them before?"

"Nah. Just stinkin' druggies, weren't they. Homeless, I reckon," Stu said.

"Well, you've got my card so if you do see anything you should let me know. If you don't, you could get into trouble."

"What for?" George said.

"Withholding information."

"Yeah right!" Stu spoke again.

They had slipped down from the wall now and with a final glance in her direction, they sauntered away pushing and jostling. George turned as they reached the corner and looked into her eyes. He gave a nod. She had the feeling she'd be seeing him again.

Betsy's door was just a little ajar. Stella knocked and walked into the hallway. "Anybody home?"

"In the kitchen. You bring cake?"

"I could only get scones. I brought some jam and cream though."

"I can make scones meself, it's easy. Still, if you brought cream."

The old woman reached out to take the bag. The teapot was on the table with a knitted cosy over it. There were two mugs with milk already poured.

"Are you expecting visitors?"

"You're here, aren't you?"

"Yes, but… the cups."

Betsy glanced up from the worktop where she was buttering the scones. She didn't speak.

"I have a couple of things I need to speak to you about." As she said it Stella wondered why she was bothering. This scary old woman seemed to know everything before it happened. Perhaps she should simply sit down, eat the food, and wait to be told.

With a small groan Betsy lowered herself onto the wooden chair. She rubbed at her arm. "That's sore. What have you done to your arm?"

"How do you mean?"

"Your arm. Got to be a bit sore. It'll heal, don't worry. Just make sure you keep it dry."

"How did you… oh never mind."

There was a huff of a laugh from Betsy as Stella picked up the mug. "Right, what is it you want me to tell you now?"

"The girls have disappeared."

"No."

"What do you mean, no?" Stella said.

"Haven't disappeared, have they? Just you don't know where they are."

"Alright then. If you want to be pedantic."

"Oh get you and your long words."

"Betsy, do you know where they are?"

"Why would I know where they are?"

"You seem to know a lot of stuff and they used to come and see you."

"Aye well, they haven't come to see me today. Leave them be, why don't you? They have enough to put up with."

"You know I can't. They might know what happened to Fee, they must know what happened to Phillip Harwood."

"And they might just be frightened women trying to survive."

"You have to tell me if you know where they are."

"Aye. Well, there we are then." And with the non-committal statement Betsy filled her mouth with food and chewed slowly.

"Listen – about my arm."

Betsy nodded and reached for the mug of tea.

"I was attacked last night. In the street outside my house."

"Nasty."

"There's something niggling at me about it. I don't think it was just a mugging. Is there a way I can sort of access my thoughts?"

"Access your thoughts? Jesus, girl, what do you think I am, some sort of trick cyclist?"

"Well, no. But you seem to know stuff and I just thought maybe there was a method I could use. Something I could do to shake it loose."

"Shake it loose." Betsy sighed. "If there's something you should know, you'll know it. Just have a bit of faith. Stop trying to force things. Just let it come. Now bugger off, I've got stuff to do."

She had been dismissed. The old woman went from the kitchen to the living room, turned on the standard lamp, and picked up one of her books. "Shut the door on the way out. There'll be no more visitors tonight."

Stella turned left at the gate and headed for George's house. The boy had something to tell her. She felt it. She tutted. Now she sounded like the old crone she'd just been with. Still she walked along the street to the Kennys'.

Chapter 58

George was perched on the saddle of a racing bike chained to the drainpipe in his garden.

"Where are your mates?"

"Gone down the brook."

"You didn't go with them?"

"Nah. Not allowed. Me mam is scared I'll drown. Some kid drowned there years ago and she's bloody paranoid."

"Don't talk about your mam like that. Anyway, listen I think you might have something to tell me."

"Is it true, what you said about getting into trouble if I don't?"

"Would I lie?"

"You're a copper, course you would."

There were so many things she could say but there was no point, so Stella held her tongue and waited.

"Don't tell the others I told you. Okay. We went down there last night. We wasn't doin' nothin'. Just like, you know, lookin'. Anyway, we saw them prossies. Them ones that used to stay there. They came past. It was dark and they were on the other side of the road, but I know it was them. One of 'em shouted at us. Told us to bugger off and have some respect. Haven't a clue what she meant. Respect of what?"

"Did you see where they went afterwards?"

"They went to that old witch's house, like. Didn't stay. Just went in for a bit and then I saw 'em later on up the main road. Probably looking for blokes to blow."

"George! You really could do with your mouth washing out. What would your mam think if she heard you?"

The boy shrugged. "Well, I told you now so I can't get into no trouble, like."

"No. You won't. Thanks for that."

She left him unlocking his bike. He was probably going to meet his mates down by the little stream, mother's warning or not. It was all well and good laying down rules but if nobody checked to see if they were followed, it was pointless. She had the feeling that inside was a small boy who wanted boundaries and guidance, but who was going to do it if it wasn't his family? She sat in the car feeling a little sad, but this wasn't her problem.

She sent a text to DS Watt confirming the women were back on Merseyside, and she would make sure all the mobile patrols were aware.

Heading back to the station a call came in from Rupert.

"Alright, mate. I'm on my way back," she said.

"Great. There's something interesting just come through from Sergeant Flowers."

"What's that?"

"Why don't I tell you when you get in? There's another thing as well, very odd, best if we have a proper talk."

"Do you know what, Rupert? You're worse than my mam, she does this."

"Does what?"

"Rings up and says, 'you'll never guess what's happened,' and then won't tell me."

"Sorry, boss. But as you're on the way in anyway."

"Yes, alright. See you in about ten minutes."

Chapter 59

Jordan and Rupert were sitting together watching the screen when Stella arrived.

"Best start it again," Jordan said, reaching out to poke at one of the buttons on the keyboard. "What time is your Zoom call?" he asked Stella.

Bugger, that hadn't been strictly true. She'd asked the Harwoods to get back to her but there had been nothing yet.

"Oh, they've had to change it. Not sure now."

"Where have you been?"

"Down the squat, like I said."

"Need a word later, Stella. When we've brought you up to date on this."

"Right. No probs, boss." He wasn't pleased, she could tell.

Rupert glanced between the two of them, coughed and started the video again from the beginning.

"Right. So, we've got the enhanced footage of the car. Much clearer," he said. "It's definitely Jewell."

Stella leaned in to watch.

"Okay, yes. I see. He doesn't look particularly scared, does he?" she said.

"That's what we thought. But there's more."

Jordan stopped the film. "There, what do you see?"

"Erm, the car, two blokes, oh one of them has a bag. Looks like a sort of sports bag. I wonder if it's the clothes missing from the flat?"

He started the film again. "Now, look into the car," Jordan said.

"I'm not sure what I'm looking for."

"There. Underneath and then inside." He pointed.

"Is it smoke?" Stella asked.

"It is, and look inside – you can see just the hint of flickering."

"But that means…"

"Yes." Rupert leaned back and crossed his arms. "It was Bob's mate who spotted it and gave us the heads-up. We'd all assumed the car had been torched by kids. Well, of course we did, they usually are. But from this it looks as if he did it himself. Jewell set fire to his own motor."

"Bloody hell. But why?"

"We might have the answer to that," Jordan said. "You should have had a report from the lab."

Stella logged onto her tablet and scrolled through the messages. "Yep. Here it is. Oh."

"Oh indeed," said Jordan. "Fee's fingerprints in Doug Jewell's car. Inside the glove compartment. So, the fire didn't destroy them. He made an attempt at cleaning it. He smudged prints elsewhere, but he missed these."

"So, he'd tried to destroy it."

"And cocked it up," Rupert said. "We've had some dashcam footage in from the van driver who raised the alarm, and the timing indicates that when the van drove off the car was well alight. The fire brigade confirmed that an accelerant was used. So, I guess he thought it was job done. They were in a hurry to get away. Parking on the hard shoulder it wouldn't have been long before someone noticed, and they didn't want a patrol checking on them seeing as the van was nicked."

"Well, this puts a whole new slant on things, doesn't it?" Stella said.

"It does and we really need to up our game now searching for him."

"I've got everyone on answering phones, emails and checking the force websites in hopes that someone has seen him. Now, if you have a minute maybe we can go for a coffee. Couple of things on my mind, Stella," Jordan said.

"Yes, of course, boss," she said. "Oh, I do have some news about the other girls. They are back in Liverpool. A witness down at the squat has seen them."

"Would this be the same witness as gave us Fee's name?" Jordan said. "The old woman?"

"No, it was one of the young lads. I just spoke to him by chance really and he said they'd seen them."

Jordan narrowed his eyes and walked out of the room. He held the door for her. He might be old-fashioned in his manners but the look he was giving her was far from friendly.

Chapter 60

They took cups of brown liquid from the machine. Neither of them started drinking and Stella knew it was just set dressing.

"Something wrong, sir?" She tried to get ahead of the game.

"I hope not, Stella. I think we have some issues we should sort out so we can move on cleanly."

"Issues?"

"I fully understand this has been difficult for you, being in charge of the case but overseen by DI Dunn and all that meant, and now you've been landed with me."

"I don't think of it like that, boss."

"Yes, you do. You must. However, I think I've made it plain I'm here to help. I'm not here to take over."

Stella opened her mouth to speak but thought better of it. He didn't look angry. If he'd looked angry, she could have been annoyed in return, but he just looked unhappy.

"You have nothing to prove. Not to me anyway, and not to your team. We're all on the same side here. All I want, like you, is to find out who killed Phillip Harwood and, if it's connected, which we both know it must be, who murdered the poor girl in London."

"Yes, of course."

"So, you need to be honest with me. You need to share all the information you have."

"I have, I did."

Jordan shook his head. "I don't think so. This information you came back with today, for example. You don't speak to a boy by accident. You had a reason to go to the squat. You should have told me what it was."

She couldn't look at him. Stella pursed her lips and blew out a puff of air. She was going to sound stupid. She really didn't want to talk about Betsy. But the woman knew stuff. She knew the girls. In fact there was no doubt she knew even more than she had already shared. But what would he think? Was there a way she could put this across without it seeming totally insane?

Rupert stuck his head round the corner of the door. "Erm, boss and boss."

They both spoke together. "Yes," Jordan said.

"Give us a minute," from Stella.

"It's the Harwoods, on the Zoom. The invitation has just come in. I haven't opened it yet. What shall I do?"

"Bugger, they were supposed to be making an appointment." Stella turned and took a step towards the incident room.

"Best go," Jordan said.

"You sitting in, sir?"

"Yes. I think so."

* * *

The older couple sat side by side on a beige settee. In the background there was a window covered with a heavy net curtain and a short row of porcelain figures on the ledge. A small white dog was curled on the cushion beside the woman. They looked haggard and worn. Phillip's father had dark circles under his eyes and the whites were red and sore-looking.

"I know we said we'd let you know when we were going to do this, but we needed our neighbour to help us to set it up."

"That's alright, Mr Harwood. I'm free now. This is DI Carr with me. He's in charge of the case."

"Oh – I thought it was you," the woman said.

"It was decided we needed a more senior person."

"So, you weren't taking it seriously before then? What's changed?" There was a flash of anger in Mr Harwood's eyes. "You said you were doing all that you could."

"We were. We are. I promise you we are. The case has been elevated." She hoped the positive vocabulary might soothe him.

"So we'll talk to him then," Phil's mother said.

There was an awkward moment, but Stella smiled into the video camera. "That's fine."

"So, Detective Inspector, what's happening? Have you done anything to find out who killed Phillip?"

Mr Harwood butted in. "And when can we have his body released? We need to get things moving. We've been in touch with his work, and they hold a will, but they reckon they can't let us have it until we have the death certificate. When can we have it?"

"Leave it with me," Jordan said. "I should be able to help there. You will be able to have an interim certificate. There will be an inquest so that could delay things. But the interim certificate will mean you can arrange his funeral."

"But what about probate? We want to get his flat on the market and what have you. We don't want this hanging over our heads."

"Yes, you can apply for probate with the certificate. I'll have someone give you a call to sort all of it out for you."

"Right. Good. Now do you know who killed him?"

"We're working on it but it's complicated. I have to ask, do you know of anyone who might have wished him harm? Anyone, even from a long time ago, whom he had problems with?" Jordan had clenched his hands into fists and the warmth had gone from his voice.

"No, we hadn't spoken to him for a long time. He'd moved away. He didn't keep in touch with anyone."

"I'd like to ask about his sister."

"Catherine. We don't know anything about her," Harwood said. "She's gone."

"My colleague did ask if you had a picture of her…"

"Oh, yes. She did. I forgot." As she spoke, Phil's mother glanced around the room and they thought maybe she had a photograph on display. "I'll have to go up into the attic. There might be something up there. It'll be old, mind you."

"That'd be really helpful. Thank you. Even if it's old it might give us something to work with."

"Do you think *she* killed him?" Phil's mother said. "That's not going to be it. You're barking up the wrong tree there. Always close, they were. That was why he went up there to Liverpool. Some silly idea that he could find her. One of her weird friends told him that she was up north. Got a transfer from his job and off he went. We told him to let her go. She was never any good, not since she was young. He wouldn't listen to us, though, would he? No, what would we know? Well, he hadn't had to sort out all the trouble she was in over the years. So, that was the last thing she did for us, wasn't it? On top of everything else she took him away. No, she won't have done it. Anyway I don't expect he did find her."

They spent another couple of minutes confirming they would keep the parents informed and then clicked off the internet chat.

Stella and Jordan sat in silence, staring at each other. Neither of them was sure what to say.

"They're a bit cold, aren't they?" Stella said.

"You could say that. How sad."

"Anyway, they weren't much help. It makes you wonder how mums and dads can care so little about their children. Have you got any?"

"Yes, a little boy. Harry. It just doesn't seem possible to me that anyone could be so uncaring."

Rupert walked across to stand beside them. "You both look a bit cheesed off, something wrong?"

"No, not really wrong, mate. Just something a bit sobering," Stella said.

"Ha, talking of which, it's end of shift. Everybody's ready to leave unless there's anything else today. We thought we might go for a bevvy if you're up for it."

"Thanks, but I'm going to get off home." Jordan glanced at his watch. "Might have time to read the bedtime story."

Stella understood. "Go on then. I'll come for a quick one."

Chapter 61

Jordan was home in time to do the bath, the cuddle, and the story.

"Everything okay, love?" Penny said.

"Yeah. Just gone about as far as we could today so…"

"It's lovely. I'll start dinner."

"It's okay. Let me do it. I'm going to make a chicken pie. You put your feet up. I have to work later but we'll have a glass of wine and a sit down while the pie cooks."

"Heaven," she said.

At two in the morning Jordan heard Penny in the kitchen and then the light from the hallway spilled into the dining room where he was working on the laptop.

"I've made you some hot chocolate, I put some rum in it," she said.

"Wow. Thanks, love. What are you doing awake?"

"I was checking on Harry, he was grizzling a bit with his sore gum. That new tooth should be through soon and it'll be a relief for the poor little thing. Anyway, your side of the bed was empty, so I sussed that I'd find you here."

She sat beside him, the silk from her dressing gown rustling on the cushion. She put her head on his shoulder. "What are you working on, can you tell me?"

"It's Kirkby. This murder enquiry is taking up all my time while I'm there and I really need to make some progress so I can report to Dave. He needs to decide whether to initiate a formal enquiry. Time's moving on."

"Have you found anything?"

"Everyone I've interacted with seems pretty straightforward. Certainly, Stella and Rupert are decent and committed. Dunn doesn't seem to me to be the sort of bloke who would have spoken out of turn. But I'm just going through internal messages and reports hoping something might pop out. It's not a very effective way to work. I'll be honest, I'm beginning to think this is not the way to deal with it. I'll hand it back to Dave and let him bring in internal affairs. It causes such bad feeling, usually, and it's always possible nobody from the station deliberately warned the den and it was moved for another reason."

"Well, try and get some sleep, love. I'll go back up. Are you in early tomorrow?"

"Yep, briefing at seven. After that I'm going to go and have a word with an old woman in Westvale. Stella has been talking to her and there's something a bit fishy going on there."

"Oh, what?"

"Dunno. Just a feeling I've got. Can't put my finger on it but she's a bit cagey when she talks about her."

"It can't be anything to do with the drugs raid, can it?"

"I don't think so. I hope not. I really like Stella. I'm also convinced she's right and her case is totally separate. But we shall see."

Laced with rum and enriched with cream, the hot chocolate was good. Jordan sat back in the chair and closed his eyes. He let his mind wander and inevitably it took him to the office and work and quite suddenly there it was. An off-the-cuff comment, the chance remark that linked to what he'd been reading and the nasty worm of an idea he really didn't want to acknowledge.

Chapter 62

Stella was already in the incident room. She smiled a little hesitantly when Jordan pulled out the chair from behind his desk. "Morning, Stella. How's the arm?"

"It's okay thanks. A bit sore if I touch it, but otherwise no problem. I can move it fine." She lifted her hand and waved it above her head.

"Have they had any luck finding out who it might have been?"

"No. I've had a look at some pictures of local scrotes but nobody I really could identify. Actually..."

"Yes?"

"Oh I don't know. Do you sometimes have a niggle in the back of your mind? Something you can't quite put your finger on?"

"Of course. They reckon most coppers do. The good ones, anyway. What is it?"

"Well, I can't put my finger on it." Stella grinned at him.

"Okay, point taken."

"It's just, there was something about him that seemed familiar. Probably just somebody I dealt with when I was on the beat."

"I would just let it stew, but don't dismiss it, and if there's something there it'll shake loose."

"Right."

"Listen, have you had coffee?" Jordan said.

"Before I came in, but I could use another one."

"I wouldn't mind a quick chat. Do you fancy the canteen?"

"We could nip up to Maccy Dees if you like. The coffee's better and I could eat a muffin."

They used Jordan's car. It wasn't discussed but Stella had walked past her own. It was time to do something about it. Maybe she'd ask Peter to do some research for her. He had a bit of knowledge about cars. He'd love it going round the showrooms, maybe having a couple of test drives. She smiled at the thought. Perhaps she'd buy him one. How would he feel about that? Chuffed at the new car but maybe thinking she was showing off. She shook the thoughts away. All of it had to wait until this case was over.

Jordan insisted on paying for their breakfast.

"I've got a bit of a difficult thing to talk to you about. It's probably best we're away from the station."

She tried to think what she could have done now. "Okay."

"As you know, there're some residual questions after the original drugs deal. You know, the one that went pear-shaped."

"Oh, right." This wasn't what she'd expected.

"We've never been able to put it to bed properly."

Stella stared at him as she crumbled the muffin between her fingers.

"Is that it, then?"

"Sorry?" Jordan said.

"Is that really why you're here? I'm not daft. I know it's not just to help out. Is it why the case was taken away from DI Dunn? I hope you're not suggesting I had anything to do with that. Not me, not Rupert. Nobody I know." She could feel the anger building but tamped it down. He was senior to her. Initially, she liked him and had already sailed a bit close to the line in their confrontations. She lifted the cup and sipped her coffee.

"It's all part of my job, Stella. I work for St Anne Street, you know that. We are still unhappy about what happened, and it needs to be explained. Anyway, we've got off to a bad start. Take a breath. Give me a chance to explain."

Stella nodded.

"I was going over some of the reports and something popped up. It could be nothing at all, but it bears looking at, I think."

"Okay."

"Your clerical team. How well do you know them?"

Stella shrugged. "I've only worked closely with them since the start of this case. Mel's lovely, keen, and talented. I did mention to you, I think, that Ruth and I didn't hit it off very well. That doesn't matter really now because it seems as if she's gone off."

"Ruth. I know you told me her surname…?"

"Cowgill."

"Okay, have a look at this." Jordan held out a copy of a statement.

"Oh, right. So, this is one of the dealers from the second raid?"

"Yeah. Gordon Cowgill," Jordan said. "How much do you know about Ruth's family?"

"Nothing much. She actually made the point she didn't want to mix her work and private life. But it's not such an unusual name, I know a couple of others from school."

"Is she on holiday now, or sick, do we know?"

"All I know is that she isn't in. We'd have to ask HR."

"You don't have her address, I don't suppose?"

"No – not a clue."

"Okay. I think we need to have a word with her. Probably best if you leave it with me but I'd like you along if you're okay with that."

She wasn't okay with it. It felt bad. She didn't want to be involved in this, suspicion, and casting doubt on the behaviour of a colleague, even one she didn't much like. There was no real choice. In fact it might look bad if she refused, might put her own motives in doubt.

"Okay. When you like."

"Great. Maybe we could call and see her and then you can take me to meet your old lady witness in Westvale."

Oh great, this morning was just getting better and better.

Chapter 63

Back at the police station Jordan went into one of the empty offices to call HR and not be overheard.

"Everything okay?" Rupert asked as Stella threw her bag on the floor under the desk and flopped onto her chair. "They said you were in, but nobody knew where you'd gone."

"Meeting with DI Carr."

"Oh right. Anything new?"

"No. Not right now."

"Okay. Well I've got a bit of news. It's probably not really important but…" He shrugged.

"Go on then."

"The tattoo. You know the one Fee had."

"Oh yeah. What was it? A bluebird or something?"

"A swallow. I was trying to find out where she had it done but with everything else that's been going on, it was difficult to fit in trawling round the shops. Anyway, I've got a couple of mates who are into ink and what have you. One of them, Jimbo, he's covered in them. Tattoos, piercings, the lot. So, he knows a lot of the shops and the styles of stuff they do. Anyway, long story short, I reckon I've found the bloke who did the design. I sent him an email last night and this morning I've had a reply and he reckons it is probably one of his. We can go and have a chat with him this morning if you like. Or I could just go myself."

"I'd like to talk to him. Surely when you're having something like that done, you chat. Blimey, even at the hairdressers you natter about all sorts of stuff. Where is he based?"

"He's only up the road. We could be there in a couple of minutes."

Stella grabbed her coat and bag and Rupert had to run to catch her.

It was a small shop in the middle of a parade of other small shops. A kebab house, a hairdresser, an off-licence. The windows were covered in adverts. The walls inside were lined with framed pictures of designs and there was a small wooden bench and a glass counter filled with pieces of jewellery and a few decorated bongs.

As they walked in, a bell jangled and a huge bloke covered in tattoos came through from the rooms at the back of the premises. "You Rupert?" he asked.

"Yeah, Jimbo said you might be able to help us. This is my boss, DS May."

"Alright, love. I'm Tony." Stella's hand was engulfed by a great paw, but the man's grip was warm and gentle. He smiled at her. "Come on in the back. I've got an appointment in quarter of an hour, but I can make you a brew."

"No, that's fine thanks. I don't want to keep you," Stella said.

Rupert had the printout and he passed it over.

"Yeah, it's one of mine. The ladies like it. It's not too big so they can have it somewhere more discreet, like. Back of the neck, hip, you know. That way it only comes out when they're in their undies or a swimsuit."

"Does it have a special meaning? I know some do," Stella said.

"It used to be a sailors' one. Used to show how far they'd sailed, depending on whether they had one or two, like. Then there was the superstition – you know how superstitious seafarers are, and swallows return home, don't they. Now some people have it to represent that, return home, some say it represents freedom. Bit of a contradiction I suppose but this stuff is often lost in stories and it's just a pretty image. I reckon it can mean whatever you want it to."

Stella took out the picture they had of Fee. "Do you recognize this woman?"

"She the one who had the tattoo?"

"Yes. We don't know how long ago?"

"Not so long, early on in the year. I remember her anyway. Good-looking bird. Bit skinny but pretty."

"What can you remember about her?" Stella said.

"Is she in bother?"

"Why do you ask?"

"Well, come on, it's obvious she's on the game. I wouldn't – well obviously. My hubby wouldn't be very pleased. I suppose she cottoned on pretty quickly because she was just relaxed with me, comfortable. Had a sensitive gaydar and whatnot. I reckon you should leave 'em be. They're fulfilling a need, aren't they?"

"I'm afraid she's dead. She was killed."

"Oh, I'm sorry about that. Yeah, that's last that is."

"We're trying to find out who might have done it, obviously, and we know so little about her. Anything you can tell us might help."

"Right." He blew out his cheeks and narrowed his eyes. "As I say she was nice. Friendly. She was with a mate. Another woman. Same as her, I think. You know – working girl. Not sure they were very close, not like lifelong friends, but they came in together. Anyway she wanted some ink as well. But I turned her down. She wasn't best pleased, but she wasn't well enough. She had scabs, you know, on her arms."

"Scabs?" Rupert said.

"Yeah. Track marks. She was a user and not very well. I don't do users. They don't heal properly and then they come back and cause trouble. In the end she had a

164

temporary one. You know like a transfer. I can do personalized ones. She had to come back the next day for it. I felt sorry for her, to be honest, she had that air about her."

"Air?"

"Yeah. Life gone wrong."

"Can you remember what it was, the tattoo?" Stella asked.

"Yeah. It was initials. P and a C and a heart with a swallow above it. It was nice. I can show you a copy. I keep all my designs. I was pleased with it. I told her, you get yourself well and I'll do you the proper one. Course she never has come back, not yet anyway."

Chapter 64

By the time Stella and Rupert arrived at the station, Jordan had texted to find out where she'd gone. He met her in the car park and clambered into her old banger as Rupert walked back inside.

"We can go in your car if you like," she said.

"This is fine. Mine's round the other side. Anyway it's already warm in here."

She was about to apologize about the condition of the vehicle but stopped herself. She really did need to be more confident if she wanted to impress him.

"Okay, HR were a bit tight-lipped at first but in the end, they did give me her address. She called in sick but hasn't sent a doctor's note," Jordan told her.

"So, where are we heading?"

Jordan took out his phone. "I've got it on Google for directions. It's Simonswood. Do you know it?"

"A bit. It's not far."

"So, tell me about this tattoo."

"Nice bloke, the tattooist. He remembered Fee. Didn't really tell us anything we didn't already know but he did say she was with someone else, another girl. I think it might be worthwhile going back with an image from the service station. Fee's was the only clear facial view, but you never know. There might be something that seems familiar with one of the others. He said she was a drug addict and not very well."

"That's not a surprise, is it?"

"No it's not, but Fee was nice-looking and not unhealthy despite her lifestyle, so there might be something to think about, you know, the difference. One theory has been the girls were escorts and not just street workers. You couldn't have someone doing that if they were spaced out and covered in track marks, could you?"

"No, possibly not. I think it's the next left?"

"Yeah. Got it. It's not bad around here, is it?" Stella said.

"No, it's nice, mind I like older houses, to be honest."

"Yes, me too. Though some of the converted old buildings are lovely. That's it up there. I suppose it's her car in the drive."

There was no response to their knock. Stella took the couple of steps to peer through the window. It was covered by vertical blinds partly closed. She tapped on the glass. "Ruth, it's DS May. Can we have a word?"

There was no movement.

"She might be in bed I suppose," Stella said. "I've got her mobile number."

She dialled. As the call went through, they heard the faint sound of the ring tone but there was no answer.

"Asleep maybe," Jordan said.

"Well, we need to speak to her." Stella banged louder on the window.

"What the hell's all the row?" The disembodied voice floated down from above and they both stepped backwards onto the grass. "I'm trying to get some kip here. I'm on nights. Go on, bugger off."

Stella took out her warrant card and held it up. She knew full well the woman leaning out of an upstairs window next door wouldn't be able to read it but assumed she would know what it was.

"Oh yeah, might have known, bizzies. You should know better."

"We're looking for Ms Cowgill. Have you seen her?"

"Snotty bitch. No. Her car's there."

"Yes, we saw," Jordan said. "But she's not answering the door."

"Aye well perhaps she doesn't want to talk to you. She doesn't want to talk to many people. Her and her no-mark son."

"Does her son live with her?"

"Now and then. Comes and goes. Anyway, leave us alone, stop making that racket. Go on, bugger off."

With that the window was slammed and the net curtain flipped back into place.

"Have we enough for a warrant?" Stella said.

"No, I don't reckon so. I've heard from St Anne Street. They confirmed Gordon Cowgill's next of kin is his brother. It didn't take long to find out Ruth is the mother to both of them but it doesn't mean she's done anything criminal."

"No wonder she didn't want to talk about her home life, eh? I wonder why it wasn't picked up in any screening."

"She's been in the job for a long time. He's only been off the rails for a couple of years. Maybe she just hid it well. But this is a bit worrying, to be honest." As he spoke Jordan reached and rattled the door handle.

"Is there any access to the back?" Stella said.

"I suppose we could get over the fence. It is odd she hasn't responded to us. Either she's out, which is naughty if she's sick, or – I don't know, maybe she's very sick indeed."

"In which case she could be in danger. We should try to get in to her."

They looked at each other for a long moment until Jordan nodded his head. He reached into his pocket and took out a medium-sized Maglite torch. It was quick to break the single-glazed window in the little porch and to reach through to the inside. There was a deadlock. The brass key was on the window ledge, and it needed the hole in the window enlarging before Stella could reach her smaller hand through. The front door was secured with a Yale lock. Jordan put his shoulder to it, and it took several tries before the wood of the frame splintered and they accessed the hallway. By now they had made so much noise with no response, they were partly prepared for the scene that greeted them in the bedroom. It was still unpleasant and shocking.

Chapter 65

They waited until the ambulance had gone. Jordan found a piece of hardboard in the shed to fix over the broken window. They'd need to make proper arrangements to secure the house.

"I'm going to get on to Serious and Organised," Jordan said. "We need to find where Gordon Cowgill is being held. I'll go and tell him what's happened."

"I'll get back to the station. Shall I take this with me?" Stella held up an evidence bag with the note inside.

"Let me get a picture of it." Jordan recorded an image of the piece of paper with the few lines scrawled across it.

I'm sorry. I had to warn him. He's my son. I didn't have any choice. I'm a mother.
Tell DS May it was nothing to do with the squat.
My boy would have told me.

* * *

The atmosphere in the incident room was hushed and tense. As Stella walked in, they all turned to her.

"Boss, is it right, what they're saying?" Rupert said.

"I don't know, what are they saying?" she said.

"Someone picked up a call to the emergency ambulance. Has Ruth Cowgill killed herself?"

Stella looked around at the expectant faces. Mel was sniffing, her eyes red and puffy.

"You all know I can't say much right now. I have to go and have a word with DI Dunn. As soon as we know just what's happened, I expect he'll come down himself and have a chat. In the meantime, just get on with what you were doing please. We've got a case here that's going nowhere fast, and it could be we have a couple of women out there at risk. Come on, do your jobs."

DI Dunn's secretary held open the office door when she saw Stella walking along the corridor. "He's expecting you. There's someone from HR in there with him."

"Thanks."

The conversation was sober and sad. They were police and details were important. Stella described the scene in the bedroom. The empty blister packs and a few pills spilled on the floor. The bottle of whisky, the dead body of Ruth Cowgill splayed across the bed under a twisted duvet. She didn't go into details of the vomit or the other stains and smell. There was no need.

"Do you have the note?" Dunn asked.

Stella placed the plastic bag on his desk. It wasn't evidence of a crime yet instinct and training meant that Dunn didn't touch it. He leaned to read the scrawled words.

"What's your thinking here, Stella? I have my own ideas, but I don't want to influence you."

"I don't see there's any doubt, sir. She was the one who warned the people at the drug den about the raid. We will be able to confirm it when we speak to her son. There'll be no point in him denying it now."

"Where is he?"

"He is supposed to be with his brother. He's on bail. DI Carr has gone to speak to them both."

Dunn nodded. "I don't think there can be any doubt really. Of course, we need a statement from the son. What a shame. She'd been with us a long time."

"Sixteen years. Always well thought of," the bloke from HR muttered.

"Well, Stella, I suppose you're pleased," Dunn said.

"Sorry, sir," she said.

"She could have been trying to cover for him, but it looks as if this is proof positive that you were right, doesn't it? We'll confirm with the son but a dying confession and all that."

For a moment Stella was actually speechless. Something she had never experienced before. She ran a hand over her face, buying time. "Sir, if Ruth's death is the price for me being right, then I would have much preferred to have been wrong. I didn't know her well, but she was a colleague. I don't know what it's like to be a mother but if it means you will put everything on the line including a job you love and your own life, then she was exemplary. Yes, she broke the rules. Yes, she let us down, but she made the decisions selflessly with her heart and, for me, that is awesome. May I go, sir? I have a report to write up and an ongoing inquiry that needs me."

Chapter 66

Stella was still shaking with emotion when she sat behind her desk. She logged onto her computer and scrolled through the reports. Rupert swivelled his chair around and began to speak but she knew rational conversation was beyond her right now. She just held up a hand and he turned away. Tears prickled at the back of her eyes. Did the DI really believe she was so cut-throat, so cold, as to think of Ruth's suicide only in terms of her own career, as some sort of confirmation she had been right all along? Is that how other people saw her? The idea was appalling. She glanced around at the others in the room; how did they see her? She had always been a team player. She was shaken by Dunn's comment.

Her phone rang.

"Stella, I've arranged to bring Gordon Cowgill in to make a statement," Jordan said. "He was out on police bail. Both brothers were at home and are pretty cut up, as you might imagine. I've given him an hour to get himself together but when he heard about his mum and saw the copy of the note, he confirmed what we thought. She gave him the heads-up about the raid."

"Do you want me to come to St Anne Street?"

"You certainly can if you want to but it's only a statement. I don't think there's going to be any problem getting him to tell us what happened. He might be a hard bastard and a low-level thug but it's his mum and he's devastated. I'll let you know what happens. Are you okay, Stella? You sound a bit subdued. It was horrible finding her like that. If you think you need to take time off, I'm sure it can be arranged. You can speak to someone as well. Trauma counselling is there if you need it."

"No. I'm fine, sir. Honestly. Thanks though. It's just sad, isn't it?"

"Yes. It might help a bit when we have all the details. I'll get back up there as soon as I can."

She put down her phone and turned back to the computer. She felt adrift and unfocussed. Perhaps she should just take a breath. Get a drink and give herself time to get herself together. She bent to pick up her bag.

"Boss." Rupert appeared at the side of her chair.

"Yeah, what is it?"

"Phil Harwood's car. It's just been picked up on the M6."

"Really?" All thoughts of coffee and a quiet corner had gone. "Tell me what you know."

"It'd been nicked. A young lad. He'd gone off on a jolly up to Newcastle to see his mates; gone on a bender, what have you. It's got false plates so it wasn't picked up by the ANPR. Anyway, on the way back the stupid sod got himself into a minor accident and when the traffic patrol checked him out, he tried to make a run for it, vaulting over the fence and off through the fields. Of course they had him. When the plates turned up false, they checked the VIN and eventually it led back to us and Phillip Harwood. I've arranged for him to be brought here and the car is on its way to the pound. I've let Sergeant Flowers know and he's sending a couple of his technicians to go over it."

"Great stuff. Thanks, Rupert. I wonder how much this lad has messed with it."

"Well, with luck not much. He won't have had it valeted, that's for sure, so we may get something."

Chapter 67

Gordon Cowgill tried to swagger but his heart wasn't in it. He lowered to the chair in the interview room with a sigh and put his head in his hands.

Jordan gave him a moment. "I am very sorry for what's happened with your mum, Gordon."

"Yeah, right."

There was no point in saying more. Even if the younger man could be convinced Jordan was sincere, nothing would make any difference today.

"Youse said youse wanted a statement. Let's get on with it. I don't want to be here long."

"You already know what you tell us will not make any difference to the old charges against you. You'll still have to answer for those."

"If I'm going to help youse there should be something in it for me."

"The charges you'll have to answer for relate to previous offences, and your involvement with what was happening in the address raided in Northbrook. We might be able to do some negotiating on the drug dealing. We're just trying to put a couple of things to bed. Draw a line under some questions. Of course, if you give us some valuable information that's another thing."

"Okay, are you recording this?"

Jordan started the machine and went through the preamble introducing himself and the constable sitting quietly beside him.

"When you're ready, Gordon."

"Right, so my mam knew what I was up to. Not all of it, and she was always on at me to get out. She didn't understand. She'd been with the police all those years and she still didn't understand. I told her I was too deep in to just walk away."

"Deep in with whom?"

Gordon looked up and pursed his lips. "Don't be a dick. I can't tell you any more than I could tell her. I know I'm probably going down for the GBH, I want to come out the other end with all my fingers and no scars."

"So, despite your mother's pleas, you stayed in the game. Selling misery."

"Look, mate. If people want to buy product that's not my fault. I just provide what they need. End of."

"We could debate that but it's probably a waste of time. Tell me what happened before the first raid in Westvale. How did you know it was going to happen?"

"My mum didn't know exactly where I was, not for sure. I kept her at arm's length, didn't I?"

"Did you not worry that her conscience would lead her to tell the people she was working with what you were doing?" Jordan said.

"As I say I never give her no details. Anyway, she was my mum, she would never drop me in it. Well, she never, did she? Silly cow went and killed herself instead. What did she have to go and do that for? Didn't think about me, did she? Didn't think how I was supposed to get over that." He couldn't speak for a while and hid his face, lowering his head so the hood fell forward. Eventually he sniffed, dragged his sleeve across under his nose and carried on.

"I went to see her one night and she got drunk. We always had a bevvy when I went round there and now and then she'd tie one on. Sometimes she drank a bit too much. Not a lot, she wasn't an alkie or nothing, but now and then. When she was stressed, I suppose. Anyway, that night she told me I should be careful. Told me they were bringing in the big guns. I suppose she meant you lot. She said there was going to be a big raid all over the city." He stopped speaking for a moment and blew his nose on a piece of scrappy tissue. "Get us a drink, will ya?"

Jordon nodded at the constable. They brought him water.

"So, I saw I could get some brownie points. If I warned people what was going down. Trouble was she only told me the day before it was due to happen. We didn't have much time. Just got me and my mates out, cleared our stuff away and cleaned the place."

"So did it work?"

"What?"

"Did you win brownie points? Did it do you some good?"

Cowgill shrugged.

"So, you betrayed your mum and got nothing out of it?" Jordan said.

"Well, I didn't have enough time to contact people, not anybody that mattered. Wasn't time, was there? You have to go through levels, like, and they go through other levels. Like the army, innit. Tell you what, whoever gave you the second address is a dead man walking. That raid's brassed off some important people. My mum, well, she was in a right state about everything. It just built up. I don't reckon it was my fault at all, to be honest."

"And are you ready to give us some names? These important people you were going to inform."

"You pissing me about? No effin' way."

"Well, in that case all we can do now is to draw a line under what happened, remove any suspicion from your mother's colleagues."

"Do you think I'm bothered about that? You soddin' coconut."

The constable shifted in his seat, clenched his fists. Jordan ignored the insult, he'd had worse.

"Okay, if you've no names for me, what about our other enquiry? If you help with that it might carry some weight with the judge."

"What other enquiry?"

"The unlawful killing of a man in a squat in Westvale. Not very far from where you and your mates were dealing. We thought there must be a connection."

Cowgill shook his head back and forth several times. "Your lot already asked me about it. I don't know nothing about that. That was something else. Nothing to do with me or anyone I know."

"Do you know either of these men?" Jordan placed a copy of the golfing picture from Jewell's flat on the table.

"No, don't know them. Look like a right pair of tits."

"Do you know this girl?" Jordan opened his file to a picture of Fee lying on the slab in London.

"Shit, man. Don't show me that, she's dead."

"Do you know her?"

"No, I don't." As he spoke the younger man pulled the file towards him. "No, poor cow. I don't know her."

"Okay. I think that's all for now," Jordan said. "I'll have your statement typed up and you can sign it for us when you report in tomorrow."

"My mum," Cowgill said.

"Yes."

"She never done nothing wrong all the time she worked with youse lot. Nothing. It was just that she knew with the GBH outstanding I'd be sent down for a long stretch if I was caught dealing."

"Yes, I see."

"Well, does it have to come out, ruin her reputation and her good name? All because of me?"

"It will go on the file, obviously. You have to know people will hear about it. She left that note after all."

Cowgill's eyes filled with tears. He swiped them away before they had time to fall. "I can't tell her, can I? I can't tell her I'm sorry. I am. She was a hard bitch at times. But me da was long gone and she had us two to deal with. She did her best."

"Maybe the best thing you could do for her would be to try and straighten yourself out. Do your time and then stay out of trouble," Jordan said.

"You've got no idea, have you? When you're in with these blokes, you're in. Unless you can get me a whole new life like you do with kiddie fiddlers and killers."

"I'm sorry, I just don't think what you've given us would be enough. Unless you want to give us some heavy hitters' names."

"Not happening. Never ever happening. I don't want to bleed to death in some skanky showers in Walton. Nah. Forget it, I'll take my chances. Anyway she's gone now, isn't she? Can't get on at me no more."

Chapter 68

Back in Kirkby, the car thief looked to be in his early twenties. Dressed in greasy jeans, trainers, and a football club top, he seemed the unlikely driver of a classic Jaguar. But then, who knew these days?

In this case, however, they did know. Darren Cooper had an address at his mum's house in Bootle and had never held down a job for more than a few months since leaving school.

Stella took Rupert with her to the interview.

Darren didn't seem particularly concerned at his situation. He slouched on the plastic chair, his legs stretched under the table – they had to ask him to move before they could sit down.

"You've been read your rights, Mr Cooper. Do you understand what you've been told?" Stella said.

He moved his gum to the side of his mouth. "No comment."

"Do you understand why you are here?"

"No comment."

"You have waived your right to legal representation, is that correct?"

"Don't need no swanky-arsed lawyer telling me what to do, do I? I haven't done nothing. Out for a run, wasn't I?"

"Out for a run, in the rain, at the side of the M6," Stella said.

"No comment."

"Well, what do you think, Detective Moon?" Stella said. "Not getting very far. I reckon we should go straight ahead and put the murder charge to the DI. I mean, twocking is one thing but it's not going to get you much more than a slap on the wrist, given the state of the prisons. But a car with false plates and a big question mark over who killed the owner, well there's a whole different kettle of fish."

"Yeah," Rupert said, "go for it, boss."

"Hey, calm down," Darren said. "Murder, what the hell are you talking about? I was out for a run, I told you. Minding my own business and them pigs saw me and thought they'd have a go. Nobody said nothing about no murder. I don't know nothing about no car."

"Well, the traffic officers didn't know. All they saw was a plonker running away," Rupert said. "Course it doesn't matter. We've got clothes from the car, we'll get fingerprints, DNA, all sorts of evidence. So, Darren, once we've taken your prints and a cheek swab, you'll be in the clear."

Now they had his attention. He straightened in the chair, his forearms on the table.

"Hey, you're out of order now, mate. I don't know nothing about no murder. Back off."

"And yet here we are, a dead bloke, his stolen car, and you, Darren. I mean, you can see how we might think you're involved in this, can't you? Especially you being so unhelpful," Stella said.

"Alright, alright. I took it. I saw it, it wasn't even locked. I was only borrowing it. I was going to put it back. My mate was ill, I needed to go and see him."

They all knew this for the lie it was, but it was progress of a sort.

When her phone rang Stella's first instinct was to ignore it. It wasn't what she needed. Not now, not when they had just started to move on. But it was Bob, he never rang her. Since he had joined the team, the older copper had simply got on with his job. All the paperwork was properly filed and recorded; all the calls were correctly logged. Tasks were allocated efficiently. He may not be out in the streets chasing bad guys, but he was invaluable doing what he did. Anyway, maybe leaving him right now could focus Darren's mind. She turned off the recording and they left the room, a uniformed officer standing silent watch by the door.

"Bob, what's happening?" she said.

"Sorry to interrupt, boss, but we've just had word. They found a laptop in the car. It's with the forensic department right now but I don't reckon it belongs to m'laddo there. It's a really expensive piece of kit, we're talking over a thousand apparently."

"Jesus. It's a wonder it's still there. You would have thought he'd have flogged it."

"Apparently it was under the front seat, effectively hidden unless you knew where to look for it. Of course, the password protection is a bitch. But with a thing that expensive it's what you would expect. Anyway, they're all of a twitch down there, it's got them excited trying to get into it."

"Thanks, Bob. Let me know if you hear anything."

"Back in there, boss?" Rupert asked.

"Nah. Let's go and get a sarnie. Let him sweat a bit."

As they walked down the corridor, Jordan came through the door from the car park.

"Stella, Rupert. I hear you've had some excitement."

"Yeah, a bit," Stella said. "We're going for a coffee. Leaving the car thief to sweat."

"Do you mind if I come with you? You can fill me in on what's been happening."

* * *

"So, I'm right in thinking this Darren isn't the sharpest tool in the box?" Jordan said.

"I think you could say that."

"He reckons the car was unlocked?"

"That's right," Stella said. "But how likely is it? A classic Jaguar."

"But he had the keys when he was picked up?"

"Yes, according to the traffic police they were in his pocket. He tried to say they'd planted them but really that's going nowhere, is it?" Rupert had bought the coffees and a packet of biscuits.

Stella had another pang of guilt at being treated by the blokes. But the biscuits were shortbread, and she did like a shortbread.

"So, either he's telling the truth and the car was unlocked or he got the keys from Phil Harwood," Jordan said.

"Well, yes, it has to be when you put it like that," Stella said.

"Which do you reckon? Do you see him as a killer? He hasn't got a record, has he?"

"Shoplifting when he was still at school and drunk and disorderly after the last derby match."

"Plonker," Rupert said, thereby letting them know just which of the teams he supported.

Jordan grinned at him.

"So, if he is just a chancer and has found the car unlocked, then what on earth was Phil Harwood thinking leaving it like that?" Jordan said. "Seems to me either he was forced to, or he was in such a panic he simply ran off and left it."

Stella remembered Betsy. *'He didn't want to be there. He was angry and he had no choice.'*

Chapter 69

"I don't think this numpty is going to tell us much. I reckon we'll end up just doing him for the car theft. We need to hang on to him for a while though. Just in case," Stella said.

"Leave it with me. If we need extra time, I should be able to swing it. He is still under suspicion for the killing, has to be. I guess we all know it's not very likely," Jordan said.

"Okay. In the meantime let's hope they get into the laptop. I reckon it could be significant. It's not Darren's, is it? So it has to have belonged to Phillip Harwood," Stella said.

Her phone rang, an unknown number. If this was the bank again, she was going to draw all the money out and stick it in her building society.

"You need to come down here."

"Sorry, who am I speaking to?" Stella said.

"Don't be so daft."

"Betsy, is it you?"

"Oh, give the girl a lollipop."

"I didn't think you had my number."

"You left me your card. Do you think I'm so daft I can't use the phone?"

"No, not at all. What is it you want, anyway?"

"I told you. Get yourself down here. There's somebody you have to speak to. And don't take too long."

This was the chance to introduce Jordan to Betsy. Of course, she could just be complaining about the pickled onions, but Stella turned to Rupert.

"I really need to get off. Could you finish the interview with Darren? Basically just put the fear of God into him, see if he gives you anything useful and then stick him in holding until we decide his future. Jordan, I wonder if you'll come with me? There's someone I want you to meet, and it sounds like this could be important."

Fair play to him he didn't ask her to clarify anything, he simply nodded and picked up his jacket.

If this was about cake or onions, there was going to be hell to pay.

* * *

"So, the squat?" Jordan said as he pulled out onto St Chad's Drive.

"Couple of houses away from there. Do you know the way?"

"I do. I went down a few days ago just so I could visualize the place. They'd just about finished processing the scene and the council were ready to board it all up. Anyway, who is this person we're going to see?"

"Okay. Her name is Betsy. She's an old woman. But she's been… erm, helpful. She knew the girls and a bit about what happened in the squat and even on the night Harwood was killed."

"How does she know this stuff? Is she mixed up in something dodgy? If she is, you really should have mentioned it."

"No, she's not. Not as far as I'm aware, anyway."

"But you haven't had her in to make an official statement."

"No, I haven't."

"Is that wise? If there's a possibility she's a material witness, we should have had it all documented."

He was right, of course, but then it had all been so odd. Stella turned to look at Jordan. "I think it's best if you meet her first and then you might understand my actions. She also said there is someone waiting to see us, so that's puzzling."

"Well, the puzzle will be solved in a couple of minutes. We're nearly there."

Chapter 70

The door was ajar, and Stella shouted through as she stepped into the hall. "Betsy, it's me, Stella. I've got somebody with me. It's DI Carr."

They turned into the lounge to find Betsy beside the fire, sipping a cup of tea, and on the settee with a glass of orange juice, George Kenny turned to them, his eyes round with anxiety.

"Hello, ma'am." Jordan crossed the room his hand held out.

Betsy took it in both of hers and patted it.

"Ah. Nice. Sit down, lad."

George shuffled along the couch and before he sat beside him, Jordan shook his hand. The boy looked ready to burst into tears and his hand shook violently, spilling his drink onto the carpet.

"Hang on, George. Don't you be messing up my rug. This man's not going to cause you any harm."

"You said as how I'd get into trouble if I didn't tell you something and you found out about it later." George directed his comment at Stella, who was now in the other easy chair.

She glanced at Jordan who had leaned back and looked totally at ease in this strange company.

"That's right, George. But I also told you not to be frightened, didn't I?"

"Stu said I'd have a record now, because I talked to you."

"Rubbish. He doesn't know what he's talking about. Anyway, we've come down to see you, so what is it you've got to tell us?"

"Them prozzies." He glanced at Jordan as he spoke, but the DI didn't react. "I've seen 'em."

"Okay. Great. Where were they?" Stella said.

"They were up on the shopping centre. They were in the café. Then later they were in the corner by the cinema. They were just sitting on the steps with their stuff."

"When was this, George?"

"This dinner time. I was going back to school. But when I saw 'em I thought I'd get into trouble if I didn't tell you. If I'd gone home my mum would have been mad, so I came to Betsy. She said I had to tell you." He nodded, satisfied he'd done his duty.

"Okay. We're going to go down there and see if we can find them. Thanks so much, George. I think those ladies will be glad you told us. Their friend in London was killed so they're probably frightened. You did a good thing." Jordan spoke quietly but in no way did he sound condescending and as he stood, he held out his hand again to shake that of the boy. "Thank you for your help."

He turned to Betsy. "Thank you as well."

The old woman just cocked her head to one side. "Your people brought you up right, didn't they? Go on, get off and find those girls before something horrible happens."

Chapter 71

The shopping centre wasn't particularly busy, it was late afternoon and things were winding down. "We don't have any decent pictures of these women, do we?" Jordan said.

"Afraid not, we've got some taken from CCTV footage but only Fee showed her face to the cameras."

"Well, the main thing, I suppose, is that we know they are still in the area. Or I should say still back in the area?" Jordan said.

They spoke to the girl behind the counter in the café, but it had been a busy Friday and she hadn't noticed anyone in particular out of place. "We get all sorts in here. If they behave and pay, I just let them get on with it."

They did a couple of circuits of the centre and the market. They peered into places where Stella knew homeless people gathered.

"Used to come here when I was on the beat. There's always been problems, beggars, down-and-outs, drug addicts, unfortunately. It's not too bad right now but I can sort of understand how they ended up here. I guess in a way there's safety in numbers. I'll make sure the patrols are given a heads-up to watch for them."

"We might as well get back to the station. I'll walk, it's pretty near and I could do with a breath of air. I'll see you in the office. Is that okay?" Jordan said.

"Yeah. Fine, boss. Actually, I can leave my car here for now, I'll have to come back later for some shopping."

"Do you live on your own, Stella?"

"I do. I have a flat out in Aintree. My mam and da live in Wavertree. Didn't you used to work there?"

"Yes. It was good."

"How are you enjoying being part of the *elite*." As she spoke Stella did air quotes around the word.

"To be honest, I haven't had much chance to get settled. I was straight into the drugs raid and that led on to this."

"Well, I'm really glad of your help. It wasn't that I couldn't manage, of course I could. But it's made a difference, getting away from DI Dunn. Oh sorry, I probably shouldn't say that. But we were coming at it from completely different places, and it was difficult."

"Yes, I understand. Trouble is, Stella, we really need to have some progress, this case is going cold."

She nodded. "I know. There seem to be so many threads and they won't knit together."

"Nothing we can do but keep pegging away at it. How's your arm by the way?"

"It's not too bad, thanks. No major damage. Actually, that's something I keep coming back to."

"How so?"

"They never found anyone to point the finger at. That's not a surprise, is it? But I have this image of the bloke running away, jumping over the fence by the railway and there's something there. I can't shake it loose. You know I never thought it was just random."

"You still think it was somebody you know, then. I know you were on the beat for a while, could it have been somebody from near where you live with a grudge?"

"I don't really see how. They'd have to follow me home, it's not likely. I mean I was just a beat bobby, nothing really particular I remember. It's just that I have the feeling I'd seen something like it somewhere else. The whole scene. Course it could just be something off the tele or simply me looking for something that's not there."

"Did you view the CCTV from the doctor's surgery?"

"I haven't had a chance. Rupert had a look at it. He didn't notice anything to really help."

"Let's do that. Maybe whatever is lurking in your memory will become obvious. Sometimes with a bit of distance, your mind's clearer."

* * *

It was after shift change and the room was almost empty, computers all powered down. It took a little while to set up the video of poor quality, grainy film.

Stella gave Jordan a commentary as they watched. "I was walking from the top of the road and the bloke came behind me. I don't know which direction because I wasn't paying proper attention. Anyway, that's out of shot. Oh, there he is. So this is after me and Keith had fought him off. He stopped to grab the weapon and then legged it down the road to the fence. We can see that. There he is. He's pretty fit, he almost vaults over, doesn't he? Not a scramble. So, I guess he's young and – oh…"

"What?" Jordan said.

"Just a sec."

Stella fired up the computer at the next desk and opened another video file.

"Bloody hell!"

"What?" Jordan came to stand behind her.

"Okay, I won't say anything because I don't want to plant any ideas in your mind but… well, just watch, yeah?"

Jordan ran the film a couple of times. "It's Jewell, isn't it? I would say almost certainly. Run them side by side."

"I don't think there's much doubt, do you?" Stella said after they'd watched both videos a couple more times.

"Jewell attacked you. But why, what would he hope to gain? If he just wanted to scare you, he must have known it wouldn't make any difference to the investigation, and even if, heaven forbid, he'd hurt you more badly–"

"Killed me, you mean," Stella said.

"Well, yes. Even then he had to know we would keep on trying to find out what happened. Killing a copper was hardly going to take the heat off."

Stella sat quietly for a while and Jordan went to buy a couple of drinks from the machine.

"I must do something about this coffee. Maybe I'll bring in a flask."

"So, that bugger beat me up and tried to cut me. Jesus," Stella said.

Chapter 72

It was shortly after seven when they left the station. There was nothing to be done about the latest discovery. Okay, so now they thought they knew who had attacked her outside the flat. They couldn't do anything about it when they didn't have any idea where Douglas Jewell was. As she drove to her mother's house, Stella mulled it over in her mind. There was some benefit, wasn't there? They had assumed he had gone to London, maybe trying to leave the country. But the attack had come after they had found his car burned out and watched him driving off in a van down the motorway. If he was back on Merseyside, had he risked going back to the flat?

She sent a message to Rupert to be ready to go with her to Albert Dock early the next morning.

It was a relief to see her grandfather sitting in the living room.

"Are you feeling better?" she asked.

"I'm alright. Just had to get used to stronger pills."

She sat beside him and gave him the news. Of course, he already knew about the money. She glanced at her mother who had the grace to blush and then shrug.

"But, Stella," her grandfather said, "I don't know how to do it."

"It's okay, I'll sort it." As she made the promise, she wondered how she would fit it in and hoped it was as simple as she was suggesting.

"Isn't it jumping the queue? Isn't it taking someone else's place?"

"No, Granda, you'll go to a private hospital. You'll not take up room in the NHS and actually it means someone else can have your place."

He didn't look totally convinced but he smiled at her and patted her hand. "You're a good lass, you are, and thank you."

In the hallway her mother hugged her close. "Thanks, love. I knew you'd help him out. I'm sorry about what I said. I was worried about him."

"Yeah. It's okay, Mam. Listen, could you ring the doctor tomorrow and see what we have to do? Only this case at work is so complicated and I want to get things moving for Granda."

"Yeah, course I will."

"And, Mam."

"What?"

"You think about what you want to do. Stay here, move away – this money, it's for all of us."

She left the house with a smile on her face. She'd been worrying needlessly. They'd had some good luck, that was all.

* * *

First thing in the morning she sent a message to Rupert telling him she was on the way and to meet her in the car park to avoid the rush hour.

He messaged back that he was in the incident room, and really thought she should come in first.

"What's going on, Rupert?" she said as she walked into the incident room. "I wanted to avoid the rush hour."

"I've been in touch with forensics. I wanted to give them a shove about the laptop."

"Oh, right."

"Seems they had a geek working till late last night and he's managed to get some information off it. Don't ask me how. He did tell me, but it was like he was speaking Dothraki."

"Doth what? Is he from Africa or…?"

"GOT."

"Gee. Oh. What the hell are you on about?"

"Sorry," he said. "Have you really no idea what I'm talking about?"

"No."

"Shit. Well, I didn't understand him. But he's sent up a report. It's probably on your computer by now."

"I haven't looked yet this morning. I wanted to make an early start."

"It's interesting, boss. Look."

She leaned in to see the list of emails and appointments.

"Okay. So, did this Dothraki bloke explain what he thinks we're looking at?"

"He's not…" Rupert started. "Oh never mind. Pull up a chair. So they have these initials, I reckon maybe they are places." He pointed with a pencil.

"Places?"

"Yeah. You know, like airports. Codes for locations."

"So, it's to do with flights?"

"Don't think so. I've made a bit of a start on checking, and they don't really make any sense. Not from John Lennon at least. So, we need to think about those. The other things are emails to him from someone else, longish threads. Now, the geek reckons he can maybe find out who they were to, given time. They've used VPNs so it's a bit complicated. We'll just have to be patient on that," Rupert said.

He continued, "It does look as though he was up to something weird, though. And there are bank accounts. The geek managed to get into those once he had access to the hard drive. Now, we know he was pretty well heeled but there's all sorts of investments and shares and stuff. And some of it is offshore. Offshore! I mean, okay, he's a banker so he knows about this stuff but he got something else going on, has to. Oh yes, and there's pictures of women. The usual thing, scantily dressed, sexy poses. Not actually hard porn, more sexy modelling. I guess the forensic department could have a go at trying to find out who the women are if it seems important."

"Okay. Well, although that's all excellent work it doesn't explain why Phillip Harwood was at the squat or why Douglas Jewell attacked me with a knife outside mine."

"What?"

"Oh yes. Last night, me and the DI sussed out what it is that's been bothering me about that night. We're pretty well convinced it was Jewell."

"Oh Jesus. This just gets more and more complicated," Rupert said.

"Well, we just have to keep going, mate. Just keep unpicking the knots."

Chapter 73

Stella had slept well. Having the money sorted was such a relief and being able to help her grandfather with his operation was really lovely. Now, she pushed it to one side again. Mum would sort the doctor. She'd done it before when they needed home visits for Nana and what have you. She wasn't to be trifled with when her family needed care.

She left Rupert going through the emails looking for any clue as to just what they meant. Not many of the civilian staff had turned in. Mel was there, she looked flustered.

"Everything okay there?" Stella said.

"Yeah. Well no. I've sent a message through to you just now with the number of Phillip Harwood's parents. They were on the phone first thing and really annoyed. Very rude, actually, when I said you weren't in yet."

"Did they say what they wanted?"

"Not really. I couldn't understand. It was something about the will and it was your fault, sorry that's what they said. About his sister, and you stirring things up. Honest, they were really mad and not making a lot of sense. Could you ring them back?"

"Yeah. Of course. I'll get on to it as soon as I've got myself a cuppa."

"Oh, DI Carr has brought in a big thermos, over there on the table. You just pump the top. It's real coffee, it's gorgeous."

"Where is he now, do you know?"

"He's with DI Dunn, I think."

* * *

Phillip Harwood's father was angry. As soon as she told him her name, he began a tirade. "I blame you for this. You looking into things and stirring things up. Haven't we had enough to put up with?"

"I'm sorry Mr Harwood, you'll have to explain what's wrong."

"We haven't heard anything from our daughter for years. Years. As far as we were concerned, we had finished with her. All the money and time you spend on your kids, and they pay you back by going off the rails and making you a laughing stock."

"It's still not clear what it is you want from me, sir."

"Just a minute. I need to let the dog in."

She was left holding the phone and listening to the palaver getting the animal inside and calming it down and then the slam of a door while it was shut away. She was tempted to hang up. But that would only delay this strange call.

"Right. The nice DI we spoke to, your boss, he arranged for us to get an interim certificate as he said he would. We contacted our solicitor and he got in touch with the bank up there."

Melanie was watching and Stella rolled her eyes. "Okay."

"Well, they have his will and apparently, Phillip, our son, has left everything – everything, mind you – to his sister. To Catherine."

"I see. But I don't know what you think I can do about that. It's an issue for you and your solicitor, and the bank. I don't know why you've called me."

"You were the one who was looking for her. You started asking questions about her."

"Yes, but as part of our enquiries. We felt it might be useful to speak to her."

"Why?"

"In case she'd seen your son recently. In case she could give us any information about his current life."

"Well of course she can't. She's gone. She's vanished. The life she was living, she's more than likely dead. We've come to terms with it."

"But, Mr Harwood, if Phillip has named her in his will, then maybe that wasn't what he believed. You told me you hadn't been in close contact with him yourself for a long time. Is it not possible they were in touch? Perhaps he knew where his sister was, and he wanted to take care of her."

"Rubbish. Just rubbish. If you'd not started stirring things up, then this would never have happened. We are his only relatives. Everything should have come to us and now it won't because of you."

"I'm sorry, I don't see how you've reached that conclusion. I don't know when he made his will, but I've

193

only been involved since his awful death. I just don't see how you have come up with the idea it's in any way my fault."

"Well this isn't going to end here, let me tell you. I shall be speaking to your superiors about the way you have handled this. What are we supposed to do now? That flat, his accounts, his car, all left to rot while the bank find his sister. It's outrageous."

As she put down the phone, Mel placed a cup of coffee on the desk.

"Brilliant, thanks," Stella said. "That was so odd. I'm still not sure what he thinks we've done. Rupert, leave that for now. We need to go down to the bank. See if they'll give us any information about Phillip Harwood's will. I'd love to know when it was made. I don't have much hope, but we'll give it a try."

"It's Saturday, boss. I don't reckon there'll be anyone there."

"Damn. Is it really? I've lost track."

"Yeah right." He laughed. "We'll have to leave it until first thing Monday. But we'll be lucky if they tell us anything without a warrant."

Chapter 74

Stella peered at the emails on Douglas Jewell's laptop.

"Mel, will you give Rupert a hand to go through these for a while? Perhaps sort them a bit. Maybe we'll get a clue as to just what was going on. Don't discount any ideas at the minute."

"You should ask Bob as well, he's really great on documentation and filing and so on," Mel said.

"Bob, did you hear?"

"I did. I'll get on to it as soon as I can," he said. "These blokes were bankers, weren't they?"

"Yes."

"So there's something to keep in mind, could be some sort of back door dealing. Have you not thought of involving the bank?"

"I think we need more than this to show them before we can even mention it. Have we heard from the financial investigator?" Stella said.

"No – not yet. I'll chase them. I do know he was well off but seems it's more than we'd expect. Can we have a go at home? Seeing it's Saturday, save me coming in tomorrow."

"I reckon so, but just between us, yeah? Sorry, Mel. You don't have to. I can't get you overtime for it, and I don't think you can do it remotely."

"It's okay, boss. Don't worry."

Mel was soon back on the phone but there was a dead weekend feel to the office. Nothing was happening.

Her phone binged with an email alert. It was from the Harwoods.

This is what we had to put up with and now more trouble because of her.

An image was attached. It was a very young teenage girl. Black Kohl rimmed her eyes, she had several piercings, purple hair and her school uniform tie was knotted to resemble a noose around her neck.

This was when she was excluded from school the second time.

Stella could see that from a parent's point of view there were problems. But she'd had her own rebellious stage and felt a tug of sympathy for the sad-eyed young woman. She printed a copy and stuck it onto the whiteboard beside the picture of the dead man.

"I'm popping out. If the DI comes in, tell him I've gone back to speak to the witness at the tattoo parlour. As soon as you've all caught up, you might as well get off. I'd be grateful for anything you can suggest with the computer stuff."

* * *

There were two people waiting in the outer room of the tattoo parlour. One, a young woman, was nervously clutching at the hand of the man with her. They muttered together as they turned the pages of a book of patterns.

They all looked up as the curtain between the front and back rooms was swept aside.

"Ready for you, Kayleigh. If you're still up for it. Oh, hello. You're the…" Tony paused and glanced at his customers.

"Just need a quick word, Tony." Stella understood he didn't want rumours about his establishment and the police. "It's about that other matter. From a couple of days ago."

"Come on through. Won't keep you a minute, Kayleigh."

Stella showed him the picture of Catherine Harwood. "If you try and imagine this person a few years older, do you think you might have seen her before?"

"Yeah. That's the girl who came with Fee. The one who wanted some ink. I told her no, she wasn't well enough. I recognize the piercings on her ear. They've not been done very well. The spacing's off."

"Blimey, I wouldn't have noticed that."

"No, well. I have a bit of a thing about it. If something's worth doing and all that. Yeah, I'd put money on it. It's her."

"Thanks, Tony. I'll let you get on."

"Cool. If you ever want a bit of work just let me know. I'll give you mates' rates."

"Right – thanks for that." Stella laughed.

* * *

Jordan rang. "Anything happening?"

She brought him up to date on the laptop messages and the email from the Harwoods. "I'm going to show it to Betsy now. The tattoo artist had no hesitation though. He was sure it was the woman with Fee."

"Okay. Keep me apprised. I'm off home. Got to get stuff sorted for tomorrow. I've got visitors for lunch. I was wondering if you'd like to come. It's DCI Griffiths, you know him already, and then just me and my family."

"That's nice of you. I'd love to, actually. Shall I bring something?"

"No, it's all under control. We'll see you about twelvish if that's okay. The satnav'll bring you straight there. Crosby it is. I'll text you the address."

She hung up the phone and immediately regretted the acceptance. She'd be out of her depth. Two senior detectives and Jordan's wife. She sighed. Maybe she'd call back and tell him something had come up. Yeah, in a while, that was what she'd do.

Betsy's door was closed and when the old woman answered the knock, she looked bleary-eyed and a little befuddled.

"Are you okay?" Stella asked.

"I was until you came round here banging and hammering. I was having a sleep. Come in, you can put the kettle on."

Once they were settled with tea and cake, Stella passed the picture over to Betsy. "Do you have any idea who this might be? Older now and maybe not quite as gothy."

She peered at the photograph and held it up to the standard lamp she'd lit while Stella was making the tea.

She sniffed and passed the paper back. "Aye. Well I reckon it could be somebody."

"How do you mean, somebody? Of course it's somebody."

"Why are you asking?" Betsy said.

"We just need to speak to her. It's the sister of Phillip Harwood and we know she was a friend of Fee's. Stands to reason you'll know her. I think he'd been in touch with her lately and that was why he was here. You do see, don't you? It's important we find her. She could well be in danger," Stella said.

"Aye, it might well be somebody's sister but anyway, that's Ceecee, isn't it. Bless her heart."

Chapter 75

"You can go now."

Stella was used to Betsy and her brusque manner, but there was something else today. The woman didn't seem as controlled as she had in the past. She wrung her hands together and gulped down the tea ignoring the slice of the cherry cake Stella had brought.

"Betsy? Are you okay?"

"Sure I'm okay. Why wouldn't I be?"

"You seem a bit anxious."

"Don't be stupid. Why would I be anxious? You come round here out of the blue interrupting my nap. Anyway, you should go and leave me alone. Go and do your job."

"That's just what I am doing," Stella said. "I need to find Ceecee. I think she might be in danger."

"Aye well, do it without me."

"Have I upset you?" It was then she heard the creak of floorboards above.

Betsy glanced up and then began to cough. It wasn't convincing.

"Have you got visitors?"

"What's it to do with you if I have?" But in spite of the snappy response the old woman's face reddened and she shuffled in her chair. "Just go. You have to when I ask you to."

She was right, of course, and Stella had no choice but to gather her things together.

The narrow hallway was gloomy in the late afternoon light. There were boots lined up by the door. On other visits Stella hadn't noticed any footwear lying about and the hat stand had held only a black vinyl shopping bag. Now there were two short jackets hanging from the hooks. The boots were nothing an old woman would wear, not even one as quirky as Betsy Minoghue. Hooker's boots, Stella's mam would call them. Long, patent leather, with high heels and tassels around the tops. She had been asked to leave and Betsy was close behind her, hustling her from the house.

Stella turned her head. "These yours, Betsy?"

"Granddaughter's. She left them here."

"I didn't know you had a granddaughter. You said you weren't married."

"Ha, you don't know everything. Now go."

"Please, Betsy, if there's something you should be telling me, let's do it. I don't want you to get into trouble."

The toilet upstairs flushed. Betsy twisted to look down the hallway towards the staircase.

"Who is it? Are you afraid? Have you a problem here?"

"No. None of your business, is it? Go on, get out."

As she left, Stella looked up in time to see the net curtain at one of the bedroom windows fall back into place.

She hated the idea, but she was going to have to consider getting a search warrant. Unless there was another way to find out who it was hiding in the old woman's house.

Chapter 76

Jordan was spending Sunday morning in the kitchen. The baby was in his highchair chewing a carrot stick, and Penny had gone for a run. He had jazz on the radio, a rib of beef ready for the oven, and a mound of vegetables to prepare. He was happy.

* * *

Dave Griffiths had brought wine and a toy for Harry.

"Thanks for this, Jordan," he said. "It's a nice change. Penny, I promise there'll be no work talk."

Penny grinned at him. "We'll see. At least you can talk about the football for a while."

"Ha, no point with your husband. I can't believe he's still more interested in cricket. I'll have to take him to a match. That'll have him then, he'll be red forever."

They sat in the living room and drank beer. Jordan turned the heat down in the oven and frowned at the pan of roast potatoes. He dialled Stella's number again. The third time. He understood things came up, family stuff or maybe she'd simply changed her mind. She should have let him know. He was surprised she hadn't. He double-checked his texts but there had been nothing.

There was no answer. He glanced at his watch, she was over half an hour late now and no word. Well, so be it.

"I reckon we'll just have to start without her."

This was going to be awkward tomorrow if she simply didn't turn up. He tried her phone again after they'd eaten. Of course by now she was probably embarrassed and cringing when she saw his name on the screen. He left another message.

"Hi, Stella. I hope you're okay. Let me know if you've got a problem. See you tomorrow."

He rang the station on the off chance there'd been a development and she'd decided to handle it on her own, knowing he had plans. But they hadn't seen her. Now he was unsettled. He'd go round later on, when David Griffiths had gone home; he'd just take a quick trip to Aintree. Better to clear the air now than have an atmosphere in the office.

* * *

Bob pushed back from the little desk in the corner of his living room. His wife brought him tea and cake. "Are you going to be sitting there all day?" she said.

"No. I'm not, but I will need to speak to the DS. I reckon I've got this sussed and it's pretty important."

"Going in to work then?"

"Maybe. Sorry, love. I've given her a ring and left a message. We'll just have to wait and see."

She shrugged. "I'm going to go and see our Vera. Just let me know what's happening."

Chapter 77

There was a car parked in the driveway of Stella's home, but it wasn't hers. Nothing unusual in that. After the attack she had told Jordan all about the parking problems. He rang the bell for the ground floor flat. When there was no answer, he tried to peer through the bay window, but the drapes were partly closed.

Jordan couldn't remember the name of the tenant of the flat upstairs, but knew they were friendly. He rang the bell.

"Sorry to bother you, mate. I work with Stella." Jordan waved a hand in the direction of the window. "She was supposed to visit me today and she never turned up. I've been trying to contact her. I'm a bit concerned."

"Come in. We'll give her a knock. She could be at her mother's."

Keith tapped on the door with his knuckles. "Hey, Stel, a mate of yours is here. Are you in, babe?"

They didn't wait long, there wasn't a sound from inside.

"Hang on." Keith pulled his phone from his pocket. "I've got her mam's number."

"Hiya, Lydia. It's Keith, I need a word with Stel. Is she at yours?" He shook his head. "Okay, love. If you see her, can you tell her…" He raised his eyebrows and opened his eyes wide.

"Jordan."

"Can you tell her Jordan was here?" He turned and stared at the door. "I don't know what to tell you. Hang on." He dragged open the front door and peered up and down the street. "Yeah, there you go. Her car's there, do you see? Behind the white van, down the end."

"Maybe she's gone to the shops," Jordan said.

"Doubt it. There's none really near that'd be open today at this time. Maybe the Indian for a takeaway, but normally she'd ring. It was raining earlier."

"I don't suppose you've got a key?" Jordan said. "I really am concerned, and I doubt she'd mind." He pulled out his warrant card.

"I'll go and get it. Shit, I hope she's okay. Somebody mugged her, oh, well you'd know about that."

The flat was dark and chilly. Jordan reached a hand to the radiator in the hall and shook his head. He turned on the light and examined the timer on the thermostat.

"Switched off over an hour ago." The small gas fire in the living room was cold. "Stella, it's Jordan. Are you okay?"

They both knew by now she wasn't there, and he was simply going through the motions.

"It's not right, this," Keith said. "Can you do something?"

"Oh yes. I'm going to have the patrols watch for her but if she doesn't turn up in the next couple of hours things will escalate quickly. You'll keep an eye out, mate?"

"Course I will. Is there anything else I can do?"

"Not just now, thanks. I'll leave you my card. If anything happens give me a ring. She's got plenty of messages on her phone, so she knows to ring me herself when she gets them."

Keith pulled his phone from his pocket again and pressed a number on the speed dial. They heard the chime of the ring tone drifting through from the living room.

The phone was in a laptop bag beside the settee. Jordan knelt on the floor and lifted it out with his fingertips.

"Okay. I'm starting an alert and then I'm going to have a word with your neighbours. Find out if anyone has seen her."

"Can I help, can I do that?" Keith asked.

"I think it's best to leave it to us, but thanks."

"Well what can I do?"

"Sorry, at the moment all you can do is wait and hope this is all a storm in a teacup."

"It's not, is it?"

"No. I don't think so. Not at all."

Chapter 78

They needed to get a search under way. Jordan should have officers out in force searching for their missing colleague. He climbed back into his car and pulled out his phone. Getting the search moving would take him back to the station. Phone calls, briefings, consultations, and other things would detain him there when really all he wanted was to be out looking for Stella. He wanted to be doing that right now.

He rang Rupert and brought him up to date.

"What do you want me to do, boss?"

"I'm going to do a quick tour of the neighbours in case anyone has seen anything. I've got her laptop here. Do you know her password?" He knew it was common to share the information with someone else, *just in case*. If she shared it with anyone surely it would be with her DC.

"I do."

"Okay, best if you come here. Have a look at it. Probably quicker than accessing her office machine and at least you'll be on the spot if I need you."

"What about, Bob? Shall I contact him?"

"We should let him know. For now I don't think there is much he can do. If I don't make any progress in the next hour, then I'm pulling out all the stops and he'll be involved anyway."

"You don't think it's best to get a search under way straight off?"

"Possibly – yes – probably. But bear with me. There is still the outside chance this is not a big deal. She'll be livid if we embarrass her. I have a couple of ideas. If they don't pan out, I'll raise the alarm. Okay, get yourself over here and speak to Keith. He'll let you in."

* * *

He canvassed the houses opposite as the ones most likely to have information. None of the neighbours had seen anything. A cold wet night in September, curtains closed and nothing to interfere with Netflix. Crossing the road, he noticed the light on the CCTV camera at the doctor's house.

The woman who answered his knock wasn't the doctor. She said she was the cleaner and caretaker and didn't have access to the CCTV.

"I really need to see it. Quick as possible," Jordan told her.

"I'm sorry, son. I don't know how to do it."

"Will you let me have a look?"

"Hang on, just a sec."

She rang the GP and he talked Jordan through the access routine. It wasn't much but there was a van double-parked for a short while. All he could see was the snub-nosed bonnet. No plates. It was grey. It was probably a Transit. It stayed for a while and then reversed rapidly up the street.

Now it was time to pull in some outside help. He phoned Bob. Rupert had brought him up to date and he was champing at the bit for something to do.

"Get on to City Watch," Jordan said. "I'm trying to find a grey Transit van." He gave him the time and the address.

"You don't know which way it went then?"

"Nope. But it's Sunday, it's miserable weather and it's the only thing I've got. Just ask them to have a look at all the roads around here. I know it's weak and probably hopeless but give it a go."

"Okay, sir. I'll get on to it straight away. Is there anything else I can do?"

"Not right now. I'll get back to you."

He jogged back to his car, pulled out onto the A59, down to the A506, and then through Fazakerley to Kirkby. This could go horribly wrong and end in catastrophe, but he was doing it anyway.

Chapter 79

There was nobody about now. Lights shone from behind curtains and blinds, but the rain and the hour had cleared the roads of all but a few cars. Jordan turned beside the school and had a moment of indecision.

If Stella was with the old woman, then the chances were she was safe. He parked at the end of the layby and walked back to the squat. The council had finished securing the place. Metal sheets were fastened across the windows. Already someone had tagged the biggest one. There was no light, no sign of life.

He walked down the narrow front path and pushed at the door. The neglected lawn was sodden and he wished he'd remembered to put his boots on, but he wouldn't be long. Just a quick look around the back of the house. As he passed the door, he bent to lift the flap of the letter box. The workmen had done a good job and it was screwed closed. No chance of rubbish being posted through, no chance of burning paper. It was good but made it impossible to peer into the empty hallway.

The wooden gate to the back garden had been screwed closed but someone had kicked it open. The bottom was splintered, and the frame split where the bolt had been. He pushed it forward and walked into the dirty, litter-strewn space.

He should stop now. Call for backup and have the place searched properly. He stepped out onto the pavement and turned his head back and forth. The road was lined with cars. He couldn't see a grey Transit van. His phone rang. It was Rupert.

"Any news, boss?"

"Nothing. I'm at the squat. It was just an idea I had, but I think I was probably wrong."

"So, call out the cavalry then?"

"I reckon so. I'll head back to the station and meet you there and we'll get on it. Just give me a few more minutes, I need to speak to someone here first."

"I'll meet you as soon as. I'll call in Bob, shall I, and will you speak to DI Dunn?"

"It's okay, Rupert. I know you're itching to get things going, I understand. I'll call Dunn."

Jordan went back to the broken gate. There was a narrow concrete path down the back of the house, it was cracked and weedy. Jordan trod carefully on the uneven surface towards the kitchen door. He stopped to try and see through the narrow window, but all he saw was his reflection.

The back door hadn't been boarded but a heavy hasp and staple had been screwed to the frame. It hung open and the chunky padlock lay in a dirty puddle on the ground.

Chapter 80

As it opened, the bottom of the door scraped across dirt and grit lying on the cracked vinyl. A little light leaked into the first metre, beyond was all darkness. Jordan's phone torch drew a bright bubble around his feet.

He knew there was someone there.

The kitchen was empty. The place stank of waste and damp. He moved into the hallway, the smell was stronger and he covered his mouth with his hand. Someone had closed all the interior doors. The first beside the kitchen opened into a cupboard with coat hooks and a couple of shelves; there was dust everywhere and the residue from the SOCO examination. Next was the living room. Cold and filthy. The blood was gone but the air was tainted with the smell of chemicals.

He moved on to the staircase.

He knew he should back off now. The right thing to do would be to get out and call in the troops. If he did that and Stella was up there, with someone else, there was no way to know what would happen. How could he walk away and leave her?

He trod at the edges of the wooden stairs. He could hear the swish of tyres on the road outside. A car horn blared. Somewhere water dripped.

He moved upwards.

The bathroom was the source of most of the smell. He wondered briefly whose job it would be to clean and repair it. He wouldn't go in there if he could avoid it. Nobody could be in that room.

As he opened the door to the front bedroom there was the creak of floorboards. The shuffle of movement. A whimper.

A quick flash around with his torch showed him nothing. Empty space, stained walls, and the torn edges of carpet where it had caught on the tacks holding it down when the house was a home, and somebody cared.

The small box room was not the source of the noise and he turned on the landing. He had no weapon, he didn't carry an ASP anymore. A detective wasn't supposed to need one. A detective inspector wasn't supposed to get himself into a situation like this. He crossed the landing and laid a hand on the doorknob.

As he turned the small, plastic handle he heard another shuffling sound, another soft sob of noise. He drew in a breath and flung the door back on the hinges. As he strode into the room, he roared out a warning. "Police, Police."

There was no shot, there was no yell of response, and there was no attack. What there was came from the corner, in the darkness.

Chapter 81

Stella was angry. She was angry with herself, she was angry that she was cold, tied up and gagged, and she was angry that she'd had to be rescued by DI Carr.

Jordan knelt beside her. First, he tore off the tape stuck across her mouth. She gulped in a breath. As he cut the zip ties around her wrists she wiped at her face with the ends of her sleeves, mopping up the tears and snot. Immediately he loosened her feet she tried to stand.

"Hang on. Hang on a minute. Take a breath."

She paused, leaned back against the wall, and breathed deeply.

"Okay, good. Now, are you hurt?" he asked.

"No. Well, not really."

"How do you mean, not really?"

"I reckon I've got some decent bruises and my wrists are…" She held out her hands and touched the raw, red lines. The skin was broken in places, and she hissed with the sting of it.

"I'm just bloody miffed," she said. "I was such an idiot. I can't believe I was such a pillock. I should know better."

"Come on, first of all, let's get you out of here. Get you somewhere warm. Are you sure you don't need a doctor?"

"No. No, I don't need a doctor. I need a pee and I'm going to have to use that stinking hole. I need my stupid head examining, that's what I need. I don't want to get warm. I want to get even. I want to go and grab that bastard by the balls."

"Okay. Right, well. Look, just take a minute. Which bastard are we talking about?"

"Bloody Douglas sodding Jewell. The evil scrote. A polythene bag, a frigging polythene bag over my head. I can't tell you what it felt like."

The anger gave way to shaking sobs and Stella slid back down to sit in the corner of the room, struggling to regain control.

"I thought I was going to die." It was just a whisper.

She raised her eyes and Jordan opened his arms and let her lean in. Physical contact rules be blowed, she needed a cuddle.

"Okay. Let's get back to the station, or your house if you'd prefer and you can fill me in."

"No, there isn't time. We need to get after him. He's vicious and he's desperate and dangerous."

"Was he on his own? How did he manage to bring you here? Can you tell me what happened?"

She took a breath. "I was up really early, I had so much on my mind. I guess it was about six o'clock. Hang on."

She ran across the landing and into the bathroom. He could hear her cursing at the smell and the condition of the place. When she came out, they moved to the lower floor and she leaned against the window ledge, getting herself together and filling Jordan in on how she'd been taken.

"I let my guard down. You'd think by now I'd know better. I should know better. Normally at night I look through the bay window. I can see my front door. I was tired and irritated because I was working, and I didn't even look. I just opened the door. The porch was empty. I stepped out and that was it."

She had felt the movement beside her and turned, but it was too late, and he was too quick. She knew she would never forget the feeling of the plastic in her mouth as it moved, slapping at her face with her panicked gasping. As she told Jordan about it now her heart began to pound and suddenly, she couldn't breathe. She began to shiver.

He pulled back and looked at her face, his eyes concerned. "You okay?"

She shook her head and turned to lean against the wall so she could stand. "Yeah. I'm fine. I'm okay, I just need some space. We need to go down the road. I reckon he could have gone from here to Betsy's and it's ages ago. Enough messing here, come on."

She staggered slightly as she walked across the room, but she was going to get Douglas Jewell and they were going to throw the book at him.

Chapter 82

There was a light showing in the living room of the house at the end of the terrace. Stella pushed at the door, but it was closed. Not surprising on a cold wet night, but you just never could tell with Betsy.

They knocked on the wood and rattled the letter box cover. Stella stepped across and tapped on the window. There was no answer.

She walked down the path and looked back and forth up and down the road. There was no van, not like the one she had been thrown into outside her own flat and dragged from at the squat. So that was good, wasn't it?

They knocked again.

"She's an old woman. She could well be asleep," Jordan said.

"Well, for one thing she told me she doesn't sleep well, spends much of the night watching out of the window. But, even if she is, how come the light is still on in the front room?"

"Security, safety. Could just be what she does. I'm not saying you're wrong, I'm just trying to think logically."

Stella scratched at her head, ruffling her hair. "It feels wrong."

"Why are you so convinced Jewell is here?"

"Because I think the girls are here. He was furious and ranting about women dropping him in it. Filthy whores, screwing everything up, he said."

"When was this?"

"It was when he was dragging me up the stairs in that filthy squat. Don't know the time, it was impossible to tell how long I'd been there. He left not long after he stuck me in the room. I was there all day. It was really early when he came to mine. Said he'd be back when he'd decided what to do with me. Hours and hours. But if Betsy's light has been on all day, I reckon someone would have noticed, wouldn't they?"

"It's rained most of the day and it's gloomy," Jordan said.

"Yes. You could be right. What are we going to do?"

"You think she's in danger, don't you?" Jordan said.

"I do. I truly do."

"In that case we have to go in. Let's look round the back, how do we get there?"

"Round the corner. The house attached is actually flats. We can probably get through."

They pushed all four buttons and heard the harsh sound of buzzers inside. Three voices answered.

"Police, I need to get in. I need to get to the rear of the houses." Jordan said.

One of the residents told them to bugger off and that he wasn't born yesterday, but the other two pressed the release for the lock.

They went along the narrow entrance hall and out through the back door. There was a small area of grass with wheelie bins and washing lines and a low fence at the end of the garden.

Jordan clambered over without too much trouble, but Stella knew she'd never be able to shin up the damp wood. She dragged a wheelie bin across the space and managed to get to the top of the fence in a two-step manoeuvre. Jordan helped her down. They were in Betsy's back garden. There was a patch of grass, a sleeping flower border, and a couple of plastic chairs. There was no light from the kitchen window, but the back bedroom threw a small patch of illumination at the end of the grass.

Jordan turned the handle, pushed inwards and the door swung open.

On the kitchen table there were three mugs, the dregs in the bottom cold and skinned over. There was a plate with the remains of the cake Stella had brought the last time she was there. There was no sound.

Chapter 83

Stella's throat had dried. She knew they had to do this, but she didn't want to move from the kitchen. She didn't want to go to the living room and see what may be there.

Jordan glanced at her. "You okay?"

She could only nod.

"Hello, Mrs Minoghue, it's Jordan Carr. Are you okay?" The rules dictated that he announce their presence, but he kept his voice low.

There was no response. He pushed open the door into the empty room as they heard the footsteps across the floor upstairs.

Jordan held out a restraining hand, but Stella was already on her way. She looked up as Betsy began to descend. She held onto the banister rail, but as far as they could see she was unhurt.

"Well you took your time," she said. She pushed past them and flopped into a chair in the living room. "Pour me a dram." She pointed at the cupboard where her liquor was kept.

"Are the girls here?" Stella asked.

Betsy shook her head. She didn't bother to deny they had been in the house. "Went this afternoon."

"Has Douglas Jewell been here? Do you know him? Did he hurt you?"

"I do now. Primped-up ponce. You missed him, not by long but a miss is as good as a mile, as they say. Tried all ways with me but couldn't get what he wanted. He didn't have the guts to do anything more than rage and threaten. Oh and this." She held out a hand to show them the bruise around her wrist. "I locked the door when he'd gone. Went back up to watch out, I had this." She pulled a knitting needle from her sleeve. "He'd not hurt me again. He's weak."

"Do you need a doctor?" Jordan said.

"No, I have some arnica in the cabinet. You can get that for me after."

"Do you know where he is now?"

"Gone after Ceecee and Pat. He'd been looking for them, he said. Been up at the shops. Been in the pubs. Hasn't got a clue."

"Do you know where they went?" Jordan asked.

"I don't know for certain, but I reckon they've gone down to the docks. Gone to her brother's place, he gave her a key. Not long ago. When he found her. She thought they'd be safe there. I tried to tell her it was the last place they should go, but she wouldn't listen. He was trying to look out for her. Trying to help her get right. Didn't do him no good at all. She feels guilty."

"Have you called the police, Betsy?" Jordan asked.

"No, I haven't. By the time I'd got someone to listen to me and they'd sent somebody round, and taken stupid statements, and all of that, it'd be a week next Wednesday before anybody did anything. Anyway, I'd seen you. Saw you from the window going into the place at the end. I knew you'd be here next. I would have unlocked the door, but you were round the back before I had the chance. Mind, I'm sorry I didn't know you were there, Stella. I wouldn't have left you if I'd known. But things were busy here what with the girls all of a twitter, and then that idiot boy. Are you alright? Take a drink. Both of you."

"No, we're on duty. We'll have to go. Do you want us to fetch someone to sit with you?"

"No, I'm alright. I'm never alone, you know that, Stella. When you find her, Ceecee, remember what she's been through. Treat her as kindly as you can. Life has made her do what she did."

Chapter 84

"Are you alright to carry on? I'm going down to Albert Dock," Jordan said, once they were back in his car.

"Yes, course I am. I know the flat, it'll be quicker together. We should let Rupert know what's going on. I haven't got my phone though."

"Sorry. Here, I brought it with me in case anyone rang while I was looking for you."

"Brilliant. Oh, you've been in my flat then?"

"Yes, your neighbour let me in. I hope that's okay."

"Yeah. It just feels a bit odd."

"We were worried about you."

"I get that, it's fine. Really, it's fine. I'm glad you did."
She turned on the mobile. "Message from Bob."

She was quiet for a while as Jordan drove through the city streets, almost deserted now.

"Right, well I can't understand it all. He left a text and then sent an email. He rambles on a bit, but he's been working bloody hard at it. It wasn't to do with banking, not all of it anyway. He reckons it's a bit strange. Some of the numbers are references to some sort of shipping or ticketing as far as he can tell – times and dates. Not planes, though. Ferries to Europe. A few to France but mostly the Netherlands. He says he thinks it could be some sort of distributing or transport. He reckons nothing else makes sense. He's been on to the ferry companies to see if he can access their manifests on the dates he's worked out. That can't happen until tomorrow. He says there a fairly simple accounting system. Money in, money out and a profit."

"What the hell can he be shipping?" Jordan said.

"Whatever it is, surely it's nothing to get them killed over. Bob says there's more work to do on it."

"Okay. Well, when we get our hands on Jewell maybe he'll be able to clarify things. It's all valuable but does it tell us anything much more about the murders?"

"I suppose not. If you park here, we can walk to the flats. Do we have a plan?"

"Not as such." Jordan grinned at her.

"Right, winging it then. I've texted Rupert to bring the key from evidence. He should be on his way soon."

* * *

A new concierge was behind the reception, and obviously in Sunday night mode. They noted the cup of coffee on his desk and spotted the magazines hastily hidden as they approached. Jordan flashed his warrant card.

"We're going up to Phillip Harwood's apartment," he said. "Is there anyone up there?"

"Not as far as I know. I've only been on half an hour, mind you. But that one's all locked up, isn't it?"

"We've got a colleague coming with a key. Tell him we've gone up," Stella said.

"Before we go, can you have a look at the CCTV feed in the car park? See if there's van or a car in Mr Jewell's parking space?" Jordan asked.

The concierge clicked a couple of buttons and leaned nearer to the screen. "No. Not right now, his space is empty."

They tried the door of the lower flat first and there was no answer to either their knock or the buzzer. On the next floor, Harwood's apartment was locked up. Stella put the side of her head against the door.

"Not sure whether I can hear anything from inside, it could just be the lift," she said.

They both turned to where the elevator doors were sliding open. Douglas Jewell, standing inside, was immobile for a moment. He gaped at them. Jordan was the first to react, striding down the corridor. Jewell pressed the button.

Jordan sprinted the last few metres, leaned and reached to get his arm between the heavy metal doors, but it was too late. He spun back and by the time he reached her, Stella was already well on her way to the fire exit at the other end of the building. She flung open the door and launched herself at the concrete stairs, Jordan a hair's breadth behind her.

Chapter 85

They clattered down the stairwell, jumping steps two at a time, and swinging themselves round the landings. The door at the bottom opened with a push bar and brought them out on the dockside.

A bright sunny afternoon would have seen the walkways thronged with sightseers, shoppers, and residents, but now there was nothing but the streaming rain and, in the distance, the figure of Douglas Jewell as he rounded the corner and ran along the Kings Parade. The security guard stood at the door peering into the deluge. Jordan flashed past him with Stella close behind. She paused briefly.

"When our mate arrives, tell him what's happened and send him up to Harwood's flat. If two women come down, try and get them to wait." She turned and scurried after the two men.

Jordan had called out, but Jewell pounded on through the puddles making for the bridge over the Canning Dock and access to the Pier Head. Once there he could turn, cross the concourse and thread between the grand buildings, on into the confusion of streets in the city. There were buses and taxis there and Jordan needed to catch him first.

The span of the bridge was slippery, the tarmac slick with running water, and Jewell skidded on the slight slope. He grabbed the railings and glanced back to see Jordan just a metre away.

"Stop. Police, wait. You're just making things worse. We need to talk to you. You can't get away. Just stop."

He ran on across the bridge. Both men were winded, and Jordan saw Jewell grip his side. A stitch?

"Don't be a fool. Just come in and talk to us. We can sort this out."

Stella had stepped onto the bridge. The air was filled with the blare of sirens. Rupert doing his thing.

They could see the flash of blue reflected on the walls of the buildings and on the undersides of the heavy cloud.

Jewell had paused on the bridge. He turned and faced Jordan.

"Come on, man. You have to know this is over for you now. Just come in and talk to us."

Uniformed officers appeared from the direction of the Pier Head running towards the Canning Dock. Jewell looked back and forth, grasped the railings, and leaned over the dark, roiling water.

"Don't be a fool." Jordan took two more steps.

Jewell climbed the low railing and without another look back he dived into the waters of the Mersey.

Chapter 86

If he had jumped feet first, he may have been okay. If he had taken longer to think, he may have been okay. As it was, he simply climbed over the railings, lifted his arms above his head and dived into the darkness.

They all heard the sound. They knew it wasn't right. A dull thud followed by a rattle was not a diver entering the water. There was a sort of splash, but it was too quiet. Jordan had thrown himself over the chain-link fence and shone the light from his torch onto the rippling surface. If Jewell's dive had come off, he would be surfacing some way further out, but he was there, just beneath the edge of the bridge, face down, unmoving. They didn't know what he had hit. In a way it didn't matter, but there had been something. Maybe the maintenance walkway, lower than the bridge proper, a metal span which was almost invisible from where they stood in the dark and the rain. Maybe he had misjudged the angle and struck the wall.

"Oh Christ," Jordan said.

Stella was leaning over, shining her torch onto the floating man. The uniformed officers were sprinting past the Pilotage Building and Rupert could be seen jogging along the Kings Parade. It was down to him. He pulled off his shoes and shrugged out of his jacket.

"Boss, don't!"

Stella had dragged the life ring from its holder and thrown it into the water, but it floated uselessly beside the man whose legs were beginning to sink, dragged down by the weight of shoes and clothes.

Jordan jumped. He didn't know what was under the bridge. He didn't have any clue how deep the water was and what there might be lurking under the surface. He thought he'd rather damage his legs than his head and at least the jump took him clear of the ironwork.

The cold shock took his breath, but he was ready for it. He drew in air as soon as he surfaced, kicking, and pulling. He wasn't far from Douglas Jewell and reached him in a few strokes. He rolled the unconscious man onto his back, and with one arm supporting the upper body, the other using an ungainly sidestroke, he dragged him through the water towards the concrete sides of the promenade.

"How the hell do I get out?" he yelled up to the little group on the walkway.

"There are steps back up near the flats." This from one of the patrol guys. "It's too far. Hang on there." With that, he climbed the gate to access the mechanism for the dock gates to open.

His mate was close behind him and they dragged open the trap door and slipped and slid down the steep slope, clinging to any handhold they could find.

Rupert and Stella shone their torches from the bridge, but the illumination was shadowy and confusing. The tide was going out and Jordan was tiring fast, fighting the cold river. He grabbed at a cable snaking down the mechanism and hung on. The other officers were close now, wet and dirty and determined. They reached to grab at Jewell's sopping clothing as Jordan pushed the unconscious body closer.

"You won't be able to pull him up. I don't think he's breathing," Jordan said.

"No other choice, is there," the nearest copper shouted.

Jordan strained to hold him as close as he could, kicking and choking in the dirty water.

It was difficult, dangerous, and confused. They were desperate to get the unconscious man onto flat ground and start CPR. Later they wouldn't have been able to say how they had done it. But the flood of adrenaline, the instinctive drive to save a life, and pure bloody-mindedness drove them on. They hauled him from the river. Rupert had grabbed the second life ring and slid it down the slope to them, wrapping the rope around his back leaning against it, gripping it with both hands. Stella took hold further along the length. The bobbies grabbed it, clung to it one-handed, as they scrabbled on the slimy surface, hanging on to Jewell between them. With all four working they managed to drag him up to the trap and lay him on the ground.

Stella and Rupert took over from the exhausted officers who now went back over the side to help Jordan out of the water and up to the top.

Jewell wasn't breathing, his lips were blue and there was no sign of life. They compressed his chest and breathed air into his flaccid lungs, on and on. They heard the scream of the ambulance heading towards them and they continued to work, pleading with him to breathe, to fight, to stay.

Chapter 87

Jordan was shivering despite the survival blanket. He was soaked and exhausted and the paramedics wanted to take him to the Royal, but he wouldn't have it. "I've some spare clothes in my car. Just let me go and get changed. I'm fine."

They couldn't force him, and they needed to leave.

"You go with them, Rupert. Someone should be there."

The detective constable nodded and turned away.

"Stella, we need to get back to the flats," Jordan said. "See if those girls are inside."

"I told the security bloke to hold them if he could. He's got no authority, but they might not know that. They might not be there, though. We didn't see them."

"No, but there was a reason Jewell came up there. Either he knew where they were, or he was hoping to find them."

"Do you want me to bring your clothes? I can run down and be back in a minute."

"No, I'll walk back. It'll help to thaw me out a bit."

They trailed back along the Kings Parade. He didn't want to wet his jacket, so he pulled the silver sheet around him. Stella folded the other garment over her arm.

"This your Superman impression, boss?"

"Ha, not really, is it? Not after what just happened."

"You did your best. You put your body on the line. You couldn't have done any more."

Jordan simply shrugged and trudged on.

He had a tracksuit in the boot of his car, some dry trainers, and a towel. He squirmed and wriggled into the outfit sitting in the back seat. He rubbed at his face and felt his body warming. His hair didn't need attention, the close curls shrugged off the water and in spite of the grit on his scalp, he didn't think he looked too bad when they went back into the flats.

"We're going up to Harwood's flat," Stella told the concierge.

"Is Mr Jewell okay? What was that all about?"

"Can't discuss it with you right now."

They left him disgruntled and frustrated as they entered the lift.

"Have you got the key?" Jordan said.

Stella held up the evidence bag. She pulled open the top and fished inside for the key ring with the whale.

They knocked. They listened. There was no sound from inside.

"Looks as though we might be out of luck here," Stella said as she pushed the key into the lock.

The flat was warm. There was a small light burning on the coffee table in the living area. Two young women sat side by side on the huge settee. One had her arm around the other who was sobbing quietly into the silence.

Chapter 88

The women didn't move as Jordan and Stella stepped into the room. Jordan introduced himself and they glanced at each other and the older one, a bottle blonde with eye make-up streaking her cheeks, nodded. The other girl could barely sit up. She was shaking, her glance shooting back and forth, sweat sheening her brow. She rubbed at her arms and leaned forward over her knees. Jordan recognized the junkie in her.

"Is Dougie with you?" she asked.

"No. There's no-one but us," Jordan said. "We need to speak to you. You're Catherine Harwood, aren't you?"

"Cat."

"I'm Pat." The other woman gave a small laugh. "Cat and Pat. We come as a pair." She wrapped her arms around her friend's shoulders and pulled her close. "This is Cat's place. Her brother left it to her. It's not all sorted yet, but it will be."

"I heard that," Jordan said. "We need to talk to you both just now."

"Is Dougie coming?" Cat asked.

"No. I'm sorry but Douglas is dead."

"Dead?" The woman screwed her eyes closed. "No, he's coming now. He said so. He said we had to wait for him, and he'd get me some stuff and get us away."

"I don't think you should say any more, Cat." This from the blonde.

"Where was he going to get you away to?" Stella had lowered herself to the other settee and she leaned forward now, speaking quietly, conversationally.

"Holland. That's where he sends people. Well, girls. He sends them there. He'll find a place for us. Someone to look out for us. Not like the men in London, not those. It's better in Europe. You get treated with respect. Phillip said we shouldn't go. He said he'd look after me but he's dead. My brother's dead."

Stella glanced at Jordan, and he nodded at her to carry on.

"Why does Douglas do that?"

"Cat, just shut it, yeah," Pat said. "You do see these here are the bizzies. Just keep your trap shut."

"No, it's alright, Pat. It's time to tell them what I did. It's time to own up. Dougie's dead, he said so." Cat waved a hand towards Jordan. "I won't be going to Amsterdam, not never. It's over and you have to own up in the end."

"Shit, babe. Please don't."

"What is it you want to tell us, Cat? If you've got something to tell us I'm ready to listen," Stella said.

"No, she's not going to. She's not saying nothing to nobody. She wants a lawyer, and she doesn't want to talk to you."

"Maybe she should just decide for herself," Stella said. "You know, just make her own mind up. Then you can have your say and we can sort everything out."

"How come Dougie's dead? What happened to him?" Pat asked.

"He had an accident. He drowned. I'm sorry."

There was a moment of quiet as the two girls absorbed the news.

"We're safe, Cat. He's gone," Pat said. "You don't need to say anything to anybody. Don't you see?"

The skinny young woman shook her head. She leaned and kissed her friend's cheek and squeezed her hand and then turned to Stella, shuffled forward on the settee, and spoke quietly.

"I killed her."

Chapter 89

They had to stop Catherine speaking. Before she said any more, she had to be sure of what she was doing. If it came to it, anything she may say right now would be thrown out of court by a defence lawyer. Jordan crouched in front of her.

"I think you need to come with us," he said. "We'll go to the police station so we can make sure everything is done properly. It's for your own good."

"Are you arresting her?" Pat said. Her voice catching on the tears in her throat.

"Not at the moment, no. We need to take care of both of you. Will you come with us, please? Catherine isn't well, I don't think. We can get her some medical help if she needs it."

In response Pat pulled out a handkerchief, blew her nose and dabbed at her eyes. She leaned over the edge of the couch and picked up their coats. "Come on, babe. Let's go and get this over with."

They had to send for a patrol car. Jordan wasn't cleared to carry a prisoner in his, and though he hadn't arrested either of them, he didn't want to risk their transport being questioned later if this ended up in court.

"She said 'her', didn't she, boss?" Stella said as they drove out of the car park. "Definitely, 'I killed her.'"

"Yep."

"Who the hell do you think she meant? You don't think she's been back to Betsy's, do you? I mean, we don't know when they got to the flat. They could have been up there in Kirkby. Should we check?"

"Give Rupert a call. See where he's up to at the hospital and if he's free, ask him to go and see Betsy. If he can't get away, we'll send a patrol car. I'd rather not if we can avoid it."

"Bloody hell, I hope she hasn't. I mean why would she? They've always gone to her for help, she's been good to them."

"Let's not jump to conclusions. I think they were already at the Albert Dock. The concierge had been there about half an hour, he said, so they probably arrived before him which is why he didn't know. So, the timing doesn't work."

"Yeah. You're right, boss. Yeah, it'll be fine."

"You've become quite attached to Mrs Minoghue, haven't you?"

"I have. She fascinates me, to be honest, and you have to admit she's funny and quirky. Thing is, though, if she isn't talking about Betsy, that Catherine, who has she killed?"

"If it's true at all. She's in a bad state, isn't she? Spaced out and obviously been addicted for a while. It could be nothing. Then again, and I'm trying not to jump to conclusions here because I want a clear mind when I interview her, but there is Fee. We know they were taken to London together and then after Fee was murdered, they ran away. Okay, they were running away from a nasty and dangerous situation, but it's something to bear in mind."

"Phew. I hadn't really thought about that. It's possible, given the timing and location, but why? Why the hell would she do that?"

Chapter 90

It was very late. They wanted to interview the women under caution so there was no other option but to set up a room and go through the legal procedure. Cat recovered a bit after a can of Coke and a burger. She refused to see a doctor. They had the duty nurse assess her and declare her fit to be questioned. "Be gentle with her, Jordan," the medic said. "She's very fragile."

She wouldn't have a lawyer because she just wanted it all to be over, she told them.

Pat caused a fuss when they said she couldn't sit in with her mate.

"I'm sorry but you are too heavily involved," Jordan said. "It's just not happening. Is there anyone else who can come and be with her?"

"She's got nobody now her brother's gone."

Jordan knew there were still the parents, but they were miles away and not interested. He tried again to get her to agree to have legal representation, but she simply shook her head.

Rupert had been to Kirkby and Betsy was fine.

"Blimey she's an odd one," he said. "Cranky as hell with me, but she asked me to tell you to be kind to Ceecee. Is that the woman, Catherine?"

"Yes. Betsy's very fond of her," Stella said.

She led Jordan into the room and started the interview.

"Catherine, you said you killed someone?" Stella said.

"Yes. I told you. I stabbed her. I'm not sorry. I just don't care. My brother's dead. He was all I had. We hadn't seen each other for years and then he found me. All he wanted was for me to get better."

"Who is it you mean? Who have you killed?" Jordan said.

"Fee. The murdering bitch."

They listened in silence as she filled in the details. The alley, the weapon, the wounds. There were no tears, just the relating of facts as if it had happened to someone else.

"Why, Cat?" Jordan asked.

"What? You don't know?" She looked at them, surprise creasing her brow. "You really don't know what she did? Why I did it?"

"No." Jordan kept it simple.

"I had to. She killed Phillip. She killed my brother. He loved me, the only one who did. She stabbed him. Well, then she found out what being stabbed felt like, didn't she?"

She dissolved in tears. Stella and Jordan were floored by the outpouring and took advantage of the woman's distress to leave her in the care of the nurse. Out in the corridor they stared at each other, lost for words.

"Shit," Stella said.

"Well, I didn't see that coming," Jordan said.

"Do you think it's true?"

"I do. Why would she say it if it wasn't true? She knew far too much for it to be a lie. I think the best thing would be for us to arrest her now on suspicion. Get her locked up safely and try to arrange some medical treatment. We'll come back tomorrow when she might be a bit calmer, more together, and go from there. I think we have to find out what Pat knows."

"Well, unless she's willing to tell us everything, it's just become a whole lot more tangled. Do you want to speak to her now?"

"I think we have to. We have nothing to hold her on and once she gets away from here, she'll make a run for it. It's been a long day, but we have to keep going now. You up for this?"

"I bloody am. I'll go and get us coffee."

Chapter 91

Pat's only concern was for her friend. She pleaded to be allowed to go to Catherine.

"I promise you we're looking after her," Jordan said. "She's told us basically what she did in London. What we really need is for you to fill in the blanks. How come you were there, what happened in Kirkby when Phillip Harwood was killed? As far as we can tell, you haven't done anything wrong."

"Yeah, but I don't trust you lot. You'd like nothing better than to fit me up for something."

"That's not true. Look at it this way, you tell us what really happened, and it could very possibly help your friend. Once we have all the facts it'll mean we can decide what comes next."

"And I'm not under the cosh for anything?"

"No. Look, why don't you start by telling us about the squat? Why you were there and what the connection is between there and two blokes who live pretty well with good jobs and nice homes?"

"Yeah, well, course they do. Jobs in banks paying them a fortune. But for him, for that Douglas even that's not enough. He had to do this other stuff. Raking it in from other rich arseholes."

"Okay. So…"

"Girls. Women is what it's all about. Well, no that's not true. Sex is what it's all about. Dirty, nasty sex."

"Prostitutes," Stella said.

Pat shook her head. "That's only part of it. Yes, he had a deal where he arranged for girls, 'suitable girls' was what he said, to go to parties and those, what do you call them, conferences. We were told we'd be escorts. Sounds great, doesn't it. Sounds posh. Well it wasn't posh. None of it. Yes, there were drinks and laughs sometimes, and food now and then, but what came after was what it was all about."

"What came after, Pat?"

"Beatings came after. Rape and assault came after. Filth, that's what came after."

"But why would you stay, why would anyone stay?" Stella asked.

"We didn't stay. Okay, I was trying to look after Cat. She's my mate. It was the stuff that happened to her made her like she is. All these posh blokes in their penguin suits, looking like some sort of James Bond, and then the drugs, the drink, and the filth. Well of course we didn't stay. After the first time we said never again but look what it did to her. She was already on the drugs and yes, she was bad, but she were nothing like as bad as she is now. But Fee, she was with them. She pretended to be our friend, pretended to care about us.

"She had a thing for that Douglas bloke. Kidded herself he was interested in her. Found women for him. She could do that. She was no better than the rest of us, but he kept her sweet. Gave her money so she could throw it around a bit."

"We could really do with speaking to some of the other women. The ones who were beaten, raped," Jordan said. "We can get them help, make sure they're okay."

Pat shook her head. "Not happening, is it? That's the whole point. They sent them away, you'll never find them now. Any that are left won't talk to you and anyway most of them have gone. It was all part of the deal. They were promised stuff to keep 'em quiet."

"What sort of stuff?" Jordan said.

"New jobs, a better life. Over in Europe, Holland mostly. There's no problem over there. It's all legal and safer. Ha, new jobs, what a laugh. Same job, somewhere else."

"Did they arrange resident visas, healthcare?" As she asked Stella thought maybe it would be a way of finding them a paper trail to give them a chance.

"It was all going to be done by people over there, Dougie said. That was why he took the money from the parties, to pay for all of it. Of course it was lies, all of it. But they didn't see that, they just wanted out. I wonder what's happened to them, the girls who went," Pat said.

"So Douglas and Phillip paid for them to go to the Netherlands?"

"No, not Phillip. He didn't do none of it. He just wanted his sister back. He'd seen her, on Douglas's pictures. We all had pictures taken. He had them like a menu. Take your pick. What's your preference? Anyway, he found her. Tried to get her to go and live with him but she wouldn't do it. She said she didn't want to bring him down. He wouldn't let it go though. Followed her around and then came to the squat. Came to make her go with him."

"And were there many others?" Jordan asked.

"Quite a lot, yeah. Fee got them to go to the parties with the promises of what they could have after. She made it sound lovely. It wasn't only the squat. They moved around, sometimes there, sometimes nicer places, sometimes just straight off the street. Depended on what it was for. Fee would get girls together and promise them things."

Pat asked for a drink. They brought her coffee and a sandwich from the canteen. They reassured her that Catherine was sleeping, and the nurse had given her something to help. She would be left alone now until later the next day.

"Cat was worried about her brother. She idolized him and didn't want him mixed up in it."

"Anyway one day Phillip turned up, he'd found out Cat was there and what a state she was in. He was furious. They had a real bust-up, him and Dougie. Screaming at each other and what have you. Then they got into it physically, proper nasty. Fee, she couldn't keep her neb out, could she. I don't know where the knife came from. I don't know how it all got so bad. Fee was high and the girls were all skryking, it was mad. Dougie was beating the hell out of Phillip. Then Fee, she just did it. She just stepped up to him and stuck the knife in him and…"

For a moment all there was in the room was the quiet noise of Pat sobbing and sniffing.

Jordan spoke quietly to her, leaning forward across the scarred tabletop. "You've done really well. Please keep going. Tell us what happened. How did you end up in London and what happened with Fee?"

Pat took a deep breath and sipped at the drink. "I didn't do nothing, you know. None of it was me. Okay, what Cat did was wrong, but she was out of her mind with grief."

"Yes, we understand that, but you need to tell us what happened. She won't help herself so it's up to you to help her as much as you can."

"Alright, but then I want to go."

"Where will you go?" Stella asked.

"I don't know. Too late for the homeless hostels now, the doors'll be locked. I'll just go find somewhere. You'll give me my stuff back, won't you? I need my stuff."

"Yes, but listen, why don't you stay here? You can sleep in one of the rooms."

"The cells, you mean? Oh no, no way."

"It won't mean anything. It'll just be somewhere safe for you to sleep. You'll even get some breakfast."

She thought for a moment. "Go on then, give me my stuff. I have to have my stuff."

They settled her for the rest of the night.

* * *

"I'll take you home, Stella," Jordan said.

"No, you're alright, boss, I'll just grab a cab."

"Nah. I think it's better if I take you. I'd feel happier."

"Oh, go on then, but only to make you happy."

"In early tomorrow to wind this up."

"Yeah. It's all a bit sad isn't it. And what's going to happen to the blokes, the rapists?"

"It's horrible, and I just don't know right now. With Douglas Jewell and Phillip Harwood both dead, where do we start?"

"Well, I guess we have to start somewhere."

Chapter 92

By the time Stella arrived the next morning, Jordan was already at his desk. There was a strange atmosphere in the room. Nobody was working, it was tense and quiet.

"Everything okay, boss?" Stella said.

"Yes, sort of. They had to take Catherine Harwood to the hospital last night. She's not in any danger but the nurse wasn't happy, and they've got her on suicide watch. If you're ready, we'll go and have a word with Pat. They've given her breakfast and she's in the interview room."

The woman looked up as they entered and managed to smile at them.

"Are you okay?" Stella asked.

"Yeah, not a bad bacon bap you put on here. I should spread the word. How's Cat?"

"She's okay," Jordan said. "They're looking after her. We need to get all this squared away this morning if we can. Are you ready to finish telling us what happened?"

After the drama of the day before she seemed drained and beaten. In a quiet, matter-of-fact voice she told them how they had been bullied into going to London. "They said we'd all be liable, the police would have us all as accessories. We didn't know what was true."

The van had delivered them like so much cargo and they were handed over to another group of males, another house, and more work on the streets.

"Fee was furious that she'd been left. She kept trying to get in touch with Dougie, saying as how he'd be coming to get her, that she was only there to make sure we didn't cause trouble. It was winding Cat up something shocking. Anyway in the end Cat just did what she did. She followed Fee. I didn't know she had a knife, not until later. When she came to find me, covered in blood, crying and hysterical, I took her back to the house. All the girls were out, and the blokes were off doing the rounds. I packed us up and we got out of there. I threw her clothes in a skip, the knife went into another bin. That was it. We didn't know where else to go so we came back here.

"Betsy helped us. She's lovely, is Betsy. She found out about Phillip's flat, how he'd left everything to his sister. I don't know how she found out but she's not daft and she knows how things work. For a bit there we thought it might all be alright. If we kept our heads down. We were going to live there together. We were going to get jobs and live with the knobs, and everything was going to turn out alright. But it didn't, did it? Dougie came, and you came and now it's all gone to hell, and I've lost my mate and everything. So that's it." She stood quite suddenly, picked up her bag and stepped away from the table.

"Where are you going, Pat?" Stella said.

"What the hell does it matter? It's crap everywhere, doesn't matter where." She walked from the room, and they heard the tap-tap of her shoe heels as she strode down the corridor.

Chapter 93

DI Dunn had provided coffee and biscuits. Stella and Jordan wanted to get away, there were drinks in the pub. It wasn't the celebration they'd hoped for. But it was better than being here.

"All a bit messy in the end," Dunn said.

"I'm afraid so, yes." Jordan nodded. "We did our best. Your team here were excellent."

"Apart from Ruth Cowgill."

"Ah well, yes. Apart from that. But it's not very satisfactory, I'm afraid. We've got Fee's killer, but whether she'll ever be fit enough to be tried remains to be seen. She's not doing too well. We have nothing to go on really in trying to find the men who attended the parties. I will have a word with David Griffiths, see if anything can be done. Now we know it's happening maybe it'll be worth looking into. All the girls are scattered. That's going to complicate things."

"So you'll be off back to St Anne Street now."

"Yes, I'll do the paperwork from there, I imagine. It's been great working with Stella and Rupert here, you're lucky to have them." Jordan looked across at Stella who was slowly going pink.

"Oh yes, I have always valued DS May," Dunn said, throwing a smile her way. "We don't really know why she was attacked, do we?"

"Not conclusively. We know it was Douglas Jewell, maybe it was a warning. But he should have known it wouldn't work. He was just desperate, I suppose.

Everything had gone wrong. It certainly didn't put her off doing her job. You'll have to watch out or she'll be getting poached. People have noticed."

* * *

"Is it true, what you said?" Stella asked as they walked down the corridor on the way to the pub.

"Yes, it is," Jordan said. "A bit more experience under your belt and they'll be lining up to have you. It's going to be fun watching you."

"Aw, stop it. I wonder where Pat is. I felt so bad for her. She seemed so lonely and lost."

"I know. Maybe Betsy will know."

"Yeah. I might go and see her. What do you think about Betsy, boss? Do you think she's – what – a witch or a medium or something?"

"Witches, well I don't think I believe in the old lady with the broomstick, that's for sure. It's about religion mostly, isn't it? The Lancashire Witches, Salem, they're just two that are really tangled up with the church and sex. Witchfinder General, torture, ducking stools and burnings. All these really used witchcraft as a cover for religious intolerance, misogyny and downright evil I think. I know that these days we have Wiccan and white witches who are actually herbalists and natural healers, so that's a good thing. At least there is freedom to explore what you want to believe without being at risk of torture and death. We can't deny that there are things that can't be explained. But on the other side there are charlatans and people who take advantage of the bereaved. All bad. I think we acknowledge that mysterious knockings on tables and Ouija boards are a bit of a scam, quite often. Blimey, they are sold as toys, really, aren't they? But, in all honesty – I don't know. There's a lot we don't understand, isn't there? My Nana Gloria, she's religious, goes to church every week, all of that, but she openly admits she believes in spirits and visits from people we've loved – dead ones, you know. In our dreams and suchlike. I think she'd like Betsy but the thought of the two of them together is a bit daunting."

"Ha. I'd like to meet her."

"Well, maybe you could. I still owe you a Sunday lunch. We'll have to arrange it."

"I'd like that."

* * *

The door was open in the house at the end of the terrace. Betsy had the kettle on. Stella called out and walked down the narrow hallway to the kitchen. The cake plate was on the table. She put the cream-filled Victoria Sponge out and cut two slices.

"She's alright," said Betsy.

"Sorry?"

"You were going to get around to asking about Pat. She's alright. She's found a place to stay. Not nice but at least it's off the streets."

"I have been thinking about her. I wish there was something I could do to help."

"Thick as two short planks."

"Sorry?"

"You. Don't you see what's under your nose. There's a house at the end empty. Up for sale, the council don't want it with that history. You've got more money than sense in the bank and you want to help. Do I need to spell it out for you? All anyone needs half the time is an address, without one you can't get anywhere. Just an address. You have the means to give a couple of them that and then another couple later and another. It doesn't need to be a big organization to offer help. All it needs is the will and the desire. Why the hell do you think you had that win? It wasn't for new clothes, and I reckon you've always known that."

Stella was silent. Her mind was racing but she liked where it was going.

List of characters

DS Stella May – Liverpool born and bred. Lives in Aintree.

Lydia May – Stella's mother. Liverpool born and bred. Lives in Wavertree.

Paul May – Stella's father.

Peter May – Stella's brother.

Shelley Frost – Engaged to Peter May. Has one baby – James (Jamie).

DI Ian Dunn – Inspector in Kirkby.

Detective Inspector Jordan Carr – Jamaican heritage. Married to Penny. They have one baby – Harry.

Nana Gloria – Jordan's granny.

Dr James Jasper – Medical examiner based in Liverpool.

DC Rupert Moon – Detective Constable in Kirkby.

Sergeant Carl Flowers – CSI.

DC Robert Street (Bob) – Experienced officer, mostly admin.

David Griffiths – Detective Chief Inspector with Serious and Organised Crime.

Melanie Sharp – Police administrative assistant.

Ruth Cowgill – Police administrative assistant.

Keith Young – Stella's neighbour. Tenant of the upstairs flat. Physiotherapist at the Royal Hospital.

Betsy Minoghue – Neighbour of the squat.

DS Watt – London contact.

Phillip Harwood – Victim.

Douglas Jewell – Friend of the victim. Blonde, fit, twenties.

If you enjoyed this book, please let others know by leaving a quick review on Amazon. Also, if you spot anything untoward in the paperback, get in touch. We strive for the best quality and appreciate reader feedback.

editor@thebookfolks.com

www.thebookfolks.com

Also by Diane Dickson:

BODY ON THE SHORE (Book 1)
BODY BY THE DOCKS (Book 2)
BODY OUT OF PLACE (Book 3)
BODY IN THE CANAL (Book 5)
BODY ON THE ESTATE (Book 6)

BURNING GREED
BRUTAL PURSUIT
BRAZEN ESCAPE
BRUTAL PURSUIT
BLURRED LINES

TWIST OF TRUTH
TANGLED TRUTH
BONE BABY
LEAVING GEORGE
WHO FOLLOWS
THE GRAVE
PICTURES OF YOU
LAYERS OF LIES
DEPTHS OF DECEPTION
YOU'RE DEAD
SINGLE TO EDINBURGH
HOPELESS

Printed in Great Britain
by Amazon